Out Of The Way Things

Kendall McNutt

Copyright © 2023 K. Kendall McNutt

All rights reserved.

Cover Design: SelfPubBookCovers.com/JohnBellArt

ISBN: 9798861263894

kendallmcnutt.com

ACKNOWLEDGMENTS

Thank you Courtney for the feedback. The world of this story is better because of it. Thank you Josh for the process. Wouldn't be finished without it. Thank you Karen for reading it! Karens get things done!

Thank you Heather for loving every word I ever wrote. I've written more words because of that. Thank you Daria for dropping everything to hear me tell the story again and again. Thank you Starla for reading, and Isaac for listening. Also, thank you both, along with Selah and LP, for being my found family. Thank you Kimberly for being one of my first fans, and the only one who remembers that linear timelines are for wimps. Thank you Shana for always supporting me. I have not always been easy to support, but you stick with me anyway, and I am grateful for it.

Thank you to all of my friends and family and friends who are family. Thanks Lisa, for telling me to go for it. Thanks Chris, not for story things but for brother things. Thank you Tru, not for story things either but for being exactly who you are and inspiring me quite regularly.

Thank you Tanja. For reading every time I asked. Like the time I said, "If you get a chance, could you re-read this part?" You graciously agreed. Or the time I said, "Stop doing your stupid job and read this important thing for me again. Pay attention to me." And you graciously agreed. Every time, without fail, you come through. Thank you for telling the truth. Thank you for believing in me. This is the story you most wanted me to tell, and I hope you love it.

And of course, Thank you, mom. I wish you could read it. I think you would have said it doesn't need the weird stuff, some parts are too scary, and there is no need to swear, but good job. I know you would be proud, and you would let me know how much, and also you would shake your head in disapproval when you learned that I got a new tattoo to celebrate completing this book. I love reading because of you. I love stories because of you. *I wish you were down here with me.*

Thank you.

XOXO, Kendall

OUT OF THE WAY THINGS

"For, you see, so many out-of-the-way things had happened lately, that Alice had begun to think that very few things indeed were really impossible."

Alice in Wonderland, Lewis Carroll

PROLOGUE

"Tell me about yourself," the man suggested, his tone interested, his eyes fixed on the paper in his hand. The office was designed to make me nervous. Books I probably should have known lined Spartan metal cases secured to the gray walls that surrounded me. The shelves gave the impression of bars. Each item on Mr. McLaughlin's desk rested just so, as if he had mapped the space with a compass and straightedge.

Mr. McLaughlin himself appeared to be designed with the same attention to detail. Straight posture. Precise attire. Definitively brown eyes. Well defined bone structure.

I am the master of my fate, I told myself. My mouth opened and my mind emptied. I counseled myself, *Just answer the question.* I smiled, "That's a big question." *Killing time.* "My undergraduate degree is in communications. I have always been interested in Marketing. I am fascinated by how consumers interact with the market and drive innovation."

He looked up from his paper, and nodded, then jotted down some notes. I felt encouraged.

Mr. McLaughlin continued the interrogation, "Right now you are cleaning houses, why aren't you working in a field that aligns with your training?"

Oh, no. Discouraged.

I held my smile, the confidence that shone through entirely fabricated. I said, "I would wonder that too, if I were you. I have struggled to decide what is next for me. To be honest, house cleaning is more lucrative than you might guess, so I don't need a change for financial reasons." *Lie.* "I want my next step to be the right one. When I saw this opportunity, I knew, this is something I can grow with, a company that I can represent well, and an opportunity that aligns with my values and my goals. That's why I am here."

He smiled. I relaxed. Fractionally. "Tell me more about that. How do you feel we align with your values and goals?"

I was prepared for this question. "I'm glad you asked that," I began. Our eyes locked. The room shifted, and his gaze seemed to slide around in my vision. I remained still and the room moved. *No!* I silently protested the sudden onset of vertigo. The confidence drained from my smile, "It is clear in your advertising," I stumbled in remembering my planned response, "That is, um," I stumbled in remembering the question. "I'm sorry, I am suddenly dizzy." In desperation I asked, "I'm sorry could you repeat the question?"

I could hear his response, but struggled to make meaning of his words. My eyes searched for a fixed point, something steady to which I could anchor.

Through the window, behind him, I caught sight of a car careening through an intersection. My eyes widened and my jaw fell slack. I felt the room shake as the car collided with a pole yards away from where we sat. I jumped out of my chair, knocking his coffee from his desk. Mr. McLaughlin did not turn around, he heard none of it, he saw nothing. Because, once again, nothing was happening. Another hallucination, with perfect timing.

He looked at me with worry. He looked at his coffee with regret.

"Sorry," I gasped, "I've had a lot of coffee and not a lot of water." Dehydration could excuse all manner of odd behavior. Probably not hallucinations, though, so I kept the vision to myself. I rescued his cup, now nearly empty. I looked around for anything that might absorb the coffee, seeing what I intended he handed me some tissue and together we kneeled and sopped up coffee.

"I think it's fine now," he said. "Someone will clean it. Are you alright, are you sure you want to continue?" There was genuine concern in his voice.

"Yes definitely," even to me it sounded too eager. I returned to my seat. "I am very nervous, this is very important to me. I apologize. Really, I am fine." But the room hadn't stopped moving. I shut it out and focused on the question. The question I could not remember.

Once they started, the hallucinations often spiraled out of control. Sometimes, the hallucinations unfolded in complex, lengthy scenes. Sometimes they flashed from vision to vision, imagery jumbled together in a cacophonous tumult, as was the case this morning. During the single most important hour, of the single most important day, of my entire year.

Also per usual, the vertigo intensified. I steadied myself by placing a hand on the arm of my chair.

The interview continued.

To get things back on track Mr. McLaughlin kindly repeated the question, "Can you tell me about how our company aligns with your values?"

I have no idea, I thought. I said, "Yes, about that…"

Mr. McLaughlin smiled patiently, while behind him, on the sidewalk outside an elderly woman tripped a teenager on a skateboard. The nausea told me that it only happened in my imagination. They promptly disappeared.

I continued, "The company's values..." I corrected, "My values…"

The car wreck returned, this time with smoke and police and a gathering crowd. I tried to look away, but the scene drew me in.

Mr. McLaughlin turned to look. Seeing nothing, his smile grew shallow. He looked at me expectantly. "I'm so sorry," I repeated, "I'm nervous this means a lot to me."

The candor worked in my favor, sympathy spread across his face. That was fine with me, I'd take a pity job.

And then the window shattered and I jumped backwards.

Only the window didn't shatter, because I imagined it, and I did jump back, which might as well have been the end of the interview.

After that, the only coherent sentences I managed contained the words "I," "am," and "sorry," mostly in that order.

We wrapped with the usual platitudes. He would reach out if I were invited to go on to the next stage of the process, blah, appreciate the time, blah-blah, have a nice life.

As I left the building I muttered, "I am the master of my fate, I am the captain of my soul. And that's the problem."

PART ONE: A HOUSE

CHAPTER 1

Alone in my car, rushing to my only source of income, I walked myself back through the interview: Dizzy spell. Spilled coffee. Limbic swearing. And that was only what was obvious to Mr. McLaughlin.

"Why, in every interview, do I sound like a psychopath?" I asked my empty car.

And then last week's interview popped into my head, "or an idiot?"

Next came the one ten days ago, "or both?"

My career prospects were bleak. With a poor interview presence, a spotty job history, chronic vertigo, and a difficult to explain tendency to experience complex hallucinations, my references were nonexistent. "I wouldn't hire me either," I conceded.

As my attention turned inward, my car drifted into the left lane. I sharply over-corrected and shook my head out of my reverie, forcing my mind back to the task at hand. *Good thing I am in the middle of nowhere.*

I raced through the bucolic tranquility that surrounded me, heedless of the unhealthy roar of my engine and cloud of sooty exhaust in my wake. I tried to focus on the soothing images surrounding me now, open pastures dotted with farm animals. Probably cows. Cows who didn't need to worry about gainful employment. "Hi cows," I said mournfully. I considered the life of the cattle. Eating and walking and hanging out with cow friends and colleagues. "Pretty charmed life out there in that field. You just wander around until…"

I realized cows may not be the best example of easy living and bright futures. "Maybe they're horses."

My impending cleaning job intruded on my thoughts, I sighed. Until I could manage to appear normal during questioning, I would be stuck cleaning the homes of strangers. Specifically, strangers who didn't meet me before I entered their homes. Interviews didn't show me to an advantage, Mr. McLaughlin could attest to that. Despite his obvious concern about my mental state, he had taken great care in ushering me out of the office. Concerned for me. Almost afraid of me. I doubted he would allow me in his home if I showed up with a mop and bucket.

On today's agenda, a house, situated far outside of town. To get there, I emptied my bank account into my gas tank. It was a big job, but the money was good.

The clock in my car was broken, I reached for my phone to find out how late I was. In my bag I found receipts, escaped sticks of gum, loose change, wallet, bobby pins, and no phone. Again, I felt the car drifting across the lane and pulled the wheel hard to stay on the road. *Good thing I am alone on this road.*

Determined, I felt in each compartment, pushing aside the accumulated purse debris, desperation rising.

Relief and disgust arrived together as I remembered. I pushed myself up in the seat and retrieved the phone from my back pocket. With one hand occupied steering, I held the phone up to try to divide my attention equally between the phone and the road. I thought, *no state troopers, please.* I pushed the on button on the side of the phone and slid my free thumb across the screen to unlock it. As soon as the lock screen disappeared, a message flashed.

Low power mode.

Good thing I am alone in the middle of nowhere.

"Damn." I made it to the center of the road this time and once again, course corrected. A second glance at the phone confirmed I was running late. Instinctively, I pressed harder on the gas pedal. The effort met with a soft clunk in the engine. The sound repeated with a small shudder, and I moved my foot to decelerate.

The clunking continued in a quiet rhythm and I whispered a curse. "Not today," I begged the car, "please just keep driving." In my present financial circumstances, car repair or replacement was as laughable as it was terrifying.

With consideration for the state of my car and the state of my phone, I ventured back into my bag, searching for my charger. The charger turned up in the first search. I ripped the charger free, and in the process, unseated my purse. It teetered at the edge of the seat. My hand shot to the right to rescue it. The phone smacked into the steering wheel, loosening my grasp, and then it fell, out of reach, and possibly under the seat. The purse spilled onto the car floor.

"Damn it! Damn every damn thing!" I pounded the offending steering wheel.

CHAPTER 2

I nearly missed the turn onto the rural driveway, unpaved and unmarked save the promised red mailbox. I turned hard and worried for my beleaguered engine.

With a deep inhalation of air, I forced myself back to the matter at hand: a paying job.

The end of the long, dusty drive, offered my reward, a large farmhouse well past its prime.

Thirty years ago, the place might have been charming. Decades of neglect left a sagging porch, overgrown foliage, and peeling paint. An equally derelict pickup truck rusted in the driveway, forgotten.

The car trembled to a grateful stop. I parked and turned it off, hoping it would start again. It was a relief to step out of the car. I hurriedly scooped everything from the car floor and shoved it back inside my purse. I took more care as I gathered my cleaning supplies, carrying as much as I could at once.

As I placed a foot carelessly on the first step, I felt it bend and groan with the weight. I cringed and took the next step with caution.

"Please, don't collapse on me," I instructed the house. At the door, I fumbled about in my bag again for the key, dropping first a mop, then a bucket, and finally, with resignation, everything but the bag. I found the key.

The door required extra effort and the power of a shoulder to push open, the wood swollen with summer heat. I burst through the door and instantly stumbled.

"Damn," I declared, rubbing my shoulder. I stepped inside and, for a moment, my head swam, the entry walls swirled through my vision. I closed my eyes and continued to step inside, hoping the dizziness passed quickly.

THUMP. Pain.

"Ow," I tripped and opened my eyes. A red toolbox sat just inside the door.

"Damn!" I repeated, frowning at my stubbed toe.

"Sorry about that," a disembodied voice replied. I jumped and dropped the bag. *Hallucination?*

My second scan of the room revealed a man, fully embodied. He stood in the parlor, the bright light from the windows cloaked him in an attractive glow. He repeated, "Sorry about the toolbox. The cleaner," he confirmed my identity with a nod, "Are you working on the landscaping as well?"

"Just a cleaner," I replied automatically. I tried to stifle the irritation I felt.

He smiled, a dimple appearing beside his mouth, that helped, "Not just." That helped more.

I attempted a return smile. Remembering my supplies, I said, "I'll be right back."

"But you just..." He interjected. I looked back to him, a question forming on my lips. He shook his head, "Never mind."

I returned to the porch and gathered my bucket of supplies, my mop, my box of cleansers. It didn't fit into my arms as easily as it had the first time and I cursed again.

As soon as I crossed the threshold, the man rushed to help, relieving me of the box and the mop. "Thank you," I sighed with genuine gratitude.

"Where would you like to start?" he asked.

"Um," I considered the options. Start with the biggest challenge, I figured. "The kitchen?"

"Great!" he returned, "Me too."

We would be spending the day together, I realized, ought to make the best of it. "What are you working on?" I asked, following him further into the house.

"A few repairs for the new owner," the man replied over his shoulder. "Sorry again about the toolbox. I shouldn't have left it that close to the door."

"No problem," I offered, but my toe throbbed in protest.

The repairman was handsome, if a little unusual. His hair fell almost to his chin, and he sported a denim jacket with a button down shirt neatly tucked into his matching jeans. Possibly trendy, sort of retro, definitely a statement. He wore work boots dotted with flecks of green, a paint spill? I surmised we were close in age.

In the kitchen, we set down all of my cleaning implements. The man waited and looked at me as an awkward silence descended.

Then we spoke at the same time.

"I suppose I'll..." I started.

"My name's..." he began.

"Oh," we said together. We each laughed nervously. Our eyes met, we waited, we each leaned in, waiting for the other to finish. I indicated with my hands that he ought to proceed.

He smiled, his dimple charmed me. "I'm Twain," he said. He flushed, "Like the old-timey writer."

He was even more endearing when he spoke. "I'm Win." I turned and showed him the back of my sweatshirt. The shirt had been a graduation present from my parents. My high school name and graduation year were printed on the front, my name appeared across the back in large block print. "In case you forget."

"Convenient," He smiled. "That's an unusual name, I haven't heard that before."

"It's a nickname. Everyone's always called me Win." I shrugged, "Which is actually deeply ironic, now that I'm an adult. Parents should have had more foresight."

Twain returned a quizzical look.

I shook my head, "Not a winner, rarely win." He opened his mouth to respond, an objection plain on his face. I held up a hand to forestall him, "Nope. You just met me. You don't know. So, don't do it. Be original." His pity would send me over the edge.

Twain took in a deep breath, measuring his response. "Well…" He began, I narrowed my eyes in warning. "At least people don't ask you about your time on the mighty Mississippi."

That assertion was correct, I conceded to myself. I smiled, "Fair enough." After a pause I asked, "But, how was it though?"

He shook his head. "Don't go there."

I wrinkled my nose at his response. "If you say so."

"You know, the worst part is that I've never even seen it. It is the only wish I have, to see the damn Mississippi River before I die."

"How about this, if we finish this house," I looked around skeptically, that definitely felt like an "*if*" after a quick look around, "If we finish, we drive across the country, straight to the damn Mississippi River."

Twain's pretty smile lit his face, he stretched his hand out and I took it. We shook hands and he agreed, "Deal." The passing fancy motivated me to start the work. Even as I recognized it for what it was: an attractive, ephemeral fantasy.

I glanced around the kitchen, and realized how true my words were. Neglect marked the kitchen as surely as it did the exterior of the house. I encouraged myself with the suggestion, "Let's do this."

"It's not so bad," Twain replied. "We can get this done." In only a few minutes, I was fond of him. Both novel and familiar, I felt instantly enchanted.

CHAPTER 3

We settled into a comfortable rhythm, an amiable silence interspersed with vibrant conversation. Despite my vertigo and my general dislike of cleaning, I found myself enjoying the job. After an hour of work, I thought, with Twain as a partner, I could get used to this career. I couldn't account for the near immediate connection I felt to him, but I began to imagine taking the cross country drive with him, starting a business together flipping houses. It was a ridiculous train of thought, I knew that. And still, I entertained the fantasy.

Occasionally, I caught myself watching him. Once, as he entered the room, I noticed that he caught the door frame, braced against it, and closed his eyes. The first time, I said nothing. The second time, I asked, "Are you all right?"

"It's a migraine, always makes me dizzy," he smiled, almost apologetic.

"Dizziness is the worst. I have vertigo. For a minute, I thought maybe it was contagious."

Twain cocked his head to one side, "If only I could blame you. I am afraid this has been pretty common, most of my life."

I offered him a sympathetic look; I understood his plight well. For a moment, I wondered if he experienced hallucinations like me. I pushed away the thought, of course he didn't. I wiped the sweat from my brow with my sleeve. And returned to my scrubbing.

The kitchen took me hours, scraping grime out of every cupboard and scrubbing away years of dirt. Twain lingered there more than the job likely required. By midday the effort of the work began to take a toll, sweat soaked through my clothes, my back ached, and my stomach growled,

Twain asked, "Did you bring a lunch?" I flushed in response. Apparently, my stomach growled loudly. And then it got worse.

I thought, *Damn*. "No. I didn't." Running late, per usual, I packed nothing. "I probably have an energy bar in my purse." *Or on my car floor.*

"I packed too much food. Do you want to split mine?"

I couldn't stop the smile, "Yeah, that'd be nice."

"I hate packing lunches in the morning. I never know what I am going to want to eat by the middle of the day. So I pack options."

"That's weird," I laughed. He smiled at my amusement. "But I am grateful. I need to get my life together, I can barely get out the door in the morning. I would be so happy if I made it out of the house with a packed lunch."

"Good thing we have each other," Twain said.

I agreed silently.

We sat on the back porch and shared a sandwich.

"This place is going to take a few days," I thought aloud.

"You think so? It doesn't seem that bad."

"Uh, yeah, it's real bad." I insisted.

He shrugged, "Well I know I have to come back because there is equipment and materials I didn't bring today. I will be sure to pack a big lunch tomorrow."

"Maybe we could carpool." I thought of my car, and realized that the suggestion might be more practical than flirtatious.

"I better get your number then." He didn't know about my car, so I took the response as strictly flirtation.

"Give me your phone." Maybe the daydreams weren't impossible.

Twain laughed, surprised and genuine. "I don't have a phone."

Another charming idiosyncrasy. "Okay, how about paper and a pen?"

A thorough search of his many pockets turned up the requested pen and a paint swatch. I took it from him and propped it on my knee to write my number.

I asked, "How are you going to call me?"

He grinned, and I thought maybe he thought the question was one of my charming idiosyncrasies. "I have a phone at my house."

"Fair enough," I handed him the paper and he returned it to his back pocket.

"You have a mobile phone?" He asked.

Cute, he probably has a record collection. I confirmed, "Yeah," I reached for my back pocket. *Damn it.* "Oh, I left it in the car."

His eyes betrayed his skepticism, but he said, "Okay."

On the porch, we were in full sun and I began to feel it. I pulled off my hoodie and tied it around my waist. This got another quizzical look from Twain. His eyes were drawn to my t-shirt, a Nirvana shirt I had picked up off of a two for $10 table.

"Oh, I love them, so cool," he remarked.

"Changed the game," I smiled. *Definitely has a record collection.*

Twain's voice was wistful, "I would love to see them live."

"Yeah, no kidding." I agreed. *Maybe he has a time machine next to his record collection.*

"Do you like concerts?" He held up an apple and a banana. I selected the apple.

"Of course," I said with a mouthful of apple.

He rewarded me with a grin. Peeling his banana he added, "We can go to one on the way to the Mississippi."

Our travel fantasies continued, became more and more elaborate as we worked our way through his lunch, and then carried on beyond the food and a lunch break.

When our conversation eventually slowed, I asked, "You ready to get back to it?"

Twain shrugged and stood. He reached out his hand to help me up. As I stood, I staggered, light-headed again. Twain winced and asked, "Are you okay?"

"The vertigo," I reminded him.

He nodded sympathetically, "Migraine."

Back at my tasks, the dizziness faded into the background. We each started packing up our tools and supplies in the kitchen to move to the next room. We had agreed the dining room would be fast. There was less to clean there, and Twain only had a jammed window to fix.

THUMP.

At the sudden noise, my head turned to the ceiling. It sounded like it came from upstairs. *A hallucination?* I wondered. My eyes darted back to Twain. He looked toward the noise as well. *Not a hallucination.*

"Be right back," Twain said. I heard him call out, "Hello? Is someone there?" I imagined him searching the front rooms. He did not immediately return and I heard no reply to his repeated greetings.

Twain appeared in the kitchen. With a shrug, he said, "There's no one."

"Is there a car outside?" I asked. I amended, "Other than mine."

"My bad, I should have looked for a car."

I stood, determined to solve the mystery. "Let's go check it out."

We returned to the front of the house and peered out the window.

"No car," I smiled slyly, "a mystery?"

He pointed out the window, "Is that your car?"

I nodded without looking.

THUMP.

"Okay, that was really creepy," I whispered.

"Was that the door?" He asked.

"It sounded like it came from upstairs."

"We were running the water, maybe it's the pipes." He suggested, "Or maybe we heard wrong?"

"Both of us?" I asked. "You said there is an interior designer coming?"

"Oh yeah," Twain smiled, "Probably. I'll go say hi. It must have been the door."

"I'll come with you." The second search of the foyer was as fruitless as the first. "Could be a vandal. We should search the house," I proposed, the idea born of intrusive curiosity as much as concern. Also, solving a mystery appealed to me more than scrubbing the floor.

Like-minded Twain beamed. "We owe it to our employer," Twain suggested.

"Start at the top?"

We made a game of sneaking up the stairs, with exaggerated movements and bursts of giggles. I enjoyed it thoroughly, knowing that eventually we would have to conclude that old houses make noises, and go back to work.

All of the doors upstairs were closed. "So many options," I whispered. Twain nudged me with his elbow. I met his eyes and then followed them up.

A trap door. An attic.

Twain's height allowed him to reach up easily and pull the door down before I could object.

"No way." I didn't bother with the whispering.

"You scared?" He smirked.

"Yes, now I am. Empty house. Weird sounds. Creepy attic."

Twain shrugged and steadied himself on the ladder, "I'll protect you."

My eyes rolled reflexively.

"You staying down there?"

"No," I muttered, "We can't split up, never split up." I followed Twain up the ladder, muttering all the way. "This is how we get murdered. It is in every single horror movie. I hope this isn't the prologue, someone always dies in the prologue."

Light accompanied us up the stairs from below but only just a step beyond the hole in the floor. Each wall, to the left and to the right, boasted a small circular window. Somehow these portals illuminated each egress enough to beckon us toward them, but too little to share with the room. I reached for my phone automatically. My hand found an empty back pocket instead. I pictured my phone, then. Laying forgotten, dying, under the driver's seat of my car.

Monstrous shapes waited in the gloom. The interloper could be standing in plain sight and still be indistinguishable from the menacing forms. Shapes, almost human, and reaching. Twain stepped forward. I followed. So close my shoulder brushed his back.

Twain jumped.

I gasped.

"Did you see something?" He whispered furiously.

"No, did you, you jumped?"

I felt Twain relax. "You startled me, when you bumped into me." He clutched his head. His migraine, still a problem, but he didn't complain.

I surveyed the room nervously, convinced of an unseen danger.

My scan confirmed my fear.

A threatening silhouette waited a few feet away. He was tall. Wide across the shoulders.

"Twain," I whispered urgently. Wisely, he did not respond.

The shadow man remained ready. I felt the tension in his stance. Prepared to attack. My breath came quick and shallow. I clapped a hand on my mouth to quiet my breathing.

"There," I whispered through my fingers, nearly too quiet to be heard. I extended my free hand and held a finger out in front of us. I sensed more than saw Twain's nodded response. His arm reached upward, at first, unsure.

I realized where his hand was going. I imagined, but did not see, the chain that connected to a light. A light that would expose the man, even as it announced us to him.

"No!" I whispered desperately.

With a click, the horrors of the room revealed themselves.

CHAPTER 4

An attic, years of accumulated junk and memorabilia. Things ignored, useless, just broken enough that in the right hands, they might be repaired.

And among it all, he stood. A pile of boxes topped with a globe.

Self-disgust laced my words, "Why did I think that was a head? It is really big."

"At least it's not Hannibal Lecter."

"Who?" I asked.

"From the movie, you know, *Silence of the Lambs*."

"Oh yeah," I agreed, but I didn't know.

I refused to feel silly. In darkness, the attic inspired nightmares. For anyone. In the light, it was an accumulation of generations, abandoned, maybe sad. Terrifying in a different way. Remnants of a life too well loved to discard, but not so well loved to keep close. It took effort for me to ignore the obvious analogy between the contents of the attic and me.

It took only a few minutes to learn that the attic harbored no mysterious visitors. Only junk.

As I returned down the ladder, Twain pulled the cord and extinguished the light. The room, again plunged into a darkness, turned immediately terrifying. I hurried on the steps. In the hallway, I held my breath until Twain appeared and pushed the ladder back into the attic, shutting the door.

Leaving the attic behind, I realized, for the first time, that starting with the attic made us vulnerable. If there really were a prowler, we could have been trapped up there, with no hope of exit.

Twain jumped to the floor in front of me. Reading my face, he asked, "You okay?"

"Yeah," I attempted to hide my worry. Twain raised an eyebrow in response. "Okay, maybe not. That was probably a bad idea. If someone is in the house, we probably shouldn't back ourselves into a corner. As far from the exit we can get."

Twain offered a reassuring smile. "I don't really think anyone is in the house. Maybe a squirrel?"

I shrugged, I wanted to play it off, but a feeling of dread remained, even in the absence of a threat.

Twain took my hand. "I promise, it's okay. We will look through the rest of the rooms, just to be sure."

If it were a real concern, Twain wouldn't suggest we search the house.

He confirmed that by adding, "If I really thought someone was here, we would get in my truck and get the hell out of here. We are only looking so that we don't jump at every sound. It's like a game." His dimple sealed the deal.

I pulled myself together.

This was a game. A contrived threat created to conceal our true purpose: flirtatious shirking. We each picked a door, Twain winked at me, we nodded to one another.

I threw open the door and discovered a bathroom. I entered the room slowly, my body turned to the side, ready to dodge, ready to run. A game. But residual fear from the attic still coursed through me.

The bathroom was empty. A yellowing shower curtain blocked my view of the bathtub and I felt a shiver down my spine.

I whispered, "Why am I doing this?" And then, "Damn it." Because I knew I wouldn't stop. A glance revealed that Twain had disappeared into his room.

I inched forward on silent feet.

I held my breath.

I counted down silently.

Three.

Two.

One.

At zero, my arm snaked out and grabbed the plastic. Before my sense of self-preservation kicked in, I ripped back the curtain. I gasped instinctively.

Nothing.

"At this rate," I sighed, "I am going to have a heart attack before we get back to the kitchen."

I rejoined Twain in the hall. "That was a little scary," he admitted.

"Oh, yeah," I agreed. We exchanged half-hearted smiles.

Without a word, we entered the next bedroom together. Twain a step ahead of me. The dizziness crested, and I was grateful that Twain stood in front of me.

Someone had cleared the room of furniture, but had left behind two small piles of rope.

The room spun and reformed itself. I blinked hard and swallowed to clear the nausea.

Stupid hallucinations.

In reality, the bedroom was minimally furnished, with a creaky metal bed in the center, pushed against the wall to the right. We both walked on the balls of our feet, but even while employing this careful step, Twain's boots softly clomped on the floor. We looked to the far side of the bed. Nothing extraordinary. Neglect left dust creatures in the corner. As the paid house cleaner, I made a mental note.

Twain indicated the closet with his head. I nodded my agreement. Through a series of gestures he signaled that I should pull back the door and move aside, he would wait to deal with anything that popped out. I might have laughed at the elaborate, silent pantomime if not for the very real fear taking advantage of my vivid imagination.

Twain positioned himself in front of the door. I took the door handle and pulled.

Empty.

I released a long breath.

"Did you think this would be fun?" I asked.

"I did." He confirmed.

"Do you still?"

Twain shrugged, "Ehhh, kinda?"

I agreed. Kinda.

We searched the last two bedrooms with less enthusiasm. I began to feel a little guilty about wasting time on the job. And not just my time. Thinking back to my pursuit of better employment, I recognized that my bad references may be due only in part to the hallucinations.

"Did you hear that?" Twain asked, jolting me out of my reverie.

"No. What?" I searched his face, "Are you joking?"

"Maybe it was nothing." But his voice remained quiet. "My hearing is kinda bad. Sometimes I hear things, and it's nothing."

"If you heard and I didn't, doesn't that make your hearing kinda good?"

"It's not bad, I guess." He looked around the hall, possibly for a better explanation because he continued, "It's inaccurate. I think I hear things that turn out to be something else or nothing at all."

I admitted, "I get that. I know that feeling." Not full disclosure, but a confession of sorts.

The admission seemed to relax Twain a bit. I wondered if this peculiar hearing isolated him. And then I knew I was projecting, but I didn't stop myself from feeling the connection that followed the wondering.

"To the bottom?" He asked.

"The cellar?" I asked in reply. At his nod I reminded him, "They told me not to go down there. I think it's not safe."

Another taunting look from Twain, "You worried about rules now? I dare you."

A game again. I thought perhaps he had changed the tone to erase the seriousness of the moment. "Okay," I agreed. "But if this is how one of us gets killed, I want my number back."

"Fair enough," he mocked gently.

"You have a record collection, don't you?" I asked.

"How did you know that?"

I grinned and shrugged in reply. He returned a coy smile.

At the foot of the stairs, we stood facing the cellar door. It was easily identified as there was only one closed door on the ground level. The owner of the house told me that it was an old, unfinished root cellar. Her uncle, who had owned the house, said the structure of the room was unstable, and no one had entered it in years.

Twain's gait was confident, but I noticed his hand shook a little. Once again, he led the way. He opened the door slowly, it creaked in protest.

I held my breath and stepped quietly after him. Twain had to duck on the stairs to keep from bumping his head, and the cellar ceiling was no higher.

Twain stopped abruptly. I ran into him and gasped. My lungs filled with stale, fetid air. "Oh god," he murmured. I peered around him searching frantically.

The cellar was small. I could stand in the center and reach each wall by leaning. The floor was uneven and unfinished.

In the center of the room lay a human figure.

CHAPTER 5

The decay that permeated the air found its source in the body entombed in the cellar. Even face down the decomposition was apparent. Little of the man's flesh remained, treated leather gathered loosely around his skeletal structure.

The bile rose in my throat and tears collected in the corners of my eyes.

I grabbed Twain's arm and felt the nausea reassert itself.

He glanced down at me and said, "We have to get out here." He spun on his heel and took my hand, pulling me up the stairs. I pushed through the spinning and the pressure in my ears to keep up.

Twain paused at the top of the stairs. His hearing again? He reached out to the door frame again, holding firm. His headache, then. What a couple we made.

He dropped his arm, and we took another step.

THUMP.

Movement drew my gaze.

Near the front door of the house.

For a moment, I saw someone, maybe two people, standing just inside the house. The pair winked in and out of existence. My hallucinations asserted themselves, then retreated on a dizzying loop.

Twain grabbed my arm, forcing my attention back to him. I saw the conflict in his eyes before he did it. Determination mixed with regret. "What..?" I whispered, "Do you see..?"

Twain opened the door to the root cellar. Before I could finish the sentence, he grabbed my shoulder and pushed me gently into the cellar. Vertigo nearly took me off my feet. My body complied before my mind had time enough to resist. When I caught up, I stood at the top of the stairs, watching his hands retreat and the door close quietly and firmly.

I reached for the door handle, twisted sharply and met resistance. *Twain's holding it closed*, I realized.

"No," Twain whispered against the door, "They'll hear."

"Who?" I asked, as quietly as I could.

"Standing in the doorway." I heard the tremor of fear in his hushed voice.

I froze. *Now what?* Did I force Twain off the door and help him? Maybe die with him? Did I hide and hope Twain did the same? Or was this still a game?

"Win, hide now," a strained, desperate whisper through the door, "Please, so that I have time to hide."

If he stood outside the door, he was in danger. That decided it. "Okay," I conceded in a whisper. I would rather be a fool than responsible for hurting Twain.

I withdrew from the door, aware that every sound threatened Twain. I lifted each foot slowly. I placed it just as carefully on the step below.

Outside, Twain quietly shuffled away. Those damn boots.

My breaths grew shorter, heavier. I forced my lungs open. Fill quietly, fill completely.

I remembered a breathing exercise. To force calm on my frayed nerves.

Deep breath in. I nearly choked on the foul air. My hands shot up to cover my mouth, stifling the sound. I prepared myself for acrid miasma, forced myself to habituate to it. I tried again.

Breathe in. Four, three, two, one.

Step.

Deep breath out. Six, five, four, three, two one.

Step.

The only light in the room entered from a small window opposite the stairs. When I reached the floor, I remembered the dominating feature of the room: the body. In the darkness, I could only make out the shape.

My heartbeat quickened as I found a path around it, stepping on the tips of my toes, avoiding direct contact with the remains. I pushed away every unpleasant sensation, the horrifying sight, the overpowering smell, the vestibular chaos.

I searched each wall, too dark to be certain of my surroundings. Three of the walls were covered in shelving. I could see the outline of mason jars, but the darkness concealed their contents.

I felt tears prick the corners of my eyes. Panic.

I closed my eyes.

Deep breath in, I thought, counting from four.

Deep breath out. The count from six.

Deep breath in, I opened my eyes.

I found a corner and crouched against it, wedging behind the end of a row of shelves.

My corner provided little cover, but remained dark enough that I wouldn't be visible with the door open. If the door opened again.

Waiting was a new horror. *How long do I wait?*

With only fear as a companion, my ears strained for sounds of life. Hoping to hear what happened outside. Hoping to hear nothing at all.

THUMP.

Not thump. Step.

My breath returned, loud, fast, ragged.

My leg cramped, I held myself still. Slowed my breathing. Forced my heart to slow.

Is it Twain? Are we out of danger?

I concentrated on listening, opening my eyes wide, closing them tight, though it was no help.

THUMP.

No, step.

THUMP.

"Step," I whispered. My eyes opened, preferring to know what was coming.

I clapped a hand over my mouth. Tears returned.

THUMP.

Too heavy for Twain? I wondered, trying to remember his shoes. Boots. Work boots. I willed the house to give me another clue.

"No!" Twain's voice. "No!" he repeated.

I lurched forward involuntarily.

Not that clue.

I tried to connect my feet to the ground.

"No," I echoed Twain. My hands came in contact with the body.

I felt fabric and bone.

"No," I repeated.

I pushed myself up and forward, heedless of noise. My foot caught on the uneven ground. I tripped. "Damn." I said it too loudly. I froze, my eyes locked onto the object that tripped me.

Boots. Work boots. A splash of green paint on the heel. On the right, laces broken and tied together again.

THUMP.

Not a step.

"Twain." I saw. "Please disappear," I whispered, hoping for the vertigo that told me it wasn't real.

My eyes scanned upward from the boots, my mind lagged a moment behind. I followed a sliver of light that escaped from the seam of the cellar door. Jeans, jean jacket.

THUMP.
I felt as well as heard the bump of the cellar door.
I stopped breathing.
I scrambled backward, to my corner, my knees to my chest. *Can I escape?*
On the wall, a small window, too high.
The only way out was the way in.
I curled up tighter.
The door flew open, bouncing off the wall.
I cried out. My hand flew to cover it.
THUMP.
No. Step, heavier than before, closer.
Again. *THUMP/Step.*

I shuddered with each beat. My left hand joined my right over my mouth. I felt tears slide down my face. Against my will, against reason, my eyes closed tight.

Slowly, the labored steps drew closer.
I stifled a sob.
THUMP. *Much louder.*
The noise reverberated off the walls, shocking my eyes open.
Twain lay next to the body. Blood flowed from his neck. His eyes were wild and weary.

Another sob rose in my throat and I held it back.

I tried to catch his gaze, but he looked through me. I watched his feet and hands slide on the floor, as though he tried to find purchase to stand. The deep tread on his green stained work boots caught in the dirt and he bucked off the ground for a second before falling again.

I remembered that the intruder remained in the cellar.
The one who deposited Twain here.

After dropping Twain, he lost interest. Sighing, he turned away from Twain, I couldn't see his face clearly. His gaze slid over me as though I was not worth his consideration. As though he did not even see me.

My fear for Twain outweighed self-preservation. Paralysis released me, I crawled to Twain, trying again to catch his eye, afraid to touch him. Wishing for a towel or a blanket, I realized my only option was my shirt. I took the sweatshirt tied around my waist and applied it to his neck.

"Twain," I whispered, "I'm here."

His mouth opened and closed. A shadow crept into his eyes. Open but unfocused. Awake, and unaware. I reached for his hand, closing my eyes to push back the tears. I found only air.

I opened my eyes. Alone. Twain was gone, the body and I remained. My shirt was gone, I could almost feel it in my hands. I reached for it at my waist, but found nothing. I shook my head, and the hallucination subsided.

Twain lay on his back, pushing up again with his boot. He managed to flip on his stomach, my shirt wedged beneath him, soaked through with blood.

Dizziness overtook me.

I fell backwards onto my hands, grabbing at the floor to stop it spinning. I sunk into the ground, my head swimming in the spinning room. On the periphery of my vision, I watched Twain become the body, and then himself again. Repeat. I clutched my head, wishing for the truth.

I closed my eyes tightly, *remember the strategy*. I inhaled deeply and counted backward from four.

Four. Did I make him up?

Three.

Two. Could I save him?

One. Is he real?

I opened my eyes, first finding Twain.

No, the body.

Twain's body. A faded strip of paper poked out of his back pocket.

"Did I make it all up?" I whispered to Twain.

Twain. Long gone. And wouldn't see the Mississippi.

CHAPTER 6

"Hello?"

A woman's greeting accompanied the opening of the cellar door. Time had passed since Twain faded into forgotten remains, but I couldn't mark how much. Minutes? Hours?

"I know you're here, no need to hide." The woman stepped quietly and I missed her descent. She stood calmly to one side, arrow straight spine, relaxed, still, as though no part of her body moved without planning and intention. She radiated ethereal serenity. Her exquisite beauty felt out of place in the primitive cellar, almost offensive.

The woman took stock of the room, her survey ending on the body. "Oh," she said, "well that's unpleasant."

I scrubbed the tears from my eyes. "Who are you?" I asked. Her presence felt intrusive, but not threatening.

"Call me Sophia," the woman offered. Even in the dimly lit room, her face was radiant, almost inhumanly beautiful. "I'm here to save you."

Surprise ripped me from confusion. I pushed myself up onto my knees. "What?"

"I'll explain on the way. Shall we?"

The last of the haze cleared from my brain. "Twain?"

Sophia ostensibly grimaced. "We can't help him now. Maybe if I'd arrived..." she considered, "Thirty years ago?" Sophia shrugged, "But then I couldn't help you. Need a hand?"

I found my feet, without the proffered assistance. "Who are you? Why are you helping me? How did you know where I was?"

Sophia smiled, slightly and patiently. I thought a greater smile might eclipse the sun. She replied, "Sophia. You need it. I'll explain in the car. Shall we?" Her voice compelled me forward.

"Thirty years?" I asked. Still lagging behind.

"Give or take a year."

I nodded. Sophia's mouth widened again, a patient almost smile.

Sophia turned and led the way out of the cellar.

I followed, skeptical, but determined. Nothing seemed real, and following her seemed as reasonable an action as any.

At the top of the stairs, I looked backed at Twain, gone for three decades.

I wondered where the hallucination started. When I entered the house? When I saw the body?

"It wasn't a hallucination," Sophia's voice echoed in the empty house.

The furniture was gone.

I revised my thinking; the furniture was never there.

Sophia's suggestion began to sink in. "What?" I continued after the woman, "Wait." became, "Ow!" As I tripped on the toolbox in the entryway, unleashing a wave of dizziness.

As I straightened, my eye caught movement in the parlor.

Twain. A translucent mist settled around him.

He shook his head slightly. He put a hand to his temple and spotted me. A headache, probably.

"Oh hi," Twain said, "Didn't see you come in. Are you the interior designer?"

At the sight of him, intact and alive, boots splattered green with paint, my heart swelled. My breath caught in my throat. And then, "Just here to clean," I replied automatically.

"Let's go!" Sophia called from outside. "You can't save him."

Twain offered, "Not just."

He didn't hear Sophia. I returned the smile, "I'll be right back."

PART TWO: THE EDGE OF THE FOREST

CHAPTER 7

I trusted Sophia, and I couldn't say why. Every movement, every sound she made communicated intention, confidence. I wanted to follow her; I wanted to get into her expensive and sedate Lexus. But I had just enough will to insist on returning to my own car.

Dread sunk in as I settled into the driver's seat. Remembering my phone, I leaned down and felt the floor underneath the seat. I caught a corner of the phone with a finger, and carefully dragged it out. A quick tap on the screen and it was clear that the phone was dead.

"It's going around," I whispered. I clapped a hand over my mouth, shocked at the easy gallows humor. An involuntary giggle escaped. I shook myself. "Get it together."

I found my keys in my pocket. With a quick entreating glance to the heavens I inserted the key into the ignition and turned it.

Nothing.

I let go of the breath I had been holding.

Calmly, I turned the key back, waited another moment, and attempted to turn over the ignition.

Still nothing.

I could see her in my rear view mirror. Sophia's face expressed both patience and irritation as she looked on, watching me try and fail, repeatedly, to start my car. Our eyes connected and her glance slid away as though she had no interest in my activities.

With another steadying breath, I stepped out of the car. I leaned in to pop the hood, and affected the same casual posture Sophia maintained. Out of sheer stubbornness I leaned over the engine, fixing my eyes on each individual component and silently appraising its fitness.

I knew nothing about car engines. Every time I checked my oil, I googled it first.

Though I heard Sophia approach, and I saw her feet, her voice still startled me.

"Win," she began. I hit my head on the hood.

"Damn it!" I exclaimed, and silently, *that's what I get for pretending.*

"Win," she started again, "It is time to go."

I had to stop myself from taking a step closer to her. I straightened. I closed the hood. "Why would I leave with you? I don't know you."

"I am here to help you. You have attracted enough attention for today. We need to go."

I took a step toward Sophia and then realizing I was in her thrall, I took a step back. I sighed, I looked like an idiot and this wasn't even a job interview.

Her expression softened, almost. Her mouth turned up at the corners in an almost smile. "They may have noticed," she spoke quietly, kindly, firmly. "They may be on their way. Get what you need from your car and let's go."

I nodded. Not because she compelled me. But because I had no alternative.

Sophia waited by me as I complied. From my car I took the essentials and a few random items from the glove compartment, mostly to draw out the departure and exert some self-determination. But also, I wanted to look like I had something of value in my car to pack. I left my cleaning supplies. Surely they would be there when I returned.

Halfway to her car, her words sunk in.

"Who is they?"

She paused, made eye contact, and said, "To the car first."

And I heeded her quiet command.

She said nothing as we buckled in. *Her* car started with no difficulty. With its start, classic rock issued from the speakers, unapologetically loud; it surrounded me and held me in comfortable detachment. Her car was immaculate. It looked as though she had never dropped an open bag of chips on the passenger seat or accidently popped the lid off of her coffee while driving. Either, no one had ever consumed food in the vehicle, or she regularly scoured the interior of the car with a toothbrush. I resisted the temptation to check the glove compartment for discarded candy wrappers and extra napkins.

We were well on our way before I remembered I had questions.

"Wait a minute," I interjected, "Who is they?" And then I realized, "How did you know my name?"

Again, the almost smile. "You told me."

I searched back through our interactions. "No, I don't think I did," I nearly shouted over the music.

"I'm sure of it."

And, that made me feel certain she was right, even as I knew she was not. No use arguing. "Who is they?"

"Those who would hurt you."

"The person who killed Twain." But he had been dead for a long time.

"Possibly," Sophia nodded.

"You don't know?"

Sophia shook her head, "Not exactly."

"You're not going to tell me a whole lot, are you?"

Sophia spared her a glance, "Not yet. Do you need anything from your home?"

That gave me pause. "What? Yes. I live there, I need to live there."

"We'll go to your house."

I nodded. I let the music envelop me once more. Sophia's words seemed to be on a time delay. It was five minutes, perhaps more, before I asked, "How do you know where I live?"

Almost smile, "Would you believe that you told me?"

It didn't sound like a joke. And I wanted to believe her. "No," I returned firmly, more for myself than for her. For the first time, it occurred to me to wonder what was happening, why I was involved, and who the woman driving the car was.

"I'm Sophia," she replied. And I realized I had wondered all of that out loud.

"That's your name, not who you are."

"Point taken," she conceded. "Do you know who you are, Win?"

Did I? But out loud, "Yeah."

"Who are you, Win?"

I opened my mouth to respond, and realized I had no answer. It wasn't that I didn't know. In my mind, I knew. I just didn't have the words to explain. "I'm Win."

"Not so easy to do. Even when you know."

"Point taken," I echoed.

Sophia drove to my apartment on the quickest route, with no help from me. Questions formed firmly in my mind, but dissolved like sugar as soon as they reached my mouth.

She parked her car on the street. I let her follow me to my apartment.

It occurred to me that I should feel self-conscious about Sophia entering my small, shabby home. The building, once a stately single family residence had been converted into five apartments, three on the ground floor and two on the second floor. Time and neglect left the building with sagging floors, doors that didn't close completely, and drafty windows. My studio sat on the second floor, immediately off the stairs to the left. The front door entered into the kitchen, and a small dining table separated the kitchen from the living room. The living room extended out farther than the kitchen to accommodate a small alcove that acted as my bedroom. I felt relieved my unmade bed was hidden from Sophia's view.

The apartment had some character, maybe even charm. Still, Sophia had no place in such humble surroundings. And I didn't care.

Nor did she seem to care as she settled into my hand-me-down sofa.

I stood in my living room, struck silent and slack jawed as I considered my next actions. Pack. She advised me to pack.

"This is insane." At her glance, I realized, I said that out loud.

She seemed unaffected by the comment. "Win, I can leave. And you can find a way back to your car and your job and your life. And maybe you will be safe. And you will forget me." She stretched with a languid indifference that made me crave her interest. "I think if you do that, you will die, and there will be consequences to others that you are not ready to understand. It is your decision."

I let my eyes drift closed as I considered her words. I fought my desire to please her, and I tried to find my own voice. I spoke before I could think, "And that sounds even more insane." And though I felt instantly embarrassed by my response, I was proud to hear my own voice.

She stood, and I felt her disappointment. She leaned forward, firmly placing a card on my coffee table. She didn't look at me again until she reached the door. From the threshold she offered, "I'll wait in town as long as you are alive."

CHAPTER 8

The comment stayed with me: "I'll wait in town as long as you are alive."

It came upon me in unexpected moments. On hold with the tow company. Negotiating with a mechanic. But most profoundly, while explaining to a homeowner that I would be unable to resume the deep clean of their abandoned house until,

1. I had reliable transportation, and
2. They removed the 30 year old remains of a handyman.

Perhaps, I expected the existential dread in that last one.

Worse than that, the more time that passed, the more I questioned whether it happened at all.

I returned to Sophia's card, repeatedly. I never moved it, never touched it. But it pulled my gaze again and again. I couldn't call her, it was too absurd, too impossible. Still, she was the only person who could confirm my experience. Unless I invented her, too. I considered approaching one of my neighbors and asking if they could read the card to me, reassure me that Sophia was real, even if everything else was imagined.

The Twain situation differed from any other hallucination I'd known. I hadn't been this confused about reality since I was a child. By this point, I was used to it. I never discussed it. I could nearly always tell the difference between a hallucination and reality. The hallucinations distracted me from time to time, or upset me. To cover it I made up explanations for my unusual behavior, but I never admitted to the hallucinations.

My condition had been present my entire life. Some of my earliest memories never happened.

As a child, it didn't take long for me to learn that there were things that happened that only I could see. Soon, I learned that when I described what I saw to others it frightened them. At first, I believe they were afraid for me. My mother would explain it away, a wild imagination. Eventually, I saw it in my family's eyes, they were afraid of me. And I learned to keep it to myself, no matter what I saw. It became difficult to be sure about what was real, but it was safer than telling the truth. My family was too embarrassed or scared to seek a medical remedy. And I learned to guard my secret in order to protect myself. Over time it became easier to discern fantasy from reality.

But Twain challenged all of that.

The hallucinations always came with a cost. I often reacted to them before I realized they were imagined. I knew how it made me look to others. I reach for something that isn't there: Win's always so forgetful. I trip over nothing: Win is such a clumsy girl. I pause mid-conversation, startled by a horror only I can see: Win never can focus. The idiosyncrasies weren't great enough to inspire pity, they were just enough to keep people at arm's length.

At the house, for a moment, I believed that Twain might understand. He was the first person I ever *wanted* to talk to about my condition. Probably because he was the result of my condition.

That thought, *Twain never existed*, that hurt me. I needed to prove that he existed. He haunted me. I thought of him. I dreamt of him. I replayed our day together. I wanted it to be real.

If I did nothing, then eventually I would accept that I imagined it. All of it. Twain never existed. And if that were true, my experience in the house acted as the catalyst for a spiral of dominos that led me farther and farther from sanity. If Twain didn't exist, it meant that my condition worsened. And if I were getting worse, it meant I would continue to deteriorate until I could no longer separate imagination from truth. And there was no one I could turn to for help.

I was left with one alternative. It happened. Twain happened.

If I could find Twain, figure out who he was and where he belonged, then there was hope for me. Maybe I would stop seeing him in my dreams. Maybe I would recover. Maybe the spell would be broken and I would live in the world everyone else seemed to enjoy.

Sophia never strayed far from my mind. Her vague threats returned to me periodically. I felt overcome remembering how her presence seemed to take up more space than her body.

Maybe I would throw away the card, and forget the enigmatic figure who lingered in town as long as I was alive. I wondered, *could it be possible that Twain is real, and she is not?* Another impossible question, with only unsatisfying answers.

Twain. I decided, focus on finding Twain and everything would go back to normal. Normal didn't have a lot to recommend it, but it was better than losing touch with reality and ending up in state custody.

I didn't start looking right away. I stalled. I felt an obligation to report what I found, even though I didn't know if it was real. The mysterious Sophia seemed to corroborate my memory. And she must have been real because she gave me a ride. Hallucinations can't drive a car. Unless, of course, my hallucinations had graduated to delusions. Delusions could do just about anything. And that led me back to the possibility of an escalating mental illness. I chose to believe it happened, and to be safe, I kept it all to myself. Surely, I reasoned, my former employer would find the body and report it to the police. Then there would be a news report and an investigation that would settle the question once and for all.

I fully expected a visit from local police, that gave me an excuse to pause. Yet, after days, no one came. The absence of police intervention brought back the doubts. *There was no Twain, there was no Sophia, and soon there would be no Win left in my mind.* A thought that scared me more than Sophia's portends of my demise.

To protect myself from that, I chose to focus on Twain's plight. Dead, hidden, forgotten. Find Twain. Prove my sanity.

Junior detective it would be. I reasoned, I had a library card. How hard could it be?

CHAPTER 9

Very hard. It turned out, it was very hard to search for a man who may or may not have lived and/or died in the area, roughly thirty years ago, with only a first name.

The internet turned up nothing of use. So I began to search through a database of periodicals, newspapers from 30 years ago. I had to acknowledge, 30 years might be an estimate provided by a woman who might not exist. And it was all I had. It took three hours of scanning headlines before I found it.

LOCAL MAN MISSING.

It wasn't the first time I had come across a promising headline. But this time, his name caught my attention even before I scanned the article. I took a deep breath.

Twain.

I looked up, slowly exhaling, instructing my heart to slow, and my mind to clear. I was so engrossed in my research, the library patrons had all been replaced since I began. There were kids playing in the children's section, noisier than the library standard. The computers were nearly all available now, there was only one other patron, seated a few stations away. I had captured the attention of a woman in a ball cap sitting in a chair across the library. She had no books, but when I caught her watching, she grabbed a book from a nearby display and began idly thumbing through it. I rolled my eyes, *pretty aggressive people watching there.*

Feeling calmer, I returned to my monitor. I read the article.

Local man, Twain Myers, was reported missing last week after failing to report to a job site. Police have uncovered no evidence explaining his disappearance. His truck and his tools are also missing, leading police to question whether Twain left town on his own or was involved in an accident on the way to a job. The man's family believes he is the victim of foul play. They are asking for anyone with information that could help locate the man to report it to the county sheriff.

I looked up again, *does that include me? I might have information.* I shook myself. The paper was decades old. Maybe there was an open investigation, but the urgency was gone by now. I realized suddenly, "Twain was real."

My statement earned a glare from a passing gentleman. I glanced around apologetically.

The woman in the hat still watched me. Her book lay ignored in her lap. This time she didn't pretend it was accidental. Her direct stare made me uncomfortable. I considered leaving, but my elation at finding evidence of Twain was too great. I returned to my database.

I searched for a paper from the following day from the newspaper, hoping for a follow up on Twain's story. But there was none. Not for the following day or the day after that. Twain appeared in their final issue, it seemed. Out of curiosity, I searched the internet for the newspaper.

The search yielded immediate results. The day after the issue containing Twain's story, the building housing the publication burnt to the ground. The owners were locals who decided not to rebuild. I considered my options. I could look for him in larger newspapers. I could search for him online. Now I had a last name and date. That would help.

I began to type his name, but slowed as I felt someone sit beside me. The place was empty, there were plenty of seats, and they picked the only seat that was directly next to me. I glanced over surreptitiously.

The woman in the ball cap. I jumped.

She watched me with interest. "Hi," she said. "You've been at that awhile."

I stared back in surprise for several seconds. This was unusual behavior. I would have believed it was a delusion if I hadn't just confirmed Twain's existence and my mental fitness. Something about her felt off. "Yeah," I agreed. I stood, "But I'm done now." I closed the browser and picked up my backpack. Hastily I logged out of the computer, suddenly aware that I didn't want her to see what I researched.

Sophia's words reappeared in my mind, unwelcome, *I'll wait in town as long as you are alive.*

The woman followed me, "What did you find out? You looked positively captivated."

"Nothing," I insisted, hurrying my steps. I felt a headache forming in the back of my head.

I thought the woman would stop me or keep following me. Instead she called out, "See you around."

CHAPTER 10

I walked home from the library on high alert, aware that the woman might follow me home. I resisted the urge to take the most direct route, I wanted the security of my apartment. I also wanted to arrive safe and alone. I followed twists and turns and took myself well out of the way. I went so far as to duck into a store, and sneak out the service entrance in the back.

Then I started feeling silly. Maybe the woman was the threat that Sophia referenced. Maybe she had found my apartment and followed me to the library. In that case, after my time consuming detours, she was probably waiting for me there.

Or maybe I needn't be concerned at all. Maybe she was poorly socialized and wanted a friend. That made me rude and dismissive.

And then, of greatest concern, maybe she didn't exist at all.

It used to be so clear. The hallucinations looked different. After years of practice, I now noticed the quiet shroud of mist that enveloped them, almost imperceptible. But in the house it was different, furniture appeared and disappeared, all the time it looked real. I still didn't know if the house was empty or furnished. In the house Twain was alive and real, and then he was a body, rotting and forgotten in the basement, and then he was back, no mists, no haze, no distinction from the real world.

Eventually, I found myself in front of my apartment. A quick visual sweep revealed nothing of note. No strangers, no strange vehicles, nothing but the ordinary activity of the block.

In my apartment, I kicked off my shoes out of habit, but entered without bothering to offload my backpack. I took stock of the room. Everything remained as I left it. Coffee cup in the sink. A pile of books on the floor by the couch. Unfolded laundry overflowing the basket that peeked out from behind the wall that hid my bedroom from the room. Nothing to worry about here.

Sophia's card sat, placidly waiting for me. I stared at it and considered calling her.

My thoughts raced: *Is calling Sophia the right decision? Can she help me? Am I in danger? Was I followed here? Would I be putting Sophia in danger? Did Sophia send the woman to scare me? Am I overreacting? Is any of this real?*

I forced myself to sit and I practiced my breathing. I picked up Sophia's card and traced the letters. I set down her card and stared at it. I tried again to practice my breathing. The woman in the library had left me feeling restless and tense.

I placed my feet firmly on the floor. I closed my eyes and forced myself through a series of relaxation exercises. *Acknowledge the panic. Feel it. Feel my body relaxing.* Time passed slowly, but the anxiety ebbed, leaving a faint feeling of dread and resolve.

Sophia's card drew my eye, its very presence a provocation.

Now calm, I removed my backpack and held it in my lap. I took Sophia's card from the table. Without reading it, I shoved it into the side pocket. I wasn't ready to throw it away, but I thought it best I stop looking at it.

I lay back on the couch, cradling my bag in my arms. The texture of the bag felt real and ordinary, a comfort. I couldn't name it, or even describe the nature of it, but something was very wrong in my life.

With careful deliberation, I cataloged events starting with the house, the place where my normal unusual escalated to unrecognizably weird.

I arrived, the dizziness hit, and I tripped over Twain's toolbox. I heard him but didn't see him. And then he was there. He looked normal, no mist, fully present. We talked, we worked, we goofed off. In the afternoon, he split his lunch with me, an action that supported the working theory that he was real.

I walked myself through exploring the house together, discovering the cellar together.

I revisited the end with pain and great effort. I attempted a clinical approach. Recall the images of Twain, remain distant, gather information. I concentrated on remembering, and soon, I could see it with clarity. Almost as though I were back in the cellar. I breathed deeply, pulling the familiar smell of my apartment through my nose and into my lungs. I felt the fabric of the backpack against my skin. *Still here, still home.*

I watched Twain hit the floor of the cellar, remembering the way he lost his breath at the impact. I watched him fight the inevitable, and I felt a resurgence of my own desperation in that moment. I told myself, *I am a researcher, I am not there, I am watching a recording.*

In the end, for moments he was fully present, with me, completely. Then mist gathered around his body and he faded, disappearing completely, leaving me with his withering remains. And then he returned. Only to vanish again.

I shook my head to clear the memories. Twain appeared as a real person, mostly, but sometimes, Twain possessed all of the characteristics of a hallucination.

I gathered myself together and considered the possibilities. Three hypotheses began to form in my mind.

1. Twain was a hallucination from the start, and none of it happened.

If Twain was the product of my imagination, then he had never suffered. Also, if Twain didn't exist, it meant that my mental state had deteriorated significantly. Brief interludes of hallucination was reason for concern. Full blown delusions that lasted for hours was a life altering escalation of my condition. I turned to a more appealing alternative:

2. Twain was real and I imagined his demise and the corpse in the cellar.

This idea felt better than the first. It meant that Twain was alive and well, possibly a little disturbed by a brief interaction with a deranged house cleaner. But otherwise no worse for the wear. Of course, if Twain was real, and still alive, that meant that I invented a gruesome end for him, then visualized it twice. Additionally it meant that I conjured up a corroborating newspaper article at the library. In comparing my first hypothesis with my second, I couldn't decide which was worse for me. Either I subjected a stranger to imagined torture in my mind, or I created a character, specifically so I could torture and murder him in my mind. And then, a third possibility occurred to me.

3. Twain was real, and Twain was a ghost.

It felt like a revelation. Maybe I had it all wrong. Maybe, they weren't hallucinations at all. Maybe I could see ghosts, and maybe they could talk to me. Twain didn't know he was dead, and he was locked in an eternal cycle, reliving his murder again and again. Maybe he needed my help, to break the cycle, to find peace.

My resolve strengthened. My desire to bring his killer to justice swelled.

I set aside theories of profound mental health concerns, and focused on a new possibility. I could see ghosts. And at least one ghost needed my help.

Thoughts of ghosts preoccupied me for the rest of the day. If I could see the dead, and talk to them, that made me a medium. Untapped potential surged through me. I imagined a new future. My power was a vehicle for helping the departed to peace, and their families to closure.

Hours later, I remembered the woman in the library. I remembered Sophia. Were they real or were they apparitions? Perhaps they needed help as well. I shrugged it off. Sophia, at least, was alive. Unless ghosts could drive cars.

I slept hard that night, where Twain dominated my dreams. I relived memories that happened days before and some that had never happened at all, the things Twain would never experience himself.

I woke suddenly, too early. I thought a noise startled me awake, but I listened and heard nothing. I picked up my phone to check the time. Two in the morning.

It felt wrong in my room. My heart raced as I found my feet. I shoved my phone in the pocket of my sweatshirt. I crept along my bedroom wall, casting about for an improvised weapon. I grabbed a heavy hardcover book from my bedside table. It was the first attention the book had gotten and far from its intended purpose. But it was the best I could do.

Thump.

I jumped.

My eyes darted to the window. Probably not high enough to kill me, but likely to result in injury. To get there I would have to run through the living room, exposing myself to the intruder.

I looked around the room, gripping the book tightly. My bed was set back in an alcove off the living area. From it I could see the television console, but not the full living room.

From the main room, I heard shuffling, movement of some kind.

Impulsively I called, "I have a gun!" I did not have a gun, I had a book.

At that all noises ceased.

And I was left to wonder.

A hallucination? I didn't think so, no accompanying symptoms.

A hasty retreat? Maybe, but if so, it was a silent one.

An ambush? They might have a real weapon.

I thought, *maybe I can surprise them.*

I crept forward, slowly and carefully placing each step on the carpet. I took each breath deeply and deliberately, calming my body and preparing myself for what lie around the corner.

I silently begged the floor to respond to my steps with the discretion the situation demanded, no creaks, no sound at all. I brandished the hardback above my head as I slinked along the wall, around the corner.

I paused there, scanning the room for the intruder.

I didn't have enough furniture to hide his substantial silhouette. He crouched near the dining table, near the window. He remained still, he hadn't seen me yet.

Frantically, I considered two options. I could attempt to club him on the head, or I could run for the door. Impetuously, I decided to do both.

I rushed him, swinging down as hard as I could with the book. I couldn't make out a face, but I assumed he was surprised because he made no effort to defend himself. The force of the blow staggered him, and though it wasn't enough to do any real damage, it did serve to knock him into the small, but mighty kitchen table.

I dropped the book on him and ran to the door.

As I raced past the couch, I had the presence of mind to grab my backpack.

I ran with no destination in mind. I traveled for several blocks before I noticed that I did not take my shoes. They waited for me by the door, where I had left them.

I slowed to a walk as I realized that I was likely clear of the danger in the apartment. Instead, I was half a mile from home, in bare feet, wearing pajama bottoms and a zippered hoodie. I had my backpack, which meant I had my wallet. I felt tremendously lucky that I had my phone. And, I remembered, I had Sophia's card.

My path had taken me out of the residences of my immediate neighborhood and toward a commercial section of town. Here there were big box stores and chain restaurants. The night lingered on, and few cars drove by. I noticed a few drivers glance in my direction. They might not be able to see my shoeless state, but my Kermit the frog pajama pants stood out.

As I walked on my bare feet, I developed a plan. I believed there was an intruder in my house, but I didn't know for sure. The lines between reality and hallucination were becoming so blurred, I couldn't trust my own senses. If I called the police, and I was wrong, I worried for what could happen next. I didn't think they could institutionalize me; I wasn't dangerous. But I didn't know for certain and I didn't want to risk it. I knew I had to call Sophia. I began to formulate an argument, why she should return, how she might help me, and what I might be able to do to help her in return.

I found myself in the parking lot of a Walmart. Open twenty four hours, and possibly filled with strange sights like myself. I had enough cash to buy a pair of flip flops. It was better than nothing. I waited as long as I could stand it before fishing Sophia's card out of my backpack.

When I called Sophia, I decided not to mention the encounter.

I said, "Sophia? I think we should talk."

"Are you at home?" She asked, her manner all business.

I sat on a bench, at a bus stop adjacent to Walmart. "No. I can send you my location."

"I'll be there soon," was her reply. And she hung up. I felt a small stab of disappointment. I prepared an argument. I wanted the chance to present it. Still, I couldn't argue with the results. I sent her my location and I waited.

Waiting increased my anxiety. I dug my nails into the bench. I forced myself to practice my breathing. I picked at Sophia's card and worked the edges until they frayed.

Sophia pulled up in her sensible, luxury vehicle. I took a deep steadying breath. She exited the car and sat next to me on the bench.

Calm settled over me instantly. Sophia. She made a face that almost smiled,

"I have questions," and before she interjected I added, "And I don't want any of your Jedi mind tricks."

She considered that. "Jedi? Is that a yoga term? I know yoga is popular these days."

"Um, no."

She shrugged gracefully. "Would you like to conduct the interview here? Or shall we find some breakfast."

My stomach rumbled, more from the temptation than real hunger.

"Sure," I muttered. She stood and I followed her back to the car.

"Excellent," her manner expressed patience, and maybe indulgence.

We said nothing as she drove to a nearby chain restaurant. We settled into a booth. Sophia ordered a sizable breakfast and coffee. I duplicated her order, mostly because I didn't want to read the menu or divert my thoughts from my purpose.

While we waited, Sophia asked, "What are your questions?"

I opened my mouth to begin, then forgot my questions. I focused, there were questions. I had questions. "Damn it! I said no mind tricks!"

"Very well," Sophia sighed, a mischievous twinkle in her eye, "You set that up yourself. You seem agitated. Did something happen?"

"No," I replied quickly, "I don't know." I didn't like lying to her. "No," I said resolutely.

"As you say. I sense urgency."

I nodded.

"Also, you appear to be wearing your pajamas."

"Something happened," I conceded.

She nodded again. "And you feel you can't go home?"

"Correct," I confirmed.

"I suggest you prioritize your questions. It seems time may not be on your side." *Your side.* Not our side? "You are the one in danger, Win."

It felt as though there was a reader board on my forehead, displaying every thought.

I pushed the fog aside. "How do you do that?"

"How do I do what?" It was impossible. And still, I grew more confident that she could read my thoughts. And because she appeared to be reading my thoughts, the request for clarification annoyed me.

You know damn well what I mean. I thought as loud as I could, *READ MY MIND.*

She sighed delicately. "How do you listen?"

Answering questions with questions seemed to be the basis of our relationship. I asked, "What do you mean? I just listen. That's how I listen."

Her reply was a single, smug head nod.

"Fine." It wasn't fine, but what alternative did I have? I asked instead, "How do you do the enthrallment thing? Where I forget what I am thinking and do as you say?"

Sophia considered the question. "That takes more effort. It feels like listening, in reverse, with more intensity."

"So, talking?"

"No." She leaned in, "Are these really the answers you want?"

"No," I admitted. "What happened in that house?"

My question was interrupted by the arrival of breakfast. Sophia thanked the server, then immediately dug into the food. As prim as she was, she ate with big, grateful bites, as though she was starving.

After a few minutes she offered, "You were there. You tell me."

I leaned in, "Was it real?"

"I think so." Her voice almost sounded kind. She delayed her bite, her fork suspending a slice of pancake halfway between her mouth and her plate. "You have a gift, Win."

I shook my head, suddenly recalling hallucination after hallucination, a parade of horrors. "Whatever it is, it is not a gift."

"Call it what you like. But they are not hallucinations."

"Can you read my mind?" It was unsettling that she seemed to be able to access my thoughts at will.

"I think so, when you think loudly. And often you do think loudly." Not a satisfying answer.

I forced myself to breathe. Inhale four seconds, exhale six seconds. The whole conversation was too incredible to believe. But I believed it. I believed her. "I can see ghosts," I agreed.

"No," Sophia dismissed my conclusion without consideration. "I believe you are looking into the past. If you are who I think you are."

My legs weakened and I was grateful to be seated already. "That's impossible." It felt like the right thing to say, even though moments before I was convinced I could talk to dead people. "Who do you think I am?"

"I think you are the seer. I might be wrong, it's not as though they label you at birth. Time will tell."

"Okay," I began, "Let's pretend this is real. There are seers who can see the past. And maybe that could explain a lot, but I didn't just see the past. I talked to Twain, I interacted with him." My nervous hands wrang the life out of my napkin.

"There is one seer who can see the past," She informed me pedantically.

At her diversion, I grew louder, "He pushed me, I ate his lunch!"

"Yes, that is very strange. I wouldn't have guessed that was possible." She watched me for a minute before suggesting, "Why don't you set down the napkin. It doesn't seem to help."

I twisted it several more steps in defiance. When she didn't seem to care, I abandoned the failed rebellion and dropped the tortured napkin. I whispered, "He was a ghost."

"Oh no," she chuckled in condescension, "ghosts aren't real."

I frowned. "Fine. I'm a time traveler."

Not condescending this time, but skeptical, "Unlikely. I don't believe I would have seen you if you had left the present."

"Okay. A seer, but one who does more than see the past."

"It would appear so." Her manner conveyed patience, compassion even, "I understand this is quite an adjustment for you. But I would like to remind you: Time may not be on *our* side." I noted the switch to our. "If I can find you so easily, others will be able to find you as well."

"Others did," I agreed. But it remained to be seen why someone would want to find me. I asked, "Why would anyone want to find me? I'm not hiding."

"You should be." I didn't believe it was meant to frighten me, but it did. "Are you ready to go?"

"One more question," I insisted.

Her relaxed posture held, but her eyes narrowed. "Proceed."

"What are you?"

CHAPTER 11

"I'll tell you on the road." Is how she replied. But she didn't, not right away.

Sophia asked if I wanted to return to the apartment before we left town. I didn't hesitate. "No," I replied.

She nodded. "Perhaps, we could stop at a store. For a change of clothes."

I hesitated. I didn't have the money for a shopping spree and I worried the only option was to return to the house. Where an angry man with a lump on the head might be waiting.

"I insist," she added. "I owe it to you, you'll be helping me solve a mystery."

"A mystery?" I asked. I thought it was a pretext to buy the clothes for me. But I accepted her explanation, because I had no alternative.

"Later," she assured me.

She insisted we start with shopping. I insisted that we choose a store within my typical price range. We agreed on Target. Sophia tried to talk me into every little thing I touched and every item I looked at for more than ten seconds. To avoid the pressure, I kept my hands at my sides and my eyes off the shelves. After thirty minutes of shopping I had enough clothes and toiletries to fill my backpack.

As we drove out of town, I silently said goodbye to the plant that would not survive my absence, admittedly it wasn't likely to survive my presence, either. Watching the familiar fade into new landscapes I thought about leaving my life behind for a mysterious trip of indeterminate length. And I realized how much, or in my case how little, there was worth holding on to in my life. I worked for myself, and most of my friendships and relationships were too short to lead to lasting attachment. So there was no one to call when we stopped to put gas in the car. That didn't stop me from calling an old friend I hadn't spoken to in months. When she didn't answer, I left a pathetic, weird message about how I would be out of town for a few weeks, helping my friend Sophia. That was done for Sophia's benefit. I wanted her to believe that I would be missed. But I didn't know if it was meant to dissuade her from killing me or merely that I wanted her to think there was someone who cared.

The summer hadn't quite taken hold yet, as the late afternoon sun crawled toward the horizon it withdrew light and warmth. While I watched Sophia pump the gas a wave of apprehension swept through me; I shivered.

I ostensibly blamed the chill that arrived with the evening, conveying my silent explanation by rubbing my arms and zipping my sweatshirt. My new traveling companion disregarded temperature completely, appearing perfectly comfortable in her thin, sleeveless dress. In the car, Sophia did not attempt to make conversation.

I battled a growing sense of distance from my real life. The farther we got from home, the greater my relief. It upset me that I discarded my entire life with ease. It upset me that I wanted to hold onto a lonely, unsatisfying life out of obstinance. It upset me that I still could not say with certainty that any of this was real. I attempted to clear my thoughts. I instructed my brain to notice physical sensations, to pay attention to the road, to refuse entry to all disturbing thoughts.

I watched Sophia drive.

Sophia handled a car like she took the driver's manual to heart. Hands at ten and two. Exact car lengths ahead, continually adjusted based on the driving conditions. Even her speed matched precisely to the legal limit, varying only as instructed by posted speed limit signs.

Noticing Sophia's idiosyncrasies unnerved me.

"So, where do we start?" I asked, eager to break the silence. I hoped the conversation chased away the disquiet. "I felt like I was getting close to something at the library." *Close to getting killed,* I thought. Realizing my thought might have been louder than intended, I snuck a glance at Sophia to see if she had heard me.

Sophia's responding look contained equal parts contempt and bewilderment. "No." She looked back to the road.

I thought, *No, not getting close to something. Or no, not close to getting killed?* I bit my lips closed as though they could contain the reckless thoughts.

Sophia said, "I know someone. A sort of private investigator."

Joy coursed through my chest. "We can find Twain's killer!"

Sophia began with compassion, "You are the priority, and I need to know who is looking for you."

I thought, *More like, who found me.* I said, "But I want to find Twain's killer."

She continued with a hint of mockery, "We will get to your star crossed lover melodrama when the time is right."

"Hey! That's mean." I was tired and defensive.

She shrugged.

I added, "And I just met him."

Another shrug.

"And he has a lot to do with why I called you. And he is dead. So no melodrama."

At that she sighed. "I believe what you experienced at the house is related to the threat against you."

"You think whoever killed Twain, wants to kill me?" That gave me pause. If everything Sophia had said was true, then Twain died three decades earlier. How old would his killer be? And what did any of it have to do with me? Sophia said I could see the past, did that mean that the past could see me? Was that why someone broke into my apartment?

Sophia answered with a hesitant nod, "I think that is likely." That stopped me outright. Which question was she answering?

I turned from Sophia to the car window, leaning my head against the cool glass. I watched the city fade into the suburbs, then the suburbs deteriorate into suburban sprawl. Houses became sparser and trees denser until I felt swallowed by the forest. Sophia's steady and stoic presence eased my rising panic. We were nowhere. Coasting sensibly toward a mysterious contact who appeared to live in a remote wilderness.

"Why does a private investigator live so far from everything?" In the dim light of the car, I saw Sophia roll her eyes. That emboldened me to continue with, "Doesn't he need to live in a city? Wear a trench coat? Carry a camera with a big flashbulb?"

"I believe I said, he is a sort of private investigator, not a film noir gumshoe." I deserved that. "And, he doesn't like to be around people, for the most part. Nor will he tolerate an inquisition. So try not to speak to him."

I took this bit of advice personally. "You are telling me, we are visiting a detective-like hermit, who doesn't like to answer questions and probably won't want to talk to us." For clarity, I added, "To get information."

"Yes," she sighed in relief, seemingly glad I finally understood.

I muttered my reply, "Good thing you waited until we're in the middle of nowhere to share that bit of information."

CHAPTER 12

Our enigmatic pseudo-sleuth lived in a clearing at the end of a long gravel drive. In the center of the clearing stood a well-kept camper, illuminated by whimsical rows of string lights arranged around a short wooden deck. A wide variety of potted plants clustered around each side of the door. A pair of Adirondack chairs completed the charming vignette, each placed precisely along a corner of a colorful rug before an attractive gas fire pit.

We stopped a few yards from the deck next to a sturdy looking pick-up truck. Sophia's face remained impassive as she turned off the car and left the vehicle. I followed without invitation. The yard surrounding the camper was neatly kept, and I could make out a garden just beyond it. "Do you think it is too late?" I asked. I feared what waited within the camper, and our previous conversation left me nervous and irritable. I wanted to be anywhere else, so I offered the excuse, "It is sort of late for visiting."

Sophia charged forward and knocked briskly on the door. "No."

I could hear his approach. My fists clenched, a sense of disquiet gripping me like the biting night air.

The door opened and my heart fell into my stomach.

Just within stood the most beautiful human I had ever seen. He was the last thing I expected. His already luminous face took advantage of the lambent glow of the deck party lanterns, to devastating effect.

Sophia smiled, fully, "Hello George."

He, George, with the face of a god, took Sophia's hand in both his. He returned her smile. He opened his mouth, but words did not follow. His glance slid past Sophia, and he locked eyes on me. The smile faded, though he remained still, I felt him retreat. I had just enough presence of mind to think, *he really doesn't like people.*

"It's fine, George," Sophia reassured him. "I doubt she is entirely human. George, this is Win."

OUT OF THE WAY THINGS

I felt my breath abandon my lungs with no plan to return. I grasped for a thought, a response, but instead I stared slack jawed at Sophia's casual revelation.

"Win," Sophia turned her attention to me. "Close your mouth, you are making everyone uncomfortable." I scowled at Sophia. Without acknowledging me, Sophia returned to George for an exchange of pleasantries. From her, polite questions and well wishes, from him, small smiles, inquisitive glances, and meaningful eye contact. I tried to listen to Sophia, but my mind raced, every question that began to form was interrupted by the phrase, "not entirely human."

Silence brought me back to the conversation. I realized, both Sophia and George were staring at me expectantly. Like they awaited the answer to a question. I shook my head, an effort to clear it. Internally, I practiced a sophisticated, *pardon me, I was miles away*, but I said, "Huh?"

"Would you care for a drink?" Sophia asked.

"Uh, yeah, sure," I managed. The stress of the day pressed down on me, sensations, jagged and vitriolic writhed under my skin.

George gestured to the two chairs, an invitation to sit. Sophia took a chair and I followed suit. George disappeared into the camper.

"Pull yourself together, Win" Sophia softly suggested, smooth and calm.

I whispered too, but not smooth, not calm, "Not entirely human?!"

"Your timing, Win, you've had all day to ask questions. We can discuss it later." Her gentle admonishment and dismissive tone incited the rage building within my chest. I took a few steadying breaths, preparing to unleash a diatribe that would set her straight.

But George reappeared. And he was not alone. He carried two wooden folding chairs under one arm, two beers in one hand, and two glasses in the other. The woman who accompanied him carried a tray of snack foods, meats and cheese and crackers, artfully arranged. I appreciated the effort. The woman was as ordinary as George was extraordinary. Her plain face wasn't enough of anything to be noteworthy. The woman set the tray down and Sophia stood to greet her, embracing her briefly.

"Hello, Jan," She smiled. "I'd like to introduce you to Win."

Jan returned her smile, "Good to see you, Sophia. Nice to meet you." She said to me, I couldn't place Jan's dialect; I was still distracted by George's objectively beautiful form, though I could now form thoughts unrelated to his face while looking directly at him. He was a large man, he had to duck through his trailer door, but on approach he seemed less than he should be. His movements were as small as he could make them, his shoulder hunched into an apologetic stance. As though he cultivated insignificance. A coping mechanism, I imagined.

George set the beers down with the glasses on the small side table, he arranged his own chair, then carefully poured each beer into a glass. He gave the first to me, then kept the second. Sophia and Jan abstained, it seemed.

The kind gesture took the edge off my fury, and I offered a quiet, "Thank you." He nodded. With my anger cooling, I began to notice the temperature again and thought with longing about my jacket back in the car.

Nearly as quickly as I thought it, George reached forward to start the gas fire pit in front of us.

"Does everyone read minds now?" It burst out of me, "Is that what I should expect?" My outburst startled George, and drew Sophia's attention. Jan ignored me.

"Win, your teeth are chattering." Sophia pointed out. "Everything you think, shows on your face. You have the most expressive face I have ever seen."

"Oh, yeah, sorry," I wasn't sure why I apologized, but it seemed the correct response. "Thank you," I added, indicating the fire. For a man who hated people, he was quite hospitable. He offered the slightest smile in response. It was breathtaking. I shook it off, hoping it looked like an energetic shiver.

Jan smiled at me, like she knew the truth and empathized.

Sophia's serenity folded around us all. My wrath settled down, remaining a quiet buzz in the back of my mind. We sat in companionable silence for a few minutes. George and I sipped beer. The warmth of the fire on my face and the alcohol in my throat offered additional comfort.

Sophia began with a sociability I found a little surprising. In my experience, Sophia cut right to the chase, never wasting time with small talk when there was business to discuss.

"It's good to see you here, Jan. How long are you visiting?" As Sophia spoke, Jan leaned toward her, watching her closely.

Jan turned her smile to George, who blushed prettily. "I moved in last month. It was the only way to make George learn sign language," Jan grinned. And I realized it wasn't an accent or a dialect, Jan couldn't hear, she was reading Sophia's lips.

In response to Jan's comment, George's hands moved carefully through a series of gestures.

Jan interpreted, "He says he was already learning."

"It seems you have improved a great deal," Sophia generously recognized.

Jan smiled, she smiled often and warmly. "I take it you're here for business; it's not a social call?"

"Unfortunately, you are correct." Gently, Sophia introduced the topic, "We've come to you for help, George."

George nodded. His expression was open, I interpreted him as willing.

"I believe that Win is in danger. Because of what she is."

The *"what"* struck my ear harshly. George nodded again, in agreement or just to indicate he heard. He looked at Jan and signed.

"Do you think she is connected to the others?" Jan's sweet voice gave life to George's question. I felt Sophia's tranquility sliding away. The hum of dark emotion grew louder inside of me.

I interrupted, "Wait, what others? What does that mean?"

Sophia extended a hand toward me, a stone striking me silent. But my composure splintered, glass marred by a sharp web, radiating from the impact. Sophia explained, "Someone out there wants a seer."

George nodded again, this time I sensed he knew already. Again he signed to Jan, and again, she spoke for him, "You think that is unrelated to the others?"

Sophia shook off the question, "I don't have any reason to believe that." Sophia leaned in and took the conversation back to her chosen path. Her intensity blanketed us all. "Have you heard anything, conversations about the seers, is there anything you can share?"

My self-control shattered. "Hold on," I interrupted for the second time, George flinched. "What others? I want to know."

"Nothing to be concerned about," Sophia's tone conveyed that she found my question tedious.

"I *am* concerned," I stood, startling George again, and gaining Jan's full attention. "*And* now I'm mad. *And* I am tempted to walk off into the woods, because I have had enough." My voice raised with each statement. The flood gates were open, and I continued. "I have no idea where we are, and I will probably get lost and die in the forest. But that option is looking better and better all the time!"

I thought Jan was proud. Sophia looked annoyed. George seemed empathetic.

Tentatively, George signed a response.

Jan interpreted, "If it is even possible Win is connected, she should know."

I sensed Sophia's reluctance. She took a moment, took hold of her own emotions. I felt her control return. "Please, sit, Win."

I sat. Angrily. The effect of her presence, cool and serene, attempted to assert its influence on me. I resisted, holding on to my displeasure, even as my body relaxed.

"George and I have been tracking some disappearances, people like you who have gone missing. Not seers, but humans with gifts. Possibly, there have been a few murders that may be connected as well. We suspect there is a ritualistic element to the deaths. I don't think it has anything to do with you."

I stared between them, open mouthed, for an indeterminate amount of time. First there were no thoughts. I forgot I was trying to stay angry. Without warning, thoughts tumbled together through my mind and out of my mouth. "Someone broke into my apartment. Is this what happened to Twain? Why do you think it *isn't* connected to me? Why didn't you tell me? Maybe it was the woman at the library. You should have told me."

"This is why I didn't want to tell her," Sophia explained to George. To me she said, "Slow down, Win. There is no evidence that any of that is connected to you. Twain died decades ago, and the disappearances began six months ago. I didn't tell you because I have no solid evidence that it has anything to do with you."

"How stupid do you think I am?" Her expression indicated that she weighed answering the question. Before she could interject, I continued, "People like me are disappearing and being murdered. Someone is looking for me and found me. But really, there is just no chance these things are related?"

Sophia shrugged, "There is a chance." She dismissed me again, "I think your situation is different. Not that you couldn't be kidnapped by the same group of people, I am sure they would take you if they had the opportunity. I don't believe they are hunting you specifically."

Jan and George watched the exchange with interest, popping snacks into their mouths like they were at the theater.

"What a relief. They would abduct and murder me, but it's good to know it's not personal."

If Sophia sensed the sarcasm, she elected to ignore it. "Not personal at all. But you would be very useful in the wrong hands, and that puts you in danger. George has heard rumors."

George's eyes widened in worry. He wanted no part of this fight.

Sophia continued, "Inquiries have been made about seers. Are they real? Where are they? The only way I can keep you safe is by finding out who wants you and why."

"So it's just a coincidence that we met. While you were investigating serious crimes against people like me?"

"Yes," She smiled slightly, I could almost hear her thinking, *finally, she gets it.* "I would say it was fate, but yes, you can call it a coincidence." I shook my head in disgust. I had no more thoughts or words, the surrounding forest seemed closer than before, encroaching on our sanctuary, held off only by the blaze of the edison bulbs strung around us in a flimsy ring of protection. I inched closer to the fire. Sophia returned her attention to George. "George, if you have any information that would help, I would be grateful."

He sighed. Reflexively, I moved my chair a little closer to him. He noticed and shot me a nervous glance. He remained quiet for several minutes. I thought he might talk. Instead, his hands moved slowly, deliberately.

He spoke through Jan's voice, "Rumors aren't enough. You need prophecy."

"No," Sophia said.

George appeared more nervous than before. First he looked to Jan. He raised his hands, but lowered them almost immediately. I thought, *he doesn't want her to know.* George leaned closer to Sophia.

"The witch," he whispered.

For a moment, my mind went blank. I saw Sophia's look, serious, almost angry. She talked to him, I heard her words, but couldn't comprehend them. I didn't hear him respond, but she paused as though she were listening. Jan looked annoyed, they were leaving her out of the conversation. I would be irritated by that as well. I thought about objecting on her behalf, but that might feel more like condescension than solidarity.

I realized I was in a stupor when Sophia stood.

"Are we leaving?" I asked.

Sophia wrinkled her nose at me. "Yes," her tone informed me that this had been established already.

I stood. "Thank you," I told George. To Jan I said, "Nice to meet you. Thanks for the snacks."

I followed Sophia, without hesitation, as though she held me on a string.

George stopped me, placing a hand on my arm. I looked up into his serious face. This time I didn't melt meeting his eyes. He held up a finger, then hurried into the trailer. I turned to Sophia. She shrugged. Jan watched the scene, only a little interested, still bothered by the exclusion.

George returned with a slip of paper. He held it out to me, and I took it, still looking between them in confusion. He nodded goodbye to Sophia, spared me a concerned look, then returned to his undersized home, with his angry girlfriend.

The paper read: *George. Text only. Just in case.* Followed by his phone number.

CHAPTER 13

"George is nice."

"Yes," Sophia agreed, "He is."

"He doesn't talk much."

"No," Sophia agreed, "He does not."

"Why not?" I asked.

"That is his story to tell."

"How can he tell it, if he doesn't talk?" Sophia smiled at my question, but said nothing. "He is also not in this car," I said to the window. I turned and watched his home grow smaller with distance until it was a dim, beckoning light in the dark forest surrounding us. "He thinks something bad is going to happen to me."

"Hmm." I didn't find her answer reassuring.

"Is George human?" I wanted to ask a different question.

"No." She confirmed.

Even though I suspected her answer, I gasped. Spoken so plainly, like I had asked about any basic demographic fact.

"Other than being impossibly beautiful, he looked human. So what is he then?" I couldn't accept what she was saying, but I wanted to hear more.

"If he wanted you to know he would have told you."

I hated that it was a fair response, George's kindness shamed me into letting the matter of his species go. "Are you human?"

"No." Just as matter of fact. Before I could ask she added, "I am not mortal. Let's leave it there for now." She spared me a look that stopped my follow up question in my throat.

"What about Jan? She is nice. Is she human?"

Sophia considered it for a moment, "Yes, I believe so."

"But she knows about George," I surmised.

"Yes."

I guessed again, "And about you."

"I imagine she knows I am not human."

I changed direction, "You doubt that I am entirely human."

"Win, people who are entirely human can't see into the past. That is not a gift of mortality." Anticipating my next move, she continued, "I don't know exactly what you are. There is speculation that seers are descendants of the Oracles. You are not the first of your kind. Try not to fixate on this. Many people are only partially human and they never even know."

"There are Oracles? Could we go see an Oracle?"

She shook her head, "I cannot promise that. No one has seen an Oracle in centuries. They may be gone." She took her eyes from the road, her driving remained steady. "An Oracle would be helpful, but your lineage doesn't matter. You are a seer. That we know. Once we have answers, once you are safe, you can pursue genetic testing."

"They test for this!?" My jaw dropped.

Sophia looked back to the road, "No."

"The Oracles are gone. Does that mean dead?"

My question earned a shrug. "Not necessarily. Is that really what you want to know?" Sophia read me with ease.

"A witch?" I asked. "There are witches."

"I'm afraid so," Sophia turned contemplative, solemn. She was always sober in her demeanor, but rarely serious in her tone. An unwelcome fear rose in my throat.

"What is a witch going to do for us? Cast some spells, I guess?" Even to me it seemed like we were grasping at straws.

"One spell in particular. Most witches, real witches can cast a spell to Read. Reading isn't an exact science, but it may help us find the threat to you."

"This isn't just regular reading, right? This is some sort of magical reading?" I never knew anymore.

"It is a magical reading, yes." Sophia confirmed, patiently. "George believes we need prophecy to learn more, not investigation. The witch will be able to see the threads of fate that connect to you. If someone has a purpose for you, a prophecy might tell us what that is. Only a witch can force a prophecy. I don't like it. But it will be worth it if I get enough information to find the threat against you."

"So we are going to visit a witch."

Sophia turned to face me, "Before we go, you need to understand," her voice was low and serious, "We are bound for the forest. Filled with shadows and monsters. The witch is only the beginning. It will be dangerous. Are you prepared?"

I definitely wasn't prepared. It occurred to me, given our conversations so far, she might mean actual monsters. I couldn't give that terror voice, instead I asked, "Do you mean a literal forest?"

She sighed, "Gods, I hope not. I am not going to sleep on the ground. I quite like this jacket." She brushed invisible dust from the arm of her stylishly tailored jacket.

"It is a really nice jacket," I agreed. "Sophia, this is a lot. Seers, witches, oracles, whatever the hell George is. Not entirely human. Kidnaping. Murder." I practiced my breathing. Decisively, I informed her "I need to go home. I can't just accept this as real, because you say so. I'm sorry for Twain, if everything you said is true, it is my fault he is dead. But I can't really help him. I'm a house cleaner."

"Why do you say that? Why do you say it is your fault? It happened before you were born."

"But I was *there*, Sophia. Twain hid me in the basement. He didn't have time to hide, he wasn't willing to run away and leave me. It is *my* fault he died."

Sophia met my eyes. I saw worry in her face. Typically, sustained eye contact with Sophia felt like falling into a pool of her will. But this time, I didn't feel the tug of her influence. Just her empathy, her uncertainty. "It's not your fault." Before I could object she added, "And I do not believe the kidnapping and the murder are related to your situation."

"But they could be. And you just want me to trust all of this, and follow you."

"You deserve to understand," she decided, "to make an informed decision."

She convinced me with a story.

CHAPTER 14

She began, "When I was young, my father told me the story of Maat. I don't know if it is true, I asked many times; he told me, many times, 'it is as true as it needs to be.'" She smiled at my grimace, a real smile. "And you think I am difficult."

I waited for her to continue. She drew in a deep breath and continued in a hypnotic tone. "Maat arrived in the world. It saw two different creatures who lived side by side but were blind to each other. One creature was a being of the Mists, the other a being of the Earth. Maat loved each of them and decided to bestow gifts of eternal life. Maat gave the beings of the Earth the ability to create life, versions of themselves who live on after death, children. It named them mortals.

"Maat wished to offer a gift of equal measure to the beings of the Mists. But, the beings of mist shifted between worlds. They could not care for new life and remain true to their nature. So Maat made a gift of Its own nature: immortality. With this gift the beings of mist would have no end to their lives. It named them immortals.

"Maat saw balance in this resolution and It lost a bit of itself, It was depleted by the loss. The mortals and immortals continued to live side by side. But with immortality, came awareness. The immortals could see the mortals, now. It was the immortals' nature to interfere. At first the immortals influenced the mortals in trivial ways, but their influence grew, to Maat's dismay. The immortals were hungry to understand the mortals. Over the millennia, as their knowledge grew, so did envy. One immortal, a favorite of Maat's, grew so envious that he sought to learn the great secret of mortality. The favored immortal took advantage of Maat's weakened state, he tricked Maat so that he might steal the secret of progeny given only to the mortals. He wished to master the gift, to share it with his own kind. His success was also his downfall.

"Maat was enraged. It did not have the strength to destroy the immortal or to take back Its gift. Instead, It named the immortal 'The Deceiver.' Maat banished him from the Mists, binding him to the Earth, immortal still, but capable of mortal death. The Deceiver offered the gift to his immortal allies. Those who accepted were cast out, Maat called them the Exiles, and doomed them to share The Deceiver's punishment.

"The Deceiver's gift proliferated among the Exiles. Many entangled themselves in the affairs of mortals, some were worshiped as gods, some feared as devils. And they created a new generation of Exiles. Earth bound and cursed from birth. Maat faded from the worlds, until only the Old Ones remembered him, The Deceiver and his contemporaries who had seen The Mists."

"And if not for The Deceiver's betrayal, neither you nor I would exist."

CHAPTER 15

I believed her story, even as doubts and questions crowded my mind. "How did your father learn this story?"

"He was there, it is his story, I take him at his word, more or less."

"Your father is The Deceiver?"

"As he tells it. Difficult to know what is literally true, what is half true, and what is metaphor with him. I haven't known him to outright lie, despite the name." She shrugged dismissively. "I know this is true: I am immortal born, to two parents, both Exiles. You are mortal born, but somewhere in your family history, there is an immortal. My guess, one of The Sisters. It is a rumor, a seer descended from an ancient Oracle. There are stories, but no certainties. And I am not a historian, I don't know much about it."

"How old are you?" If the story was to be believed her father was thousands of years old.

"Old. Very old by your standards."

"Then why don't you know the history?" I demanded.

"I witnessed history, I did not study it. If I wasn't there, I likely don't know. Would you like me to quiz you on current events around the world?"

"Point taken." I let the story sit between us for several minutes, before asking, "Why did you tell me all of that?"

"Win, there are those who see us, progeny of immortals, as abominations. A threat to the order in the universe established by Maat. I have been tracking some of these zealots, but they hide in shadows, they strike and disappear. You are the only one of your kind, a seer who sees the past, and you would be a powerful weapon in their arsenal. If they let you live. You must decide if you want to continue. You can go home. But you are who you are. And I fear that your fate will find you, wherever you hide."

"How do you know they aren't the same people who are kidnapping people like me? If they want me dead. It seems like you have your answer."

Sophia shook her head. "I don't know. It seems logical, but somehow, it doesn't fit. There is more to it."

"But how do you know that?" I insisted.

"The zealots are almost all humans. They are well organized, but reckless, and…" She seemed at a loss for words, "…human."

"I don't understand what that means." I lay my head back against the seat and closed my eyes. I pushed away the confusion and reached for indifference.

"Whoever is abducting people, I'm almost certain they are not human. If I believed there was a connection, I would pursue it. It would be quite convenient, to be honest. I don't have endless time to take a detour through your crisis."

"Aren't you immortal? Sounds like endless time to me." My tone communicated my increasingly sullen attitude. "I don't need your help, you know." I did, but I didn't want to need her help, especially as it became more and more clear that helping me burdened Sophia.

"You do. And I need to help you."

I let go of the argument. Fatigue began to replace all other feelings in my body, and I temporarily surrendered the will to resist.

We sat in silence for some time. She continued our path out of the forest, returning to the highway for another hour before calling an end to the day. We stopped at a non-descript motel near the highway. She went in alone and returned with two room keys. "We're right there," She pointed across the courtyard. We took our bags from the trunk and walked to our rooms.

Before I disappeared into my room she said, "Think about it. I won't try to influence you. Tomorrow, we secure payment for the witch. After that, if you want to go home, I will take you."

I thought of all sorts of things, alone in my room. Convinced myself to carry on, convinced myself to run away home in the night, convinced myself to do nothing. Fruitless thoughts slowly became restless sleep. My dreams were troubled, filled with hazy, monstrous figures. I saw Twain in my nightmares, he was afraid. He tried to warn me, but his voice was stolen from his throat, like George, and he was helpless. I was doomed, and he could see it, too.

PART THREE: THE ROAD

CHAPTER 16

I woke in the bright light of day, with the sensation that I had slept too long.

My mind started in the place it always started lately, and progressed through a familiar pattern.

First, disoriented, uncertain where I was.

Next stop, skeptical, almost certain I'd dreamt Sophia and her fantasy world.

Final destination, terrified, quite certain that whether imagined or not, it all spelled trouble for me.

I glanced at the clock. The time barely qualified as morning. We would miss checkout if I didn't hurry. I sighed, grateful that Sophia allowed me to sleep in, but not wishing to delay us more than necessary. I quickly showered and dressed.

I found her leaning against the car, waiting.

"How are you feeling this morning?" She asked.

"Fine," I replied automatically. I amended, "Tired."

After about an hour on the road she let me decide where we would eat. Today, I felt anxious. I wanted to be done, I wanted to go home. I chose a speedy drive through option.

Then there was more driving. Sophia rarely initiated conversation, though she always participated when I started a conversation.

"Thank you for letting me sleep," I said.

Sophia explained, "I thought you might need it. We are waiting on George to find the witch, there is no need to hurry."

I nodded. I believed Sophia and yet I couldn't quite believe in witches and magical creatures. "Where are we going then?"

"If you are going to approach a witch, you will need payment." Sophia appeared displeased with the notion. "Witches are, first and foremost, capitalists."

I frowned, confused, "Are we talking about a Wiccan, or a creepy old lady in a candy house, or scapegoated women who are marginalized and persecuted for nonconformity?"

Sophia turned a near smile on me. It either expressed her patience with my asinine questions or true amusement. I could never tell. "None of those. The term witch is applied broadly in modern languages."

I pointed out, "Not an answer."

"Witches are a lot of different things, the way the word is used. A full range from healers to monsters. In the old worlds, witches were humans who traded part of their humanity for power. Most people who make the trade are corrupted by it. The more they give of themselves, the more power they get, and the less human they become. People feared them. The term began to be applied to individuals who were feared for other reasons, or as you said, scapegoated women on the margins of society."

I absorbed this slowly. "Are the real ones green, with pointy hats?"

"I've never seen a green one, that seems unlikely." She continued to consider the question. "I am sure I have seen some in hats, but I did not take note of what kind."

My sarcasm had gone unnoticed. "That was a joke."

Sophia nodded, "I see. I couldn't tell because it wasn't funny."

"Wow. Solid burn," I acknowledged. Occasionally, Sophia reminded me that she was the smart one in this relationship.

She smiled. "The 'real ones' as you say are not to be trusted. They surrender a part of their humanity in exchange for their power. And they do not get to choose which part. The experience leaves them with a very transactional nature. They may offer to help you. They will exact payment. You may not know what that is until it is too late. I understand you use humor to cope with stressful situations. Make jokes if that helps. But understand how serious I am when I tell you: Witches are dangerous. If I had any other leads, I would not pursue this one."

She wasn't admonishing me. Her tone lacked reproach. Instead, I knew she worried about me. She wanted to protect me. And this morning, her maternal manner provoked me.

"You will need powerful currency," Sophia informed me. "Something the witch can't resist."

"Like a Starbucks gift card?"

"No." It was her usual "no," the one that said, you might be serious, so I will answer you seriously.

My restless night had left me with little patience. "Are you going to tell me?" I asked brusquely. "Do we need eye of newt or something?"

She considered it, "Why would anyone want that?"

I shrugged and leaned back into my seat.

Sophia chose to ignore my prickly mood. "There are substances with mystical properties, sought after by spell casters. We will acquire one."

"Are they expensive? Is there a specialty shop? How do we get one?"

Her almost smiling response annoyed me more. "You're not going to like it."

"Great," I mumbled.

She drew in a long breath, a tendril of unease pierced my irritation. Sophia explained, "I told you there would be monsters."

I turned to her in shock, looking for any hint of humor. "I thought they weren't literal ones!"

"I never said that. I fully expect, both literal and figurative monsters." Sophia seemed perplexed by my response. "Our best chance is a fungus that grows in a cave system nearby. It will likely be protected by a monster. A monster, by your standards."

"A monster in a cave? By my standards? What?"

Her calm was directly and inversely proportionate to my aggravation. "I am sure it doesn't think of itself as a monster."

"Are you fucking kidding me?"

I did not expect a reply, but I got, "No." She spared me a glance and a reassuring smile, "Try not to worry there may be no monster, at all, and then there would be no reason to worry." My relief was short-lived. She added, "However, unguarded, magical substances tend not to last long. So I do hope there is a monster, best chance of finding the fungus. As I said, no need to worry, I'll tell you how to avoid it."

"You'll tell me?!"

"Yes, of course, I wouldn't ask you to go in blind." She went so far as to reach across the car and pat my hand, her eyes steadily on the road ahead.

I pulled back. "Where are you going to be?"

"I'll wait outside."

CHAPTER 17

Reaching the cave system required a long drive into woods, followed by a short, strenuous hike up an overgrown trail. Sophia did not complain, nor did her breath quicken, nor did she show any sign of strain. I puffed along after her, occasionally caught on underbrush or struck by the sting of disturbed branch.

We had been over everything. Sophia explained why it must be me, some stupid notion about only offering what I could rightly claim. We discussed how I would find the rare mycological artifact. Still, I hesitated when at last we stood before the cave entrance.

"What if I get lost?" I disliked the slight whine in my voice. I cleared my throat to hide it.

"Remember the plan, always go left on the way in. Always go right on the way out. You can do this." I took her smile as encouraging, even as it appeared patronizing.

I muttered, "This is insane. Probably won't even find it."

"You will. You will know it when you see it." She gave my shoulder a reassuring pat. "There are rules. You must remember them."

"Rules? This gets better and better," I frowned.

"Rule 1. Stay close to the cave wall. Rule 2. Stay quiet. And, most important of all, Rule 3. Don't talk to anyone."

My eyes widened in astonishment. "Who do you think is in there?"

"No time to lose." Her mouth quirked up at one end.

And then I did it. I walked alone into a dark cave with just a flashlight. To find an arcane fungus. Guarded by a monster. The nature of which was not disclosed. "I've lost my mind," I whispered.

As I stepped carefully on the rocky floor, a list of every horror movie I had ever seen scrolled through my mind. At least a few had caves. *Definitely going to die.*

The cave mouth opened widely allowing the light of the morning to stretch several yards into the interior. The light's end made a hard line across the ground. I stared at that line for seconds before I mustered the courage to cross into the black cave beyond. I turned back to make sure Sophia waited for me, as promised. Her head nodded, a gesture that said, *keep going*. I clicked the flashlight on and made my way to the wall on the far left of the stone enclosure. I held onto the wall as I made my way slowly forward.

A trickle of water connected with my bare hand and I jumped. "Neat, dark *and* dank," I murmured.

I followed my beam of light forward, avoiding drips of water where I could.

Dread grew heavy in my chest with each deliberate step.

My foot slipped on the wet cave floor. Panic infiltrated my thoughts. I gasped and braced myself against the wall. *Breathe*, I reminded myself. I whispered, "There are no such things as monsters," *whatever Sophia says*, "Monsters aren't real." And then a tiny voice within answered, *bears are real*.

As I continued, my fear gained an unwelcome companion, a creeping sense of absurdity. I was acting like a fool. I forced my steps to become more natural, and I let go of the wall, keeping it close to my left, but with reduced vigilance. Every so often I felt an unpleasant squish under my foot or felt the splash of a puddle. I held tightly to my resolve, *I can do this*.

My mind returned immediately and suddenly to my peril. I set my right foot down. It found only air. Moments stretched as I felt myself falling forward. *This is the end*.

The ground met my sneaker after a harrowing twelve inch freefall. My left foot lurched forward to catch up and I found myself half in and half out of a small hole in the ground. I looked almost as foolish as I felt. I stepped out of the hole, deliberately calming the rush of frenzied emotion that flooded my brain.

That tiny voice returned with, *You could fall in a pit*.

I sighed. "I am going to fall and break my neck. Or be eaten by a bear. Or both." I shook my head, now as annoyed as I was afraid, "I'm going to die in this cave for a magic fucking mushroom."

I considered turning back, more than the fear of danger, I began to feel deceived, like a rube duped into a snipe hunt.

Two words moved me deeper into the cave: *What if?*

There were so many things I couldn't explain. If half of what Sophia shared was true, I couldn't walk away. Or perhaps I needed to continue because I had already sunk so much time and energy into this ridiculous quest. I knew I had to continue, whatever the real reason. So I continued. More carefully on the uneven ground, now. I followed the plan. Every time

OUT OF THE WAY THINGS

I came to a fork in the cave, I stayed on the left, and I felt even more foolish. But I kept going.

After walking in the dark for an eternity, and selecting several branching tunnels to the left, the cave narrowed. I hesitated before moving into the cramped passage, propelled now by force of obstinacy. I was all in on this venture, already.

After several yards, the stone corridor opened out into a large earthen room. I breathed a sigh of relief, more comfortable now with a bit of space to move.

And then I saw it. A blue glow emanated from the walls, illuminating the room. I broke Rule 1 and stepped into the center of the cavern.

Though the blue haze surrounded me, a prominent cluster of light issued from the back wall where a gnarled, old stump grew from the stone floor. Behind the stump, I spotted distinctive, glowing mushrooms of a deep sapphire. *That's it*, I thought, *know it when I see it*. Sophia was right about that.

I approached the wall cautiously. As I grew closer, the stump took on the appearance of a man. I shook myself, *Another imaginary danger*. The longer I looked, the more I saw it. Someone had carved the stump into the shape of a withered old man. I smiled at the craftsmanship, such detail for a carving no one would see. *Except me*, I amended.

I reached behind the stump and grabbed the mushroom stalk. It resisted. I pulled harder to no avail. I let go, braced myself against the stump, and this time pulled down hard on the stalk.

CRACK.

The sound echoed through the cavern. I broke Rules 2 and 3 in rapid succession.

The stump's wooden eyelids snapped open.

Without thinking I said, "I'm so sorry." I removed my foot from his knee and backed away.

His eyes widened in rage, a florid, raw umber threat in the darkness. He screamed his fury. I clutched the mushroom to my chest and bolted for the narrow passage back into the cave system.

He moved behind me with alarming speed. My jacket snagged on something and I felt a tug. I ran harder. My jacket ripped free, knocking me off balance. I went to my knees, the impact of the hard rock jolted through my body. His clawed hands sunk into my shoe, scraping my skin beneath. His brown, wizened face pulled back into a stiff sneer, revealing jagged, broken teeth. He pulled me closer. He smelled of decay, like moldering leaves.

I screamed, "I'm not dying in a cave!"

I drew my free foot to my chest. Taking aim at his twisted face, I kicked out with all of my strength. I felt the crunch of his long, thin nose. His grip loosened and I pulled away, scrambling to my feet.

I put my head down, sprinting forward.

With my eyes fixed to the ground directly in front of my feet, I quickly lost my bearings and ran straight into a wall. I shook myself, not a wall, didn't hurt enough for a wall. I looked up to see Sophia regarding me with concern.

"Run!" I shouted directly in her face. Sophia calmly ushered me behind her.

A sound split the cave apart. I covered my ears with my arms, curling to the ground, but could do little to block the deafening sound.

Then nothing. Silence. I looked carefully around. Sophia watched me with interest. "You got the fungus."

I didn't know which grievance to voice first. I spilled the contents of my head into the stale, subterranean air. "You said I had to come in alone. What the hell was that thing? Where did it go? Shouldn't we get out of here?"

"I scared him away." Her expression offered pity. "And yes we should probably go."

"You made that sound?"

"I did," She walked around me, leaving me to follow.

"What the hell are you?"

Her voice dropped, "Something monsters fear."

I stopped. "That is scary as fuck. Why would you say that?"

She shrugged and continued. I trailed behind her, because I had no other choice.

Alone, the silence was menacing. With Sophia and her natural stillness, the quiet comforted me. I felt my body relaxing, even as my attitude remained sullen. My grip on the mystical mushroom loosened. I began to study it as I walked. I didn't know if it had supernatural properties, but it looked weird. Sophia caught me scrutinizing the mushroom. She said, "You realize, there were some mushrooms about ½ a mile back toward the entrance, right?"

CHAPTER 18

"I have questions." I waited to talk to Sophia until we were back in the car. I was nonplussed by her casual revelation that if I had been paying more attention to my surroundings and less to my mortal terror, I might have avoided the anthropomorphic tree attack. It took the walk back to sort through my surprise and indignation.

"Of course you do."

I started with my greatest vexation. "You said I had to do it alone. In the cave I learned that you can scream loud enough to shatter my eardrums- I think I suffered permanent damage to my hearing. Can you also run at lightning speed? Read my mind from a mile away?"

"In response to your first question: No. I am quick, but not that quick. To the second question: Maybe, I have never tried." She paused, I thought she would leave it there, but after some consideration she continued, "I followed you. I wanted to see how you would do."

"You wanted to see what I would do?!" I shouted back.

"Yes. It may get much harder from here. I wanted to know if you were up to it."

"What about, 'you can only offer what you can rightly claim?'"

She nodded, "That's just a good policy."

I dropped my face into my hands and considered releasing a cathartic scream.

Sophia continued, "You did well. You *might have* gotten away on your own. I was not ready to take that risk."

"*You* weren't ready to take that risk?"

She spared me a glance. "You seem to be falling into a pattern of restating my responses as questions. I do not care for it."

I growled in exasperation. "Good thing I'm not driving, I would drive us straight into a tree."

"Thank you for that information. I will not ask you to drive."

It took nearly an hour of resentful silence for me to introduce the next topic of concern. Sophia had a way of closing conversational doors I didn't know existed. Until they closed. And then they were barred to me.

"What was that thing that attacked me? I can't believe it was human."

"No," she agreed, "It was not. My guess is that it was a spriggan. Notoriously territorial, unfriendly, murderous. But there was very little light, and I could hardly see it."

"I'm surprised you need light to see," I murmured.

"Everything requires light to see," She sounded confused by my comment, "that is how sight works."

I would not be deterred. "Did you know it was in there?"

"I knew it was possible. Many types of creatures are drawn to such places. It might have been any number of things; I suspected there would be something. And I told you as much." I accepted what she said, as much as I could, but each answer inspired a hundred more questions.

"How is it that no one has ever seen these things before?"

"Win," her tone became patronizing, "You just saw one. They are seen from time to time. But most eternal and magical creatures hide. Like George. And most are only seen when they choose to be."

It overwhelmed me. The ordeal in the cave. The new world that unfolded before me. I yawned, my body succumbing to the weariness of revelation. "One more question," I insisted. "Then I am going to lay my head back and take a nap."

Sophia smiled a little.

"I haven't been hallucinating…" A sharp look from Sophia stopped my words, I revised, "having visions. Not since we left. Why?"

Her smile slipped. "I am uncertain. My presence affects humans. If I am calm, and I am usually calm, it seems to pacify them. You are partially human." She hesitated, "I am speculating. I think what you see and when you see it is tied into your emotional state. I also think you can control it, if you learn how."

I nodded. It didn't explain everything. It didn't explain Twain. Yet, it felt true.

CHAPTER 19

"Are we going back to see George?" I asked. I didn't mean to be optimistic, I hoped Sophia didn't hear it in my voice. "So he can tell us how to find the witch?"

"No, he emailed her profile and contact information."

Moments like these ones still surprised me. I wondered if they always would. I asked, "You are a magical, immortal being. Hundreds of years old?" I paused for confirmation.

"More."

"Right. And you have email?" I asked.

"Everyone has email, Win."

"Why isn't there some magical means of communication between magical creatures across space and time?"

Sophia agreed, "There is. It's called WiFi."

I sniffed. "I expected something cooler."

"I've seen a lot. It's pretty cool."

The conversation launched a comfortable pattern:

I ask a deep, existential question, seeking to understand the mysteries of the universe, "What happens when you die?"

She responds with a question, or a literal interpretation, or both, "When I die?"

I clarify, "When anyone dies."

She supplies an unsatisfying answer, "I don't know."

The answers were delivered in one of two ways: either interest, it was a question worth pondering, or disdain, only an idiot would ask such a thing. In the case exemplified, it was disdain.

Sometimes, as I did in this case, I pressed on. "How do you *not* know that?"

And she became mildly irritated, which was sort of my goal. "How *would* I know that? I am not dead."

Which forced me to concede. I never won these contests. But I felt like I could, so I kept trying. Sophia tolerated my diversions to a point.

Exploring mystical truths that did not lay directly in my path brought greater comfort than discussing our next endeavor: the witch. Vicious and dangerous if Sophia was to be believed.

It would take more than a day on the road to reach the witch. Though Sophia approached our task with a sense of urgency, she also did not wish to travel long hours every day or travel through the night. She explained we were about two days away from our destination.

When I wasn't asking important questions about the nature of the universe, I watched out the window, enjoying the changing landscapes on display. Sophia had charted our path, and decided where we would stop for the night.

We left the highway and expected that we would soon stop, either she found a restaurant she wanted to visit or we were approaching our evenings lodging. But we didn't stop. I sensed something unusual in Sophia's demeanor. She seemed frustrated.

"We're lost, aren't we?" I asked.

"I know where we are." Sophia answered easily.

I sensed an evasion, I asked, "Are we where we're supposed to be?"

"We are always where we are supposed to be."

Recognizing that I was on to something, I continued "Did you take the wrong exit?"

After a pause, Sophia returned a quiet, "Yes."

I smiled out the window. We were well away from the highway. It was probably just as easy to find the next road back to the highway as it was to turn around. A roadside sign caught my attention. "State fair!" I shouted.

"Pardon me?"

"We are where we're supposed to be!" I explained.

"No, I already admitted that we are not." Sophia's voice hinted at irritation.

"We are," I insisted. "The state fair is on. We have to go. We were meant to be here."

Sophia heaved a sigh. "Win, this isn't a vacation."

"You're right," I agreed solemnly, "it's fate."

Sophia took a deep breath in, "Fine." Sophia didn't mess with fate.

"I'm getting a corndog," I grinned. I tasted it already. Ketchup and mustard and grease.

Sophia asked, "What's a corndog?"

I gasped. "You're getting a corndog, too."

Sophia approached the state fair as though she faced a battlefield. Her body moved with a graceful readiness, her eyes scanned the scene, deliberate and thorough. I wondered about her history, I asked, "Have you ever fought in a war?"

"Yes," Sophia answered simply. She didn't elaborate, I took that to mean that she didn't wish to discuss it and left it alone.

"Have you ever been to a state fair?" I asked, hoping to lighten the mood.

"No," she responded just as simply as before.

"You're going to love it," I promised.

Sophia paid for our entrance to the fair. She wasn't thrilled with the detour, but she seemed willing to make the best of it. She asked, "Is it like a village fair?"

I considered the question. I pictured a medieval scene with a Maypole and meat pies for sale. "I'm going to say, no. But you can tell me later if I am wrong."

Sophia reacted surprisingly well to the state fair experience. I realized, some of her attitude could be attributed to her desire to placate me. I also thought that she genuinely enjoyed the spectacle.

We walked through the farm animals. Sophia found the exhibition odd, she noted none of them were for sale and she did not see the point in displaying them. She enjoyed the local arts exhibits and the vendors. I forced her to eat corndogs and cotton candy. She preferred the condiments to the actual corndog. The cotton candy fascinated Sophia.

She told me, "This tastes terrible." But she continued to eat it, and after she'd finished the bag, she purchased another.

I warned, "You're going to get sick."

She laughed at that. "I don't get sick."

"Have you ever eaten two bags of cotton candy before? I'm not going to help you clean blue vomit out of your car." She scoffed at that, and also slowed down a bit on the second bag.

Without question, Sophia's favorite part of the fair were the games. She wanted to try each and every one. I won a stuffed horse at the *Roll a Ball Horse Race*. She won several games. A few prizes she held onto, including a ceramic unicorn and a stuffed panda. Most prizes, she handed to another player in the game before walking away.

"You like carnival games," I teased.

She nodded, with great dignity she concurred, "It appears that I do."

"There is something else that you have to try."

Sophia agreed, "You were right about the fair. I trust your judgment."

I smiled at the image she projected. Sophia dressed well, always slightly formal. She stood straight, with the posture of a dancer. Tucked under one arm, sat a darling stuffed panda with overly large eyes. I said, "That's quite an admission. I'm right? You trust my judgment?"

Sophia followed me as I led her to our next attraction. "Or it was only your luck, again," she suggested.

"What luck?" I asked. I tripped on nothing.

Her jaw dropped. Really, her mouth only opened slightly, but the slight movement proved she was gobsmacked. "Have you never noticed how lucky you are?" She asked.

It was my turn to be shocked. "Uh, no. Kinda the opposite, actually."

"It is well established that born beings who are part human and extremely lucky," Sophia instructed. "I am surprised you have never noticed."

Sophia presented herself with extraordinary sophistication and decorum. I nearly questioned her belief in luck and in fate. I knew if I opened the conversation, it would end in me feeling like a fool, so I let it be. We remained silent until we stood in front of our destination: the towering wooden roller coaster.

"Why would anyone choose to do this?" Sophia asked, truly perplexed.

I smiled up at the rollercoaster. "Because it's fun."

"It's fun?" Sophia repeated.

"Mm-hmm," I confirmed. "It's fun."

"And people pay to do this?"

"We're going to pay to do this," I told her.

She shook her head, "No."

"Sophia," I said, "you took a wrong turn. That never happens. Your wrong turn led us to a state fair. A state fair that just happened to be running at the time of our wrong turn. These things only operate once a year. It's fate. You believe in that sort of thing. We were meant to ride this rollercoaster."

Sophia wanted to object, I could see it in her eyes, but she took the concept of fate seriously. She couldn't dismiss me outright.

"We're doing this," I reiterated. Given that I was coercing Sophia into riding the rollercoaster, I couldn't, in good conscience, ask her to pay. I purchased enough tickets for one ride. I didn't press my luck that I could convince her to get on any other rides. No matter how lucky I might. The roller coaster looked like the sturdiest option available, and I couldn't leave a state fair without riding a ride.

The roller coaster did not disappoint. Me. It did not disappoint me. Sophia, however, gripped the bar as though it was her only hope of survival. Her face remained impassive. After three minutes climbing and diving and flying around corners, the ride jerked to the stop. Sophia said, "That was terrible."

"You hated it?" I was honestly surprised.

"I do not understand why anyone would do that intentionally."

"All right, no more rides."

OUT OF THE WAY THINGS

"No," Sophia concurred. "I would like another bag of candy."

"Cotton candy?" I clarified.

"Yes."

I waited while Sophia bought another colorful treat. We wandered through tents of vendors selling a wide variety of wares. Sophia browsed casually. I had very little money, and didn't bother to browse. While Sophia examined handcrafted jewelry, a booth caught my eye. The sign read, "Tarot Reading: The Future Is Yours." I elbowed Sophia.

She returned a look of affront.

"Maybe I should do that? Instead of the witch."

The expression fell from her face and she stared at me blankly.

"It could work," I said.

Without breaking eye contact, Sophia held up a twenty. "Go for it."

I went for it. I approached the booth.

In the booth, a woman sat behind a table, looking as though she had no place at a state fair. She seemed almost otherworldly, with skin too smooth for her apparent age. Her flowing white dress invoked music festivals and youth. But something about her hinted at age and wisdom. She watched me serenely as I approached. I was stopped by a young man before I reached the table.

"Hello," he said. He moved to stand behind me. I turned to face him. "Are you interested in a reading?" he inquired.

"Yes," I confirmed. "I am interested in a reading."

He offered an inviting smile. "Please have a seat. I will take your donation, and Cassandra will share your future with you."

I held up the twenty dollar bill. The man took it from my hand.

As I took a seat, I noticed a small sign displaying a disclaimer that belied the authenticity of the experience. I admitted to myself, probably will still need to see the witch. Cassandra offered me a gentle smile.

"Cassandra, huh?" I asked.

She nodded sweetly.

"That's unfortunate. Even I know that story."

"What questions can I answer for you?" I heard impatience in her voice.

"Can you tell me my future?" I glanced behind me, quickly. Sophia watched us as though we were theater. Cassandra delicately shuffled her deck of cards.

"Please cut the deck."

I did as instructed.

She smiled. "I will share what I see, but I may not be able to explain it to you."

"Great." I echoed Sophia, "Go for it."

Cassandra laid three cards in front of me. I didn't know the first thing about Tarot cards, I was at her mercy. The first card was some sort of clergy. "The Hierophant," she declared.

The second card featured a spire.

"The Tower," Cassandra informed me.

The third card contained an illustration of an old man.

"The Hermit." Cassandra considered the three images. "I see a bridge between worlds. You are in a state of transformation. Change can come with danger. Beware. The danger is hidden."

I heard a cough behind me. I turned to the sound and saw a plain young woman who had escaped my notice before. She stood at the edge of the booth opposite the man who took my money. I thought I saw a warning looking pass from the plain woman to the beautiful one named for the ill-fated Cassandra.

"I'm afraid, that is all I see."

I looked back to Cassandra, "Seriously? That's it."

Cassandra gestured to the sign next to the disclaimer. "All Sales Final. No Refunds."

Sophia stepped forward. "Let's go."

I frowned at the trio in disapproval and followed Sophia.

As I walked past her, the plain woman grabbed my arm. "Your impulsivity is a problem," she spoke with a slight, almost imperceptible accent. "You should take more care."

I replied automatically, "Okay."

She held my gaze a moment longer, still gripping my arm. I could almost feel what she felt, concern, disapproval.

Sophia moved toward us as though she intended to break the woman's hold on my arm. The woman released me and retreated into the booth.

Sophia and I left the stall. Evidently, Sophia was done with the fair, and so was I.

I said to her, "That was weird."

"Yes," Sophia's voice was dark and cold. She sounded worried. "Time to get back on the road."

CHAPTER 20

The days of travel intensified my apprehension, distilling into something closer to terror. My mind raced with all that I had seen and all that I began to anticipate.

The fair contained too many unexpected revelations for me to ignore. From Sophia, a hint at her own past. She'd spent time in wars. I wanted to ask, but felt certain she wouldn't answer. She still avoided the topic of her own species. I didn't even know if species was the right word. Also from Sophia, her belief in luck to begin with, and my propensity of luck, as a follow up. Her belief in my luck could have been superstition, it could have been firsthand knowledge. I struggled to distinguish belief from expertise when Sophia spoke.

Every time I slowed down for a minute, it felt like a stranger approached who knew more about me than I did.

Sophia advised me to ignore the tarot card reader. She assured me that readings were always vague enough to apply to anyone but with enough details to cause alarm. We didn't mention the strange woman who warned me that I was too impulsive. I thought about her anyway. The woman looked at me with recognition. I was certain I'd never seen her before. She spoke like she knew me. Like she had a right to give me advice.

I still had yet to fully process the experience of being chased by a tree.

Sophia never expressed emotions in words. But I saw tension in her posture, I heard it in her voice.

As our destination grew nearer, Sophia's demeanor grew dark and dour.

I did my part to distract Sophia with engaging conversation. My best entry point was always a question.

"Are The Mists real? Where the immortals are from?" I asked.

"Yes, but not all immortals are from the Mists."

"Are there still people..." I corrected, "Immortals there?"

"There are. And they might consider themselves people based on the definition. Not everyone followed my father. Some remain behind, some can move between worlds." Her hand left the wheel, making a fluid gesture, like she was imagining moving between worlds.

"But the exiles can't go back, right?"

"Correct," She confirmed. I sensed she was happy for the distraction.

"So you've never been there?" I continued the interview.

"I have not, and I likely will not."

"Bummer." She wasn't making it easy.

"There's a story," Sophia offered.

Without thinking I said, "There's always a story."

"I don't have to share it." Her voice revealed a sliver of vulnerability, hurt feelings maybe.

"I want to hear it," I insisted, "That was a joke, we know I am not funny." Sophia nodded, which seemed unnecessary to me. I stayed my course and said, "Please tell me the story."

Sophia's voice adjusted, and once again the world around me faded and she pulled me into her narrative. "I am told the Mists are beautiful and wondrous, unimaginable sights. I wish I could describe them, but those who have lived there speak little of their lives there. What I have learned is that the people there are protective of their lands. They distrust outsiders, they dislike change. Many refuse to leave, they do not want to be influenced by other worlds, they see outside knowledge as corrosive, dangerous. Those who journey out, the Travelers, are not accepted by all who remain. Travelers are considered a threat to the Mists by the most devout residents. After the exile, some insisted that Travelers ought to be regarded as exiles. But Travelers do not bear the curse, and they live by the rules of the Mists.

"Before the exile, there was a story told in the Mists, meant to frighten people into following rules they might otherwise question. A story of a looming devastation that threatened their realm. After the exile, the story became popular with my father's people. Some of the old ones," Sophia caught my questioning look. I thought *she* was one of the old ones. "The first generation exiles," she clarified. "The first exiles told the story to their children, as a story of hope, not fear. They spoke of a child born in another world. His father was a powerful immortal, his mother was the descendant of mystics, humans who could touch the veil between the Mists and the Earth. As a boy, his parents cast him out. They feared him, for they saw his true potential, they believed he could unmake the world they knew. He wandered the Earth alone, awaiting his destiny."

"What was his destiny?" I prompted.

"To burn down the veil. To destroy the barrier between worlds." Sophia spoke with longing, admiration.

"Did that happen?"

"No, the barriers are still very much in place." Sophia's eyes scanned the horizon, as though she could see the barriers that held her in this world. "It is an ancient prophecy. The chosen one will come and lead the people to whatever seems desirable to the people telling the story. In the mists, it was a horror story, a cautionary tale about the cost of leaving the realm. Among the exiles it was the chance for vindication, the chance to return home and live by a different set of rules."

"Do you think it's you?" I liked the idea that Sophia had a great destiny, even if I didn't understand it. "Do you think you are the chosen one? It kind of fits."

It wasn't meant as a joke, but it earned a genuine laugh from Sophia. The first I could remember.

"Many of the old ones use '*he*' to tell that story."

I questioned, "Because their chosen one is male or because they use male pronouns in place of gender neutral pronouns?"

"I always thought it was patrilineal misogyny. But you could be right, it could be either of those." The smile lingered, and her tension eased some.

"I would have thought that immortals would be beyond sexism. They have had a lot of time to think things through."

Sophia shrugged, "Matters how you spend the time." She added, "And I told you, they are people, people are individuals. Individuals think all kinds of things."

"I guess that's true." I considered Sophia's story. "It would be cool though, if it *was* you."

"Why is that?"

"Because you'd be famous, and I would be able to say I knew you before you were the chosen one."

"I don't hope it's true. Sounds like pressure, duty, and sacrifice to me. Not areas of strength for me."

I tried out Sophia's trademark shrug. I had a feeling it looked ordinary on me.

"At any rate, I don't think it's me. I think this one is just a story. Even if it is real, stories are tricky; the truth in them can be hard to find. They say it was told in the Mists, before the exile. How would they know of immortals born before the exile?"

"I thought it was a prophecy. Wouldn't that explain it?"

"Prophecies are even trickier." Sophia's tension returned as a flood. I could feel myself carried away by it. "Prophecies are riddles, traps set by fate."

I couldn't resist asking, "Then why are we on our way to force one out of someone you don't trust?"

"Because it is the only way I know of that gives us a glimpse of what is coming. Do you have any other ideas about how we do that?" The edge in her voice was almost imperceptible, but after so many hours together, I sensed her subtle shifts in attitude.

"I don't know, you're the font of knowledge around here." And I noticed that when I didn't intentionally fight it, her mood could affect mine.

With the topic reintroduced, Sophia felt obligated to prepare me for the next trial. "This time, when you go in to meet the witch, I will not follow you. You will be alone."

Clearly she believed approaching the witch to be perilous. I sputtered my indignation, "You are sending me alone? To face something that scares you."

"Caution is different from fear," Sophia explained. "But that is not the reason. The witch won't talk to my kind."

"Your kind?" I stared at her until she gave me the courtesy of meeting my eye. "What kind are you?"

She held my gaze longer than I expected. But did not answer.

"You said you would tell me," I reminded her.

"I will." But she didn't, not then.

Instead she returned to her lecture. "Witches are not to be trusted," Sophia advised.

"They can't all be bad," I objected. It still seemed like a damaging stereotype, more importantly, my anger made me contrary.

Sophia sighed, communicating to me that I had offered another naive opinion. "We discussed this. They are not all bad, most are. And you will not know the difference. Many would find you useful. Promise nothing, agree to nothing." Her voice began to raise, sounding nearly emotional, "Take the bag, offer that, nothing more. Nothing. Do you understand?"

"I do, yes. Very clear." She worried for me, I thought.

"I mean it, Win. She is not your friend; she may be charming, she may offer you more than you ask. Do not give in to temptation." I reconsidered. Her adamance landed as a lack of confidence rather than an abundance of concern.

"Got it." I tried to douse the flare of anger that tightened my chest.

"She may live in a metaphorical forest, but the danger is real. She will use what she learns about you to her own advantage."

"Got it!" My shout had the desired effect of ending the tirade. Silence consumed the car. I tried to find serenity somewhere in my mind. It eluded me. I tried for detachment. When that didn't work, I settled for distraction. I wondered, if witches existed, and tree people existed, and seers, and Sophia, and George, what else existed?

Sophia remained my only source of information and the distance between us proved uncomfortable. Assuming we both needed the distraction, I broke the silence.

I inquired, "So what other things exist?"

"What do you mean?" I appreciated her calm, normal tone. No grudges, no pettiness of any kind.

"Immortal creatures and mythical beasts, that sort of thing. What else is out there? I know about the tree people, whatever you called them…"

"Spriggans," she supplied.

"Yeah, what else is there? Besides spriggans. And seers. And whatever it is you are that is so mysterious."

She did not take the opening to tell me about herself. "All sorts of things."

"Like what? Are there vampires? Or unicorns? Or bigfoot?"

"There is something like vampires. Unicorns, maybe, I don't know. Bigfoot, did you say?"

I nodded.

"I haven't heard of that."

I thought of the figurine she'd kept from the fair. "How about mermaids or the Loch Ness monster? Are they real?"

"I do not know."

"How do you not know that?"

"Do you know all of the animals that exist?" She countered.

"No, but I know some." I continued, "And you are immortal, you have had time. Haven't you learned this stuff?"

She smiled in appreciation. "That is a fair point." I made a good argument. "Let's prorate this body of knowledge based on the amount of time you have had, how many mortal creatures can you name?"

Maybe, not a good argument after all. "I don't know," I admitted, "I have never tried to do that."

Sophia nodded thoughtfully. "Why not?" She asked.

"Because, I don't care, I guess."

She nodded, again. "Yes," she agreed, "exactly."

"Fine." So much for conversation. Soon, my thoughts returned to the task that lay ahead: The meeting with a witch.

Why do I have to see a witch, I thought, *why can't it be something fun, like fairies?*

"Fairies are not fun," Sophia informed me.

"No," I replied. Her intrusion into my thoughts irked me, especially as she seemed determined to close down my efforts to have a conversation. "We will come back to the existence of fairies, and why you think they aren't fun. But first, I want you out of my head."

"Sometimes it's unavoidable," her voice indicated she was chastened, slightly.

"Try harder," I told her.

"Sometimes it is in your interests."

"I don't care," I told her. "I should at least get privacy in my own head. I should get to choose what I share with you. You get to choose what you share with me."

Sophia nodded solemnly. "You are right. I apologize." She took a deep, fortifying breath and added, "I will avoid listening to your thoughts."

"Thank you." Her contrition surprised me. And it impressed me. As mysterious, and secretive as Sophia was, she was also generous and open in our interactions. Somehow, that made her more bewildering. "Now," I let go of the topic and returned to her earlier statement, "Tell me about fairies."

CHAPTER 21

The metaphorical forest turned out to be a ubiquitous, suburban subdivision. Sophia navigated the labyrinthine streets with relative ease, only twice turning around when a road unexpectedly terminated in a cul-de-sac.

For the first time in our acquaintance, Sophia seemed nervous. Not maybe nervous, or almost nervous, fully nervous. From what I had witnessed, it was her first fully formed emotion.

We stopped at an ordinary house, on an ordinary street. There was nothing magical or menacing about it. Sophia checked the address against a slip of paper. Twice.

I waited with her. I knew she wasn't ready for me to leave the car.

We sat for ten minutes before she spoke.

"Please, Win. Take this seriously."

I expected more confidence from Sophia, and her entreaty bothered me. "Got it," I replied curtly.

"It is unlikely that I will be able to hear you at that distance. She has probably protected the house from unwelcome entry."

I reminded her, "You said you would stay out of my head."

"I would break that promise to keep you safe." Her eyes openly communicated her fear for me. "I'm sorry, but I would."

I nodded; I didn't like it, but I couldn't fault her for it.

She continued, "This time I can't follow you, you will be lost to me once you enter. You must take care."

"I understand," I left the car to preempt a new series of lectures on the risks of bargaining with witches. I grabbed the un-mystical reusable shopping bag containing very mystical trade goods.

I mumbled to myself, "Why ask me to do it if you think I am so stupid."

I approached the conventional, boring house. A neat rambler, with taupe plastic siding and an accent of faux bricks framing the garage. It matched the tracks of houses surrounding it. The yard was in decent shape, the lawn a little overgrown, and a few weeds stood tall along the line of the driveway. Neither notably perfect nor conspicuously imperfect.

I looked back at Sophia once. She leaned into the passenger seat to watch my progress. *She must be worried.* It was the least dignified posture I had ever seen her take. "How bad can it be?" I whispered.

I knocked at the unremarkable door and held my breath.

No answer.

I knocked again, this time louder.

Nothing. I started to turn back to the car.

"Yes," A phantom voice spoke to me. I looked around in panic. It continued, "Can I help you?"

I spotted the video doorbell a moment later. Maybe I was too stupid to do this. Remembering Sophia's precise wording, I said, "I am here to request a service."

The tension stretched the seconds out, anxiety blooming in my gut. I looked back to the car, wishing I could return and forget the whole thing.

The door opened.

The woman beyond the threshold appeared in strident contrast to her comfortable surroundings. Her body arranged itself in a collection of angles, somehow compact and yet still overwhelming in its presence. She wore her dark hair back in a severe, thin ponytail. At a glance she looked nearly featureless, it took a moment of study to distinguish a pinched mouth, a narrow nose, a sharp chin. Her eyes were too pale for her colorless face, set prominently in front of incongruent round cheekbones. If I didn't know she was a witch, I would have thought she was a tired mom, outfitted in overpriced joggers and designer sandals. Looking around the neighborhood again, I realized she was probably both.

"Enter," she instructed. She held her mouth pursed, as though trying to stifle laughter. It twitched restlessly to the left and right and back again. I hitched the shopping bag on my shoulder and obeyed.

The witch ushered me into her living room. The room shared evidence of a family, pictures with a spouse and children. The room was tidy, yet lived in, a few half completed chores told the story of an ordinary day interrupted. Candles crowded the shelves. As I maneuvered to the indicated couch for our interview, I noted most of the candles were the scented variety with cute sayings and timeless quotes.

I heard Sophia's voice in my head, *Knowledge is power. Say nothing more than is needed to complete the transaction.*

The witch's mouth jerked open. "Do you have currency?"

I patted the bag under my arm.

She tittered with glee. My skin crawled. "Let me see it."

I removed the bag from my shoulder and held it open. She peered inside, her eyes growing wider with want. Her arm snaked out toward the bag. I pulled it back into my lap smoothly. Sophia would be proud of my composure.

Irritation flashed on the witch's face. "What is your name?" she spoke in quick clipped words, intermittently interrupted by abrupt unnerving laughter.

"It doesn't matter." I replied coolly. *Give nothing more than necessary.*

She sighed and rolled her eyes. "Someone from the Old World giving you advice," that statement she managed without the bone chilling giggle, but her lips still twitched. I nearly confirmed her guess without thinking. I held back.

"I am here to request a service," I repeated a phrase I knew to be safe.

Another eye roll from the witch, "Yes, yes. A service. Tell me your request, and I will tell you if the terms are agreeable to me."

Once again, I quoted Sophia verbatim, "I require a reading. You have seen my offer."

She laughed, aggressively. "Aren't you a lot of fun?" She screwed up her face and shook her head. "Whoever prepared you is paranoid and old fashioned."

I relaxed a little. "A reading," I reminded her.

"You know, if you tell me more about who you are, I can read you more accurately." She chuckled, "You get out what you put in."

"I…" nearly introduced myself. I remembered Sophia's hesitation. "I require a reading."

The witch scowled. "Fine. But don't complain to me if it makes no sense."

I nodded.

The witch began her preparations with care and deliberation. Carefully, she unrolled a simple black cloth over the coffee table.

"To protect the table," she informed me.

She selected candles from a shelf, plain candles with no clever commentary, and set them carefully on top of the cloth. She left me alone in the room, I assumed while she gathered more objects.

I took the opportunity to look around from my seat on the edge of the couch. Nothing distinguished this room from any suburban living room. Sedate, beige walls, textured curtains of a darker beige, carpet in a shade exactly halfway between the walls and the drapery. The bookshelf contained a handful of popular paperbacks, the aforementioned candle collection, family photos, and few participation trophies. Someone collected clear glass figurines. A few too many of the figurines were frogs. I looked earnestly for any evidence of spells or witchcraft. Nothing.

The witch returned with a brightly colored makeup case, a sauté pan, and a small box covered with a towel.

She opened the case, it held herbs and rocks and what appeared to be animal bones. Her hands moved in swift staccato gestures, a familiar ritual, enacted with confidence. Each item she laid out precisely. In the middle of the table, she placed the pan, and beside it a wicked looking knife.

The scene was hardly mystical at all. The table looked like a spooky vignette created as a Halloween decoration. With a non-stick pan in the center.

The witch muttered unintelligible sounds as she lit each candle. With great reverence she added a selection of odds and ends to the pan. Mumbling ceaselessly.

I leaned in, listening for recognizable words. I caught nothing. Until I heard, "Readings are interpretations." I realized she spoke to me directly, and I looked up. "The more information I have the more accurate the interpretations will be."

I stared, with a look that I hope evoked impatience and boredom. *Provide nothing.*

She shrugged. "Many who request a reading are disturbed to glimpse their fate. Are you certain this is what you want?"

I nodded. For the first time in days, I felt certain.

The witch knelt across the table from me. She indicated the floor opposite her. I wedged myself between the couch and the table, careful not to touch the table.

She pulled the towel from the box uncovering a small cage. A sizable guinea pig squealed upon reveal. I frowned. The witch pulled the guinea pig from the cage, giving it a comforting scratch under the chin.

The witch sighed regretfully, picked up the knife. She positioned the guinea pig over the pan, then split it open.

The blood splashed into the pan. I covered my mouth with both hands, giving up on any attempt to appear calm and collected.

The witch held the animal as its life drained into the pan. When the flow stopped, she squeezed a bit more blood from the poor exsanguinated creature. "I'll need to go to the pet store this afternoon. Sorry, Buttons." She shook off the regret, and set the tiny body aside.

The witch's face changed as she stared into the blood, her eyes turned hazy and unfocused. The silence lasted minutes and I began to wonder if Buttons' sacrifice was really necessary.

I shifted my weight awkwardly. I tried to avoid looking at the body of the discarded pet.

The witch's sudden stream of words startled me, more breath than voice; I shivered. "I see three." Her fingernails gripped the cloth. "Soldiers,

I think. One faces forward, scouts the path ahead. Two is still, he sees everything. Three faces away, always looking back."

"That's me," I whispered. The witch's eyes cleared and locked on mine. Her thin mouth twitched. I realized my mistake.

She turned back to her task. She continued, "You will find what you want to find, it will not satisfy you."

Her words drew me in and I felt myself sinking into her, seeing everything she said. Stronger than my vertigo, more real than my visions. I thought, *Twain*. Her eyes darkened, and I realized I spoke his name aloud.

The witch grabbed my arm. Once again our eyes met. I felt her fear and disgust. "You are being hunted."

I gasped, for a moment I shadow loomed behind the witch.

"You are hunted, even as you search for what you need. But what you need to find may destroy you." The declaration stopped my breath. I saw a face, familiar but unknown. "You are trapped by your destiny. You need the other, you're intertwined and inseparable." She pulled me toward her.

"Who?" I asked.

Her face was her own and something else, something dark and unnatural. "Together, you threaten the world." Her nails bit into my arm. "What is your name?" She demanded.

I obeyed, "Win."

"Win," her voice crackled with malice. "It is you. You are the center, they are all tied to you."

"Who?" I repeated, frustration and desperation wound inextricably together. "Who are they?"

"I see you surrounded by liars. And one of them will betray you."

I pulled back, upsetting the pan, splashing blood on the table and carpet. Her clawed fingers left angry streaks across my arm.

"Oh, gosh, not the carpet," Her voice returned to normal. Her furrowed brow expressed worry of the state of her floor.

I stood, "Sorry, hydrogen peroxide helps with blood stains." I backed away from her.

"There could be more to tell. I can see more, you could help me interpret it."

I hesitated.

She didn't seem evil. Frightening perhaps, but not evil. And she warned me. I considered asking her every question I had. Something held me back. Sophia's worried face appeared in my mind. The woman who screamed down a monster, probably feared very little. But this strange woman made her nervous. "No, thank you," I decided. "I have to go."

I turned to the door.

"Wait!" I held the door knob, but looked back at the witch crouching on the floor. "The old one. It's using you."

I gasped. She had to mean Sophia. And I wondered, *will Sophia betray me? Is she a liar?* It didn't feel true. I asked, "How do you know that?"

"It is their nature."

CHAPTER 22

"She murdered a guinea pig. I think it was her kid's."

Sophia said, "I don't think you are stupid. I think you are new. And kind."

"Huh?" My brow wrinkled in confusion.

"You suggested that I think you are stupid. I do not."

"Oh," I remembered, "Well *that* is good. Thanks." *Did she think about that the whole time I was gone?*

I tried to avoid thinking about what happened in the house. I believed Sophia planned to honor her promise to stay out of my thoughts. However, she once told me I thought so loud it was hard not to hear me. And I wanted time alone with this information.

In an effort to change the direction of my thoughts, I informed her, "I'm hungry."

Sophia started the car, and lost no time leaving the house. She clearly sensed I wasn't ready to talk, and she left me to the privacy of my thoughts.

I tried to focus on my hunger. I tried to contemplate the food Sophia would select for us. A diner. She always opted for a diner.

Eventually, I abandoned the effort to repress my thoughts. I reviewed everything the witch told me.

She identified three soldiers. Somehow I knew I was the third one. The one who looks back. Logic would dictate that if I could see the past, the one who scouts ahead could see the future. I couldn't fathom what the other one might do. I wanted to speculate, to guess, to ask Sophia.

The last words the witch offered stopped me from questioning Sophia.

No surprise that Sophia despised and distrusted witches. The witch introduced insidious doubt into our relationship. I didn't know if I could believe Sophia, but somehow, I knew the witch revealed the truth. A conflict developed in my mind, trusting Sophia came easily, almost without my input, but why? The ease of it forced skepticism.

Based on the distance we drove, Sophia's priority was to get far away from the witch. I couldn't fault her for that. I felt the same, even if I arrived at that conclusion for a different reason.

Sophia finally stopped the car after more than an hour on the highway. She selected an unimpressive diner in an undistinguished town, as anticipated. My stomach growled, suddenly ravenous.

Neither of us spoke as we selected a table. We perused menus, ordered, and even waited for food before Sophia addressed me directly. "Are you well?" She asked.

I nodded, "Tired. It was a lot."

Sophia accepted my response. Our food arrived swiftly and we tucked into it without hesitation. Per usual, I finished eating first. Sophia didn't eat as often as I did, but she always ate a feast. When I pushed away my plate, she asked, "What did you learn from her?"

I didn't tell Sophia everything. I didn't mention my lapses in secrecy. I told her that I would find what I wanted but I probably wouldn't want it anymore. I told her that what I needed to find might kill me. Sophia's expression darkened with distress.

Finally I recounted the witch's first revelation: there were three of us.

I noticed, Sophia only nodded as I shared the last. She nodded as though I confirmed what she already knew to be true. I saw it on her face. So I guessed, "But you already knew that, didn't you?"

Sophia nodded thoughtfully.

I felt a chill burrow under my skin. "Why didn't you tell me?"

"About the other two?" The question reflected curiosity. "Was it important?"

"Yes," I replied firmly, my outrage barely contained. "You said I was the only one of my kind. But that's not true. They could help me. They could need me."

"Perhaps, but they are not like you. You are connected, related in a sense, but each different. A different gift." Sophia seemed genuinely confused by my anger. "We do not know that they could help you. You might just endanger them."

"What else do you know about me? About us?" I demanded.

She considered the question carefully. "There are always three. Three seers, each with a different gift, tied together in life and death."

"I don't understand what that means." I didn't believe she was intentionally cryptic, more that she didn't know how to explain the arcane knowledge she took for granted.

"A cycle started thousands of years ago. Three were born within three years of each other. Each a seer. Some stories say they were sisters. Some stories say they were strangers. Most stories described them as magical, maybe demigods, probably immortals blessed with prophetic gifts, possibly descended from oracles. People sought them out for wisdom, for clarity, for divination. Monarchs, priests, commoners desired their counsel. Some people worshiped them. As the seers' renown grew, it is said they gained the notice of the Fates. The prophecies the seers shared offended the Fates because it gave mortals greater control over their destiny, mortals learned to resist, even defy the Fates. The fates can be generous, even kind, but they are also unpredictable, arrogant, and powerful. It is with good reason that wise ones caution against tempting the fates." She continued.

"The Fates punished the seers. First, the fates bound the seers' lives together. When one seer died, the other two followed. Then, the Fates cast them apart, separated them with mountains and oceans. The separation weakened them. The Fates' rage was not sated. They wanted to punish the seers with eternity. And so the seers were sewn into time, to be born, die, and reborn, endlessly, without rest. Bound together, but always alone."

The story captivated me. I shook myself free of it. The story did not inform me. "This is not helpful Sophia," The pity in her eyes strengthened my resolve. "I need to know who I am, I don't want another fairy tale."

"They are stories, Win, I wasn't there. It is impossible to know how much is truth, how much is manipulation, how much is entertainment." She reached a hand toward my arm. I pulled back before she could touch me. "You asked me what I know. That is it. I know the stories that are told."

Nothing about Sophia added up. I scolded myself for my naivety. After days of blindly following her, I began to realize that Sophia could have good intentions, and still be a liar. Just as the witch could be malicious, and honest. I felt like a child. "Why were you looking for me? How did you know I would be at that house?"

Sophia looked grave, and maybe apologetic. "I wasn't looking for you. You were not what I expected to find in that house."

"Goddamn it," I cursed, "What were you looking for?"

"The homeowner."

I felt her reluctance, I pushed harder. "Who is the homeowner to you, Sophia?"

"I told you before, there are zealots. Fanatics who live outside of reality. I believe that the person who owns that house is one of these zealots. A particularly dangerous one. I observed you in the house. It was clear you were interacting with someone, someone real. But I could not sense him."

I interrupted, "How could you tell that he was real? If you couldn't see him or hear him?"

She watched me, a new caution entering her eyes. "I saw you sitting on the back porch. Talking to yourself. You reached out your empty hand. An apple appeared in it, and you ate it. So I continued to observe. I saw you. I could sense your thoughts, your feelings, even the images you had of him in your brain, but I could not sense him at all. When I saw his body in the cellar, I suspected you were seeing the past."

"Why didn't you tell me then what I was?"

"I didn't know," she confessed. "In the spirit of full disclosure, had I known, I probably wouldn't have told you right away. I think you would have dismissed it."

"Why did you try to convince me to go with you? What do you really want from me?"

Sophia's manner changed, she appeared offended. "I thought you were important. If you were there when I arrived, I was meant to find you. I believe that you can help me."

"I want the truth, damn it!" the whispered shout surprised her. I turned away from her and watched out the window. I wished it would rain.

"It is the truth. I didn't know why you mattered, but I knew you did. I wanted to keep you close in case I needed you. And you clearly needed help." Sophia was nearly angry too, now. "When you refused, I contacted George. I asked him to look into you. I asked him to figure out what you are. George is the one who determined that you are a seer. And he told me that his network was buzzing with inquiries about seers. His words," She assured me. "Someone is looking for you. I don't know what they know about you. And now we know they may want to kill you." Her voice held no apology. "This is mutually beneficial. I can protect you. And you can draw the threat into the open."

I nodded. There it was. "You *are* using me."

"Yes. And you are using me. What difference does that make?"

"I don't know." It hurt, I didn't say it, but I thought she heard it anyway.

"Win, I didn't want to scare you, but I may know who is looking for you. Someone who associates with the fanatics. The ones I warned you about. There are a lot of them, and they have a great many resources. It is why I told you, give the witch nothing about yourself. I don't want her to sell the information."

I kept my gaze fixed on the horizon, I didn't want her to see the fear in my eyes. I told the witch what I was. And I told her my name. The clouds looked heavy and dark. *It might rain.*

"I don't know why they want you. The witch said the possibility of death. Maybe they are looking for a powerful sacrifice. That may be why your friend died."

I whispered, "He wasn't my friend, I barely knew him."

Sophia shrugged, disregarding my pathetic assertion. "They are dangerous. I told you, there are zealots. I don't know them to be murderers, but I also know they won't hesitate to further their cause. You are not safe. They want you and we can use that to our advantage."

"Right," I agreed, "You keep saying that. And nothing else. Nothing that would actually help. Because if I know, I don't need you anymore. Then who are you going to use to draw the fanatics into the open?"

"I have been attempting to protect you, Win," she insisted. We sat in silence for minutes. The server approached, silently refilled Sophia's coffee, and left without a word. We were each of us uncertain what happened next.

Sophia broke the silence. "They call themselves The Order. I think it is in honor of their god. They wish to remake the world, to fix what they see as wrong with it. They might think they can use you to do it." Sophia's voice grew in desperation.

"Maybe they just want to recruit me."

Sophia shook her head, "I very much doubt that. Please, Win. You don't understand. *You* are more than you know. There are always seers. Always three. Their abilities are always the same, more or less. Some are stronger than others. But they are seers Win, they just see."

I shrugged, "I know. You told me. The witch told me."

Sophia leaned in, she said softly, "I've never heard of a seer doing what you did in that house. You said the two of you were together for hours. You are special. Maybe he was, too. If The Order knows what you can do, they will stop at nothing to get you."

"Wait," the meaning of her words unlocked inside my mind. "What do you mean, 'maybe he was, too?'"

Sophia appeared reluctant, she must have seen that we were beyond any reticence or omissions, she continued, "I told you George did some research. He found evidence that Twain was a seer. If you are both seers, it might explain why you could see each other. But I don't think that would be enough for you to physically, directly contact each other, to pass items across time. You are a great temptation for them." I wished I wasn't bothered by her motives. But if she saw me as a way to get to her enemy, as bait, I couldn't trust her any more than the witch.

"How do I know anything you tell me is true?"

She paused, her face turned sad, "You don't."

"I thought you just cared about me." I stood, "And it does make a difference. Probably shouldn't. But it does." I left the restaurant. I considered leaving the parking lot, the town, the state. Instead I waited by the car. I didn't know what my next move was. But I knew what it wasn't.

CHAPTER 23

Sophia didn't follow me out immediately. Presumably, she finished her coffee and paid for the meal. When she arrived at the car, she seemed ready to put the conversation behind her. I felt differently.

"I need my bag," I told her.

She regarded me with suspicion. "Win, what are you doing?"

"I trusted you. And I realize now that was foolish."

"Win," she interrupted, her voice gentle, an entreaty.

"New, is that what you called me? New and kind. Maybe I am, but I am learning. I can't trust you."

"I have protected you." She insisted, "I will protect you."

I shook my head. "And you have put me in harm's way. I'll find my own way from here. I'll protect myself."

"I could influence your decision," her heart wasn't in it, I could hear the hollow echo of the threat.

Her hold on me ended with my soft reply, "I hope you don't."

She said nothing more as she walked to the trunk of the car to retrieve my bag. She took longer than necessary, probably hoping I would change my mind.

When she handed off my backpack she stared hard into me. Whatever she saw was enough to convince her to walk away. To drive away. I refused to watch her go. Instead I held onto the witch's words, *you will be betrayed.* That one didn't take long to come true. It was a minor betrayal, maybe it did not rise to the treachery the witch implied. There might be even more to come.

I found myself alone in front of a crappy diner, in a random town, with no transportation, and very little money. Possibly being pursued by a dangerous cult who planned to hurt me. A snort of laughter escaped, *at least I have my pride.*

I admitted to myself, "Probably should have thought this through."

I returned to the diner to decide my next steps. I chose a new booth, in the farthest corner. I had enough cash for a cup of coffee, at least. And an emergency credit card if I decided to splurge on anything more.

My impulse to part with Sophia left me lonely and afraid. As I acknowledged I was friendless and alone, I told myself it was the right choice.

I considered my options carefully.

First, I could go home. Maybe it was dangerous, but I could go home and put the whole impossible ordeal behind me. Unless fate caught up to me, as Sophia almost promised that it would. Sophia believed there were two threatening factions, one that was mostly indifferent but would be happy to take the opportunity to abduct and or kill me, and one that specifically wanted to use me to enact an insane apocalyptic plan because of my unique abilities. Going home was impossible, there were still too many questions.

I considered another option. Find the other seers. They were my best chance at understanding my identity. They were my kind. They might be able to teach me how to control my visions. I equated them with hope, maybe even with family. No one could understand me as well as they could.

A wave of dizziness reminded me of the comfort I had lost with Sophia's departure.

I watched a young man seat himself at the next booth. He adjusted his body to sit sideways in the booth, his back against the wall. I had a good view of his profile. We were about the same age. He looked lonely. I watched as he unfolded a newspaper, with precise, furtive movements. He looked at a fixed spot on the paper. I wondered if he was hiding behind the newspaper rather than reading it. The man seemed familiar, and I knew we had never met.

My nausea increased and I wondered what I was about to witness. I noticed the headline on the front page of the newspaper, *Local Man Vanishes, Foul Play Suspected*. I wondered, *one of Sophia's abductions?* With effort I cleared my mind.

However, if I heeded Sophia's story, they could be anywhere in the world. Finding the others might be a good long term goal, and it might take years. Especially on my own.

Then there was Twain. Finding his killer. I wasn't sure what I would do even if I figured out who murdered him, but I owed it to him to find out what I could. Of course, I had no leads, and no way of getting any leads.

There was no way to help him, unless I really could change the past. Sophia believed that someone wanted me for just that purpose. If I could figure out how to control my power, maybe I could change things for him.

At the very least, if I couldn't save him I could make the world notice he was gone. He deserved to be mourned.

But that meant controlling my power. That meant finding out more about who I was, what I was. Without Sophia, I had no one to ask.

I watched the man in the next booth pretend to read his paper. He didn't turn the page. Good plan. He would run out of pages to pretend to read. I couldn't tell if was there or if he was the past; he lacked the typical markers of visions, no haze, not all faded. But he had coffee now, and I didn't remember the server approaching him. I wondered if he was different, not entirely human.

I suddenly remembered, "George!"

In the next booth, the young man's hand twitched, he peaked around his newspaper, shook his head a bit and went back to his reading. Or rather, his staring.

I realized, if Sophia knew about me, then so did someone else. And that decided it. I would solve the mystery of me. Then I could look for Twain's killer, or stop his killer. I could find the people who wanted to find me, and stop them. Then I could find the other seers.

George had given me his number, *just in case*.

I opened my pack to search for the slip of paper George had given me. The instant I opened the bag, I learned that Sophia interfered even when she was miles away, getting farther all the time. I found thousands of dollars in cash. I wanted to be angry, but mostly the sight eased my concern. I wouldn't have to sleep on a park bench after all. I reminded myself, she could be generous, and still a liar.

I found George's number. I thought carefully about the message to send.

I began, *Hi George, It's Win, I was at your house with Sophia.*

It had only been a few days, certainly he would remember me. *I need your help. I am on my own now.* I hesitated to include that, it felt like admitting vulnerability. *I would like to find someone who can help me understand who I am. If you have any ideas, I would really appreciate the help. Thx.*

I sat for an hour. I ordered a milkshake. I drank it slowly. I watched my phone. And the man in the next booth.

A woman joined him on the seat opposite him. He appeared unhappy about it, I thought I heard him quietly and tersely inquire what she wanted. He remained behind his newspaper. I divided my attention between the couple and my phone. They ignored me. She talked more than he did, their voices were low, I couldn't hear much, just words here and there. They were so engrossed, they didn't notice me openly watching them.

A notification flashed on my phone. My hands shook as I unlocked the phone and opened my text messages.

George's reply appeared: *The Sleeping Dragon.*

CHAPTER 24

Being on my own was not great.

Over text George offered three words, in person he'd given only two; that felt like relationship progress. However, now I was left to decipher his meaning without Sophia's knowledge and experience. The couple I was spying on disappeared while I was preoccupied by George's text, I ran out of viable distractions. Loneliness and despair welled up in my chest. I pushed it back down. "I'm a capable person," I whispered. And I would figure this out.

The Sleeping Dragon.

Based on experience so far, it could mean anything. It could be a vape shop, a theme motel, a comatose serpent monster. I considered returning to the witch, but even if I could find her, I had nothing to barter with. Other than information. Sophia may have deceived me, but I believed her warnings about the witch.

I returned to my phone, my only connection to information. George. He owed me nothing, but he seemed nice, and he was the option I had. Surely, he knew what he meant by "The Sleeping Dragon." I typed and erased several replies, each written with varied levels of urgency and demand. I decided on, *I don't understand what that means.*

Fifteen minutes passed with no reply.

I faced the facts. I was more or less stranded and I couldn't live at the diner. Sophia and I had passed a motel. I estimated it was about a half a mile away. I wasn't great at judging distances, but half a mile seemed like a perfectly reasonable, pleasant walk, so I stuck with the estimate. I decided on the motel as my next step.

I paid my tab. The server looked at me with doubt, as though she expected me to return again after a brief stop in the parking lot. I smiled, thanked her, and left.

The clouds had grown angry, they crowded the sky, threatening rain. The setting fit my mood, but not my circumstances. I hurried my pace. Rain started after ten minutes of walking, but I arrived after five minutes of rain. I congratulated myself on what felt like a pretty accurate guess about the motel's location. Two wins in an hour, I decided. One bit of luck in an otherwise troubling day.

The motel was just seedy enough to take cash without a credit hold. I attempted to explain away the wad of bills I handed to the person behind the counter. The clerk made it clear she did not care for me or why I was there. After Sophia's dire warnings about my safety, the disregard came as a relief.

The room looked like any cheap motel, vaguely uncomfortable furniture, sparse, aging decor. It was tidier than expected. I sat heavily on the bed and waited.

George was either busy or finished with me. I feared the latter. In desperation, I employed my only research tool: The internet.

A quick search turned up numerous impractical possibilities, including several novels, a land formation in Scotland, and the entire country of China. I sighed, "Definitely going to need help on this one."

Watching my phone for a reply increased my anxiety. I forced back the question, *What if he doesn't reply?*

I curled up on top of the scratchy comforter and turned on the TV, scrolling restlessly through a handful of channels. Boredom posed a credible threat when mixed with dread. I stared at the illuminated screen of the TV, watching shapes and shifting colors rather than people and stories. The news caught my attention.

A composed, attractive couple sat behind the news desk. Each with perfect hair and perfect clothes that hinted at perfect lives. They had never hid from a cult in a dingy motel waiting for a text from a mysterious supernatural being. I noticed their ease as they transitioned from a local founder's day festival to a story of menace and tragedy. A local man who had vanished had been found dead.

I sat up. I whispered, "The man from the newspaper?" I didn't know that it was connected to Sophia's mystery, but I wondered. She never said where the disappearances were happening.

The news anchors went on to describe the gruesome scene with as much tact as possible. Sophia had said the murders seemed ritualistic. I shivered.

The reports promised more information as it developed, and broke for commercials.

It was like hearing a word for the first time, and then hearing it regularly after that. Was I noticing what was already there? Or had Sophia put the idea in my mind, and now saw connections where there were none.

I turned off the TV. I forcefully cleared my mind by practicing every breathing exercise I had ever learned.

Eventually I fell asleep. I don't remember being sleepy, but I jolted awake in a dark, cold room feeling disoriented. I forgot for a moment that Sophia was not a wall away, but possibly a hundred miles away by now. I disliked how much I'd grown to rely on her in our short acquaintance.

The clock informed me that it was late, too late to be awake. I wanted to roll over and go back to sleep. I couldn't resist a look at my phone.

George had replied. Just an address.

Exactly what I needed, and no real information.

I rolled onto my side and curled my knees into my chest, determined to return to sleep. "What is with these people?" I muttered

CHAPTER 25

The emotional turmoil of the last day with Sophia took a toll. I slept well into the morning. With only an hour until check out, I hurriedly showered and gathered my things. By the time I was ready, there were only 30 minutes left before I had to vacate my temporary sanctuary. I didn't know where I was going, but based on the address it would take a few days to get there. As my morning deadline approached, I forced myself to stop stalling and I looked up the address.

The search result provided me with two key pieces of information. First, *The Sleeping Dragon* was a bar. I couldn't dismiss the possibility that it was built on top of an actual dragon, but maybe it was just what it seemed. Second, the bar was more than a thousand miles away. I knew I would have to travel to get there, I knew it was out of state, but looking at the actual distance in hours and minutes disheartened me.

I missed Sophia. She made the plans, I followed. She drove, I asked annoying questions to pass the time. I realized that I might have overreacted to her secrecy. Maybe I should have stayed with her and simply treated her with more skepticism. She seemed earnest in her desire to keep me safe. Or that concern was a pretense to keep me close. To bring the enemy into the open.

Then it occurred to me that Sophia might be following me, waiting nearby for me to regret ending the association, and beg her to let me rejoin. *That* I would not do. I didn't trust her and I had some pride.

After indulging the thought for a moment, I had to acknowledge, it was unlikely that an eternal being with great and terrible power was following me hoping I would miss her. Sophia didn't need me. She had connections and money and eternity to solve her problems. Based on her story, she could just wait for the next me. Maybe the next me would be more gullible.

I left the motel room with minutes to spare.

I had plans to make and nowhere to make them so I found myself back at the diner. I almost hoped to see Sophia parked outside. She was not.

There were only a few patrons in the restaurant. The server gave me a knowing look as I made my way to my usual table. I ordered a substantial breakfast, hoping it would buy me adequate time to make a plan. I searched my bag. Somewhere there was a notepad from one of the hotels Sophia and I had stayed in. I found it in the front pocket, slightly crumpled, but perfectly serviceable. The pen was easier to find.

I didn't know where to start.

I had no car. I had a lot of money. Renting a car with cash was out of the question. I wasn't sure that I could buy a plane ticket with cash. I could buy a car, but that would require the ongoing purchase of gas. My funds were ample, but not that ample. Only one option remained, the bus. I wrinkled my nose.

My food arrived before I could chart my bus path. I divided my attention between eating and searching bus routes, jotting down notes and looking for the fastest routes.

It took four buses to get to a bus that would take me out of the state. I assumed, when I got close, I could find local transportation to the bar.

Once I had a sketch of a plan I stowed my notes in my backpack, careful to ensure that my money remained present and hidden. Having a plan relaxed me some. I took more time in finishing my meal than I had in starting it.

With time on my hands, I enjoyed a little people-watching. Most of the diners held themselves with an ease that communicated they were regulars. I watched a mother admonishing her child for playing with his food. I watched a couple bicker about the tip. I watched as a new man entered the restaurant. He searched the room looking for a seat. Between his perusal and my unabashed staring, our eyes met. For a moment, recognition flashed there, he took a step toward me. My eyes widened in panic, I looked immediately at my plate. I kept my head down, but carefully raised my eyes. He looked at me a moment longer, then chose a seat near the door. Not for the first time, I wished for Sophia.

I couldn't look directly at the man, and I had to walk past him to leave. I reached into my pack and extracted more than enough to cover the bill and the tip. I tried to ready myself quietly, without drawing attention. I slipped my backpack on, the cash I held in my hand. I refused to look at the man as I approached the cashier. I set the money and the counter and muttered, "No change."

I walked straight through the door without looking back, and then hurried on through the parking lot, and then continued down the street. I didn't turn until I was halfway to the bus stop. No one followed me.

CHAPTER 26

Within minutes of the first bus trip, I remembered how much I hated public transportation.

On the first bus I picked a seat near the back. The back of the bus promised some anonymity. It fit the image that seemed appropriate. Several of us sought these seats, and it looked like at least a few had the same idea. Not sure how many of them were trying to discern their true identity and outrun some unknown occult threat, possibly the man two seats away in a bowler hat. The hat was a bold choice and there had to be an explanation. Through mutual, unspoken agreement, there was no conversation in the back and no eye contact. We exchanged plenty of surreptitious glances and undoubtedly a lot of judgment, but no communication. The ease of the experience offered me a false sense of comfort.

This bus got me about an hour closer to my destination. It was a local bus, and stopped frequently to exchange passengers, but the line terminated at a bus station, where I transferred to a bus that would get me out of town.

The second bus was less inviting, it had fewer stops and followed a long stretch of highway. The back was full, forcing me to the middle. The middle section of the bus stood as a kind of demilitarized zone between the front, serious riders with short distances or important destinations, and the back, ne'er do wells and malingerers who wished to avoid society. For two stops, I remained the only intrepid soul in the middle. But then we stopped a third time. A woman, heavily laden with reusable shopping bags, took the seat directly next to me. An unforgivable breach of bus etiquette. Internally, I conceded, maybe I sat in her usual seat. Maybe I was the interloper. She smiled at me, forcing me to smile back. And then she talked. And I listened. Her current boyfriend had a lot of promise. They had been together for nearly six weeks, and, the woman, she felt they should move in together. Her last boyfriend had been a disaster, she still wanted to get her dog back. Of course, her health concerns made the dog situation so much worse. And then there was her job. She thought she might want a new one, she knew for certain her boss disliked her and tried to make her miserable on purpose. Our time together included a long stretch of highway driving, and in those minutes I knew there was no hope for escape. Nearing the end of our journey, she asked for my advice three times. First about the new boyfriend. It felt disingenuous to advise caution when about a week ago I hopped into a car with a stranger and left my life behind. But I advised caution. The second time she asked for my opinion was on the old boyfriend. I paused long enough that she continued without me. Lucky. And responding to her final question, about her job, I got no farther than, "Well," before her stop came up and she bid me goodbye with an awkward side hug. On the whole, I hated it, it was a terrible bus ride. However, I couldn't say it was a complete disaster because I found a nickel on the seat as I exited the bus. Lucky, again. Once more, my ride ended at a bus depot. And there I transferred to another bus.

On the third bus, I returned to the back. My relief survived only a few minutes. All of the gregarious riders congregated in the back of the bus. The air resonated with community and camaraderie. I unwittingly placed myself right in the center of it. The bus moved, it would have been churlish to select a different seat. So I smiled and engaged, responded to questions with plausible fake answers and feigned interest in the lives of passing strangers. Under normal circumstances, I might have enjoyed my new bus friends. However, between my brutal travel itinerary and my growing apprehension about my destination I couldn't muster any real enthusiasm. I bid farewell to my new travel companions at the bus station and hoped for peace as I waited for the next bus. The long haul east.

On the fourth bus, I stopped trying to control my experience. I sat directly behind the driver and let fate take the wheel. This bus traveled distances. It would take me through the night, and get me within 20 miles of my final destination. Rather than stowing my backpack overhead, I held onto it. The last thing I needed was to lose my worldly possessions and all of my money.

I settled into the seat by the window. The bus had numerous open seats, and fortunately the one beside me remained empty. When we were well underway, I fluffed up my backpack, wedged it between my head and the window, and fell into a restless sleep.

CHAPTER 27

From the outside, it looked like any dive bar. A sandwich board advertised karaoke on Saturdays and a job opening. As I stood in the parking lot, it occurred to me, for the first time, I didn't know what to do when I found The Sleeping Dragon. I didn't have a name. I didn't have a clear question. I didn't know if I was looking for the owner, or a patron, or a tunnel to a dragon's lair.

According to the illuminated sign in the window they were open. I took a deep breath and went inside.

The bar was nearly empty. Probably to be expected at 5:00 on a Tuesday evening. An older gentleman sat at the bar nursing a beer. A couple sat together at a booth in the corner. And a woman sat alone at a table in the middle of the room.

Like most bars, the cavernous main room remained dark, the stained glass chandeliers receiving little assistance from the small windows near the door. The decor was understated and unremarkable, with worn shiplap panels and maroon upholstered furniture. A series of paintings depicting classical Greek scenes stood out as an exception to the understated and unremarkable. The paintings reflected opulent Greek revival art that had no place in a hole in the wall like this one. Their placement on the walls might have been garish, but somehow, instead I interpreted their arrangement as reverent, each painting illuminated by a single sconce.

Behind the bar, a woman changed out a tap. The woman had a pretty face, of an indeterminate age, she looked like she could take any comers in a fight.

The bartender looked up at me. "Hi Win," She said. I started.

"Hi," I replied automatically. I scanned the room, maybe there was another Win.

She smiled, "I'm talking to you." She grabbed a glass, selected a tap, and poured a beer. She set it on the bar, pushing it toward me. "On the house."

"Take it," The customer at the bar suggested, "She never offers drinks on the house."

I sat in front of the drink and gave it a sip. I didn't drink a lot of beer, but I appreciated the gesture.

"You can't say that anymore, Angus," the bartender told him.

I thought of Sophia's murderous hordes who, purportedly, wanted to abduct or maim me. No one in the bar seemed to care about my appearance. I leaned closer to the bartender and whispered, "How did you know my name?"

She considered the question for a moment. Then, she leaned in until we were inches apart. "George texted me," she said, startling me with the volume of her voice. I nodded, It still surprised me when magical networks operated using normal, modern means of communication. "You ditched the ancient one, bold move."

I looked around nervously. The open discussion challenged my low profile plan. "Um," I wasn't sure how to ask her to keep her voice down, "Could you keep your voice down?" Maybe not diplomatic, but nor was the request open to interpretation.

"Oh, they can't hear us." I looked around, wondering why she thought they couldn't hear us. "Angus!" She called, "Free beer for life!" The woman looked at him in anticipation. "I'm going to torch this dump for the insurance money! Who's with me?" She shrugged. "Nothing. We can talk. I'm Delphine."

I started to introduce myself, but remembered Sophia's warnings. "I'm not supposed to use my name."

"Okay, Win." She went back to her tap, "I just said it, but okay."

"What are you?" I asked.

She reeled back. "Wow. Clearly the ancient one did not teach you proper etiquette. You do not ask people that question."

"I'm sorry. I didn't know."

Delphine sighed, "If I am going to help you, you need to understand, you have no right to my story."

"Understood," I agreed.

"That wasn't mean," she added.

"Okay," I agreed again.

"You ever wait tables?"

The conversation took an unexpected turn. "No, but I'm not here for the job."

Delphine nodded. "I know, but you'll take it." She paused, "Because you need money." She filled another glass. "And because you want my help learning how to control your power." She set the glass in front of Angus. He acknowledged it with a grunt. Delphine continued, "Not to mention, you are hoping that I will help you understand what you are and what your purpose is."

"You got all of that from George?"

She smiled at the idea. "No. Not George."

"Sophia then, you have been talking to Sophia." I sat up straighter. I couldn't escape Sophia.

"Sophia?" I saw the understanding on her face as it occurred. "Right, Sophia. Your ancient friend. No, not from Sophia. I'm sure major players like that one don't have time for the likes of me." Delphine paused in her work and looked at me directly. "Are you going to take the job or not?"

I considered it. I was afraid to stop in one place. Afraid I would be found. But I couldn't run forever and I needed to understand more in order to survive. Delphine had answers. Possibly she could teach me. I reasoned that if she meant me harm, she wouldn't bother to offer me a job, or even spare the time for a conversation. I didn't know if I could trust her, but I didn't know I couldn't. More importantly I had no other options. Sophia's money wouldn't last forever. One last time I wondered if I should go home. I wondered how long it would take before I was missed. That saddened me.

I decided, "I'll take the job."

PART FOUR: THE SANCTUARY

CHAPTER 28

Delphine wasted no time introducing me to the bar. "Your hearing is bad, Angus," Delphine said loudly, "I said, Gin. As in Ginny, my new waitress. Fitting name, huh?"

Angus murmured his agreement. I appreciated the new name. My real name was noteworthy, and I didn't need anyone else knowing I was here.

"You can put your things in the office." Delphine told me, "Then I will show you around the place."

I followed Delphine's directions to the office. It might have been my strangest job interview; it was also my first successful one. The office was tidy and small. In addition to the door to the bar, there were two additional doors leading out of the office. I found a corner and stashed my backpack. I considered attempting to conceal my cash in my pockets, but it felt too ridiculous to try it. Instead, I made certain my backpack couldn't be seen from the door.

When I reappeared, Delphine set an apron on the bar. "You can start now. Clean the tables." She pointed to a room behind the bar, "Kitchen's there."

I wrapped the apron around my waist and followed her directions. I completed the first task and was swiftly assigned another, to be followed by another and another. The tasks were easy, clean this, take a drink to that table, refill the snack bowls. Remembering to respond to the name "Ginny" challenged me more than the work. Delphine agreed I should keep a low profile.

After a few hours of work my pace began to slow, and Delphine took note. "Not used to hard work?" she asked.

"I've spent the last two days on buses." I replied, trying to sound neutral.

"Oh yeah, that would do it." She reached into her pocket and extracted a set of keys. "My apartment is upstairs, why don't you go get some sleep? You can have the couch."

I thought of a dozen objections I should have voiced. Instead I asked, "Really?"

"Yeah, go on. I wasn't expecting anyone to help out tonight, anyway. Should be able to keep these crowds under control." I looked around, at this point in the evening our customers had nearly doubled to a total of seven. "The door across from the office will take you upstairs. There are blankets in the ottoman by the couch."

I gratefully took the keys. I retrieved my backpack before unlocking the door to the stairs that led to her apartment. I spared only a moment to take in her neat, well-appointed home. The furnishings were luxurious and the art on the walls looked expensive. I shrugged, more mysteries to unravel.

I found the promised blankets, nestled into the couch, and promptly lost consciousness.

CHAPTER 29

I slept through the night, with no offending nightmares. When I woke, I felt rested for the first time since the ordeal at the house. Delphine sat at the dining room table, eating and watching me.

"Hi," I said nervously.

"Good morning," She continued to watch me. I wondered how long that had gone on. "Of course." she said, "you're hungry." I couldn't tell if it was a question or a statement. "There is oatmeal. You just have to add hot water. There are different flavors."

"Yes, I've had oatmeal before."

"You've had the kind that cooks when you add hot water? It's ready in a few minutes. It's amazing." Excluding my conversation with the witch, this might have been the strangest conversation I had ever had. And I had a lot of recent conversations to compare it too.

"It's pretty great," I agreed.

"Kitchen's through there," she pointed with her spoon.

I didn't love oatmeal, but given Delphine's enthusiastic endorsement I felt obligated to make some and enjoy it. I chose a packet with cinnamon and started the kettle.

Delphine called to me, "There is milk in the refrigerator. And cream, if you prefer it."

"Thanks," I replied.

I was grateful for Delphine's hospitality. And relieved that she planned to help me learn more about myself. But she was a little strange. From the kitchen I could hear her talking to herself. She spoke quietly, but I caught the phrase, "...told her about the flavors..." I worried that I had not adequately displayed my appreciation for breakfast.

My meal readied itself within the promised timeframe and I returned to the table with it. Delphine watched with interest. I took a bite, "Mmm, that is really good."

Delphine nodded, satisfied. "I saw an advertisement on television, so I decided to give it a try. I've been eating it for breakfast ever since."

I smiled nervously, "We live in an age of wonders." I had no idea where to go with this conversation. I focused on eating with evident enjoyment.

"You can stay here for as long as you need," Delphine informed me.

I smiled in genuine gratitude. "That is really kind," I added, "and generous. I will try to find a place soon. You've already given me a job and I wouldn't feel right about inconveniencing you."

"Well, there is no pressure. I have some chores in the bar. When you are done with your breakfast, you can use the shower if you want. When you are ready, come down and we can set up a schedule."

I relaxed a bit when Delphine left. I finished my oatmeal with less enthusiasm. After I showered and changed into my clean shirt, I tried to erase my visit from the apartment. I tidied the bathroom. I washed the dishes I used. I folded the blanket on the couch and put it away.

Delphine toiled away in the stock room off of the kitchen, carefully shelving bottles of liquor.

"Thank you for letting me stay in your apartment. I really appreciate it."

"Yeah," she said, "It's no problem."

"I'll look around today, to see if there is somewhere I can stay."

"Like I said, you don't need to hurry. I don't mind."

I changed the subject. "Did you have a schedule for me?"

"I do." She handed me a photocopied page of a calendar. She had written hours on six evenings within each week. "We're closed Mondays. Does that schedule work for you?"

"Sure," I agreed.

"I have two other employees. You will meet them this week."

"Cool," I said, "I look forward to that."

"And as for our little side project," She began, I held my breath, "We can work on that when the bar is closed."

"That sounds great." I started breathing again. "Thank you, Delphine, I am really grateful."

"I figured that out by now," she smiled. "If you stay in this office, I am going to put you to work."

"I am going," I smiled back. I left the storeroom and then the bar. And then I realized, "I don't know where I am going."

CHAPTER 30

I wandered town aimlessly. Though I longed for the predictability and safety of life at home, I didn't feel home sick. I selected a new life with surprising ease. I had to hide, so I needed a new home. Someone dangerous pursued me, so I had to have a new name. Delphine offered me a steady income and a new name. It all worked out.

And I had no idea how a person assumed a new life. To get an apartment, I needed my real name. The thought of getting an apartment reminded me that I had one. In a few weeks the month would end and a new cycle of bills would begin. I wasn't sure I would be back to pay them. Which meant that a thousand miles away, "Win" would accumulate massive debt, while "Ginny" started fresh, with no identification, credit history, or documentation of existence of any kind. Getting an apartment seemed like a challenge.

I found a coffee shop I could occupy for a few hours. I bought coffee and a pastry and I settled into a seat in the corner. I tried to return to my early state of excitement, to think about the adventure and the opportunity. Instead, questions besieged my mind. I thought about what happened to my stuff, to my furniture, my broken car. I wondered if any of my regular clients would report me missing. I considered how long my rent could go unpaid before they broke open the apartment to find me gone.

When I left, I ran without thinking. I left the door open and an injured man on the floor. I might be missing already. But there were no headlines. At this point, I was far enough that the local news featured different reporters and different reports than home. I wasn't anyone important, my disappearance wouldn't make national news. Would they look for me or just pick through my personal possessions? Would anyone care?

My mood plummeted, as I feared the answer was no, no one would care that I disappeared. It occurred to me too that that wasn't entirely true. People who wanted to use me or harm me would care that I disappeared.

And I wondered, was there any way to track me? With that question, my self-pity turned to fear.

I took out my phone and began to search, *how to disappear*. And then I realized it. Opening my phone actively created a record of my location. At least, I thought it did. I turned off my phone. One thing became unbearably clear: I sucked at being a fugitive.

I spent the afternoon shopping, picking up essentials like a new toothbrush and a prepaid phone. I was no closer to solving my apartment problem. I did not want to sleep on Delphine's couch any longer than necessary. Both because I did not wish to wear out my welcome and because the roommate experience with Delphine was awkward as hell. I had a feeling, I would be eating a lot of oatmeal waiting for a solution to present itself.

I arrived thirty minutes early for my shift. I dropped my bag in the office and tied on an apron.

Angus occupied the same seat as the night before, drinking a beer and idly working his way through a bowl of bar snacks.

"How did the apartment hunt go?" Delphine asked.

"Not great," I admitted. "But I will keep trying." By that I meant, I might buy a camper van and live in the parking lot.

"You looking for an apartment?" Angus asked.

"Yeah," I smiled, "I haven't quite figured that part out yet."

"Hmm," he said. "You into drugs?"

"No…" I added, "No, thank you?" Because I wasn't sure if that was an offer.

"You listen to loud music?" He asked.

"I have headphones," I assured him. I shot a questioning look to Delphine. She shrugged.

"I have a place you can rent. A mother-in-law apartment over the garage."

And I almost jumped up and down. If he didn't require an application or proof of identification, it might be the solution to my problem. I kept a calm demeanor and an even tone. "Your mother-in-law doesn't need it?"

"Nah, my wife hates her mother. Anyway, her mother is too good to live over a garage, that's for damn sure." He took a card and a pen out of his pocket. He jotted a quick note and handed me the card. "You too good to live over a garage?"

"No sir," I assured him.

"Come by tomorrow afternoon and you can see the place."

"Sounds good," I smiled politely. Internally, I smiled and laughed and danced.

Delphine looked at the card over my shoulder, "That's lucky."

I nodded. The card read "Angus's Auto Body Shop." On the back he had written an address.

It was shaping up to be a good day after all.

CHAPTER 31

After my shift, I spent another night on Delphine's couch. The couch was deeper than the average couch and I was shortish, overall it was quite comfortable. I considered my haste in finding a different arrangement, long term. I didn't know if Angus's apartment would work out. It might be a traditional rental agreement that involved telling him my real name. It might be cost prohibitive. It might be unlivable, maybe I was too good to live above a garage, and I didn't know it.

For the second day in a row, I woke up to Delphine watching me sleep. Whatever Angus offered, I prepared myself to take it. Delphine and I enjoyed our oatmeal together. It took some effort to convince her that I had eaten the kind with the dehydrated peaches before and I did not need a bite of hers to know how delicious it tasted. After breakfast, she went about her morning chores in the bar.

Once I showered, dressed, and tidied, I set out for the day. I decided to learn more about the town, and find important locations like the library and Angus's house. By the time of my appointment with Angus I had acquired a working knowledge of town and its amenities. I found Angus's home within walking distance of the bar, which might explain his regular patronage.

His house was old and well maintained. A lush garden surrounded the house, bursting with cheerful colors. The garage stood apart, a separate building at the end of the driveway, extending behind the house.

As I approached, I saw a woman on her knees in the garden. She saw me, and smiled.

I returned the smile. Before I could introduce myself, she said, "You must be Ginny."

Surprise tightened my chest, chased away by relief. I nearly introduced myself as Win. "Yes," I agreed. "Angus said to meet him here at two o'clock."

"He's probably held up at the shop. He's always late," she said, with an indulgent exasperation. "I'm Kya. Angus's my husband. Why don't we sit, have something cold to drink?"

"I don't want to put you out."

"Nonsense. I could use a break and some company. Angus will want to show the apartment himself, so that you can compliment him on the fixtures and the decorations." She escorted me through the house to the kitchen. The house was as beautiful inside as it was out, made more charming by the clutter of a full life. In the kitchen, Kya put together a serving tray with iced tea and cookies.

"Angus decorated the apartment?" I asked.

"Yes, he is very proud of it. When he decided to make an apartment above the garage, I told him he would be on his own with it. I am useless at indoor spaces." She picked up a bottle from the counter. "You want some bourbon in yours?"

"No, thank you." I resisted the urge to check the time. Kya shrugged and added a generous pour into one of the glasses.

Kya waved away my attempt to carry the tray and led me out onto the back patio. The backyard was even more beautiful than the front. The garden looked a bit wilder, more natural, though clearly just as well cared for.

"Did you do all of this?" I asked.

"Oh yes, this is my retirement plan." She grinned.

"It's beautiful. I can't even keep a houseplant alive."

She took a long drink from her tea. "We all have our gifts."

I thought, *most people don't have mine*. I remembered Sophia's words and amended, *no one has mine*.

Kya talked me through her plans for the garden. I attempted to ask polite probing questions about gardening, but my ignorance asserted itself immediately. She let me off the hook by asking questions about what I did. I answered by sharing my new place of employment, and shifting the focus back to her, and what she did before retirement. She shared about her work as a research chemist. Her description started out interesting, but began to be too technical for me to follow and once again my ignorance appeared.

Angus's arrival spared me the opportunity to prove myself ignorant for a third time. Upon approach he asked, "You ready?"

Kya sighed, "Would you like to join us, Angus? I could make you some tea."

"Tea?" Angus snorted, "Is this tea?" He picked her glass and took a drink.

She raised her eyebrows at me and shook her head.

"Yeah, I'll have some of that tea. Hold the ice. And the tea."

Kya replied, "Incorrigible."

OUT OF THE WAY THINGS

"Come on Ginny," He said to me, "You don't want to hang out with this drunk old lady."

Before I could object, I heard Kya laugh. She called after us, "Everyone likes hanging out with drunk old ladies, Angus."

I liked their teasing relationship. Angus had a cantankerous, gruff charm and Kya offered an ease and likeability. Already the experience provided a good alternative to Delphine's couch.

The apartment entrance stood at the top of a flight of stairs on the side of the garage. Angus led me up the stairs and opened the apartment door for me. Knowing that Angus made the space himself, I was prepared to look and act impressed.

We entered into a bright, welcoming space and I didn't have to act. The size was modest, but larger than my real apartment. The furniture was sturdy and comfortable, simple and well crafted. I loved it at once.

"We could take the furniture out, if you have your own or want something different."

"No," I told him. "It's perfect. I wouldn't change a thing."

The tour continued. The apartment was open plan, so the living room met the dining room which became the kitchen. The bedroom was in a separate room, a luxury I hadn't enjoyed since childhood. There was even a small study, with a neat little desk and a bookshelf. All together more than I hoped for and better than living in a van by a mile. I prepared myself for negotiations, for terms I could not meet, and disappointment.

Angus asked me, "So you want it?"

I responded, "Yes, please."

He said, "Great."

And I had a home. Lucky.

CHAPTER 32

Moving into the apartment was easy. I had a backpack and two shopping bags filled with recent acquisitions. Kya offered to help, but I assured her I could manage. Angus only asked for the first month's rent. He said he felt better with it occupied. The rate was beyond reasonable, and he added it might be nice for Kya to have company from time to time. I enthusiastically agreed to the terms, but insisted on paying a deposit.

Just like that I had a job and a home. Possibly, I had friends.

Kya and Angus made excellent neighbors. They checked on me often enough that I felt like they cared, but not so often that it felt intrusive. They included me, but they didn't ask too many questions. It was ideal.

I finally had a job I liked. And I had coworkers. And they were nice to me.

I loved learning the rhythm of the bar. I knew that if Angus noticed me after his fourth drink on a Saturday night, I would be compelled into a karaoke duet, most likely "Nothing's Gonna Stop Us Now" by Starship. I memorized the words, just in case. Kya only came to the bar on Saturdays. She would not sing with Angus, but she occasionally sang alone in a haunting, sweet voice. Though I had begun to regard Kya and Angus as friends, there remained a mystery surrounding them that I was reluctant to explore. Angus impressed me as old when we met, and though he wore iron gray hair and lines etched around his eyes and mouth, he didn't look old. He carried himself with a physical confidence that spoke of youth, a surety that whatever he asked of his body, it would comply readily. I placed his age somewhere between forty and seventy. Delphine dismissed him as a self-interested, old drunk. But I caught him paying attention, even when he looked to be absorbed with watching the line of his beer sink toward the bottom of his glass. He listened to whispered conversations and leaned in to decipher the coded exchanges between Delphine and me about my predicament. Kya was a complete enigma, nothing special in her outward appearance, but on occasion, she chose words and phrases that hinted at some deep insight or arcane knowledge. After so many months in the world of mystics and immortals I wondered if I was beginning to imagine magic everywhere, or if there was magic everywhere.

Angus and Kya were the most interesting patrons of the bar, easy to watch and wonder about. But they were not the only ones I subjected to scrutiny. I learned the habits of a few dozen regulars, each with their own preferred dates, times, seats, and drinks. Sometimes, when evenings were quiet and the most important tasks were complete Delphine deliberately ignored me while I played board games with a group of regulars who were close to my age. I always made up the time, though she never asked me to.

I started to feel normal. My hallucinations became less and less frequent. They almost never happened in the bar. And they rarely happened at home. Occasionally they happened while I was out and about running errands. They were infrequent enough that when they happened, it caught me off guard. I almost jumped into traffic to stop a man from being hit by a car before I noticed the unnatural fog around him and he disappeared.

Delphine waited nearly a month before she reminded me that she knew about my affliction. She asked me, "Are you about ready to start your training?"

"My training?" I asked. "Do I get to learn to make drinks?"

"I don't mean in the bar."

"Oh," I remembered. "Yeah, I guess so." A part of me wished I could live this life, without any special abilities or gifts. I wished I could forget all of the past.

"We can start tomorrow. I want you in my home gym at least three days a week. And then three days a week we will work on your other skills."

I had questions. I started to ask about the gym, but she cut me off.

"You want my help, you do it my way."

"Okay," I agreed because I had no alternatives.

I spent the evening nervous and distracted. Delphine's training announcement acted as a reminder of what I was, and the reminder arrived with a looming threat I wanted to forget. My real life tumbled into the present. Abandoned property, mounting bills, past due rent, murderous cult.

Eventually Delphine grew tired of my subpar job performance and sent me home for the evening.

"Get some rest," she instructed me. "You're going to need it."

Probably because she told me I needed sleep, it became impossible for me to obtain it. I spent the night tossing and turning. Eventually, I got up and laid on the couch in front of the television. I surfed through channels, lingering on news reports. I watched for my own disappearance, I watched for abductions and murders and the sorts of things Sophia investigated. For the first time, I wondered if that was her job. I wondered if she was an investigator, like George. It explained her secrecy, and her interest in me. We met because she was tracking a cult. And she indicated that she had an interest in the disappearances George mentioned. I asked Sophia so many questions, and though I was curious about her past and the nature of her existence, I never really asked about her day to day life.

The television had no answers for me. After scanning through all of the channels I decided on a rerun of old an sitcom, hoping the banality would lull me to sleep.

When I finally slept, I dreamt of Twain. They were new dreams. I wasn't afraid and he wasn't afraid and we talked.

I woke up tired and sad. I missed a person I barely knew, and I felt foolish. I took my time getting ready. I dressed for physical activity, because I wasn't certain what Delphine had in mind, but I imagined a lot of running on treadmills and possibly getting duped into washing her car.

When I got to the bar, Delphine sat me down. "Today, we will work on your visions, tomorrow we will work on your strength and endurance. And we will continue every other day. Mondays, the bar is closed, so we rest."

"Got it," I agreed. "So what do I do?"

"Have a vision," she suggested.

"I don't actually know how to do that."

"Try something. Think about the last time you had one. What did you do?"

I thought back, it had been a few days. I was at the grocery store. I was thinking about buying a car, but spending the money made me nervous. Then I turned a corner and I watched a fight that wasn't happening. "I didn't really do anything. It just happened."

"What was your state of mind?" She asked, grasping at straws.

"I was anxious. About money."

Delphine looked surprised. "Do you need money?"

"No," I told her, "I'm fine. I was thinking about a big purchase, that's all."

"I hope you would tell me if you needed money."

I furrowed my brow, why did immortal beings always want to give away money. "Sure," I said.

"I have an idea, come on." She beckoned me to follow her upstairs. She set me down on the couch and began searching her streaming services. The television was placed on a wall adjacent to the couch. I sat sideways in order to face the tv. "Here we are," she said, satisfaction clear in her voice. "Watch this motion picture. It is very frightening."

"Why..?" I asked. "I don't like scary movies."

"We need to make you nervous. Then you will have a vision, then you will begin to understand how your gift works." She headed for the door.

"Where are you going?"

Delphine paused, "I don't enjoy this program. It's very disturbing. Come down when you're done."

I waited until I heard her close the door at the bottom of the stairs, then I turned the movie off. I could make myself nervous, I didn't need a horror movie. Just sitting there worrying about whether or not I would ever be able to control my ability made me nervous. "Did it." I told the empty room. I attempted to will a vision. Nothing happened.

I closed my eyes and focused. For a moment, I thought I saw something at the edge of my field of vision. I opened my eyes widely and tried to see. Nothing.

I tried a few more times, but after twenty solid minutes of effort, I gave up and went downstairs.

CHAPTER 33

With sustained effort, I improved very little. I had moments, moments in which I thought something might happen. However, as soon as I felt close, the sensation skittered away. I felt the loss keenly. I tried picturing myself having a vision, I imagined plucking one out of the air, I relaxed and invited a vision. The closest I came was when I slowed my mind and reached out for it. Then I felt something, at least.

Delphine felt frustration, and she expressed it. "I don't understand why you can't do this. I feel like you are not really trying."

"I'm trying," I insisted.

"Try more," she offered. I "tried more," as Delphine suggested. It felt like plunging my hands into icy water. My fingers stiffened and I lost sensation. I tried to latch on to something, I could see it, a vision, just at the edge of my reach, but I couldn't close my fingers around it. It slipped away as soon as I grasped it in my mind. The more I tried, the more elusive the visions became.

"I feel like I am getting worse at it," I complained.

Delphine cringed. "Enough with the whining. It's annoying,"

I prepared to deny it, but I was whining. "It isn't working. And I don't know what to do differently."

She shrugged, "Do *something* differently. It's not working."

I walked away. Walking away was something different.

"Let me know when you are ready to try something that will work," She called after me.

The attempts to use my power were so unpleasant, I began to look forward to training in Delphine's home gym. She preferred this training as well. Sometimes she gave up on the other early and sentenced me to more gym time. I didn't mind.

We began with basic cardio and strength training. I wasn't really the workout type, but she motivated me by making it a condition of her assistance in harnessing my visions. At least this training I felt like I could control. She wanted me to run, I knew how to make my body do that. She wanted me to pick up something heavy, my arms didn't have to figure it out. I didn't question any of it until she told me I was ready to learn to fight.

"What?" I asked, certain I heard her wrong.

"You need to learn to fight."

"Why?" I asked. I witnessed enough violence, random violence that appeared in front of me without warning. I didn't want to participate in it. "What does that have to do with my power?"

"Nothing," Delphine responded.

"So, why am I learning to fight? When am I going to use it?" I asked.

Delphine looked puzzled, "You work in a bar."

I couldn't argue with that logic.

Delphine liked teaching me to fight best. We practiced punches, jabs, kicks, holding, breaking holds. Everything she knew, she wanted me to learn. I hesitated at first, holding back, afraid to fully engage. Delphine alternated between encouragement and taunts, eventually breaking through my reluctance. As I began to feel successful in hand to hand combat, I noticed I felt generally more confident. I noticed that I improved in all areas, except the one that was most important: My visions.

CHAPTER 34

My job, my training, my friends, they acted together as an easy escape from the reality of my situation. The reasons I hid in a town far from home, the reasons I needed a new identity, they lurked quietly in the background of every interaction, every conversation, every decision. I became obsessed. I searched the news for stories, stories of Twain's body, stories of kidnapping and murder, stories of my disappearance.

Nothing appeared about Twain. Nothing I could find. And my disappearance had gone unnoticed. But I started to see patterns of disappearances. I didn't have Sophia's resources or knowledge, but I had the internet and a knack for creative search terms.

I started with news reports, searching randomly across the country, looking for abductions, missing persons, or murders. Sometimes I could follow those to court proceedings or other public documents. The search was broad, and there were a lot of dead ends, but eventually I learned that each state posted lists of the missing. I followed names to social media posts. Sometimes people who knew the victims shared conjecture and facts. I couldn't be sure that they were connected, but I found a number of missing persons reported who were men, late twenties or early thirties, and many reports described them as loners. Once I saw the pattern, it was easier to find more. In many cases the victims showed up dead within a few weeks. When bodies were found, I looked for references to cults and rituals. I filled a notebook with names and descriptions and possible connections. It made for a good distraction.

I attempted to share my research with Delphine, but she shrugged me off and said, "Aren't you supposed to be focused on your visions?"

In response, I spent ten to fifteen minutes each day earnestly trying to summon a vision. But they continued to come and go on their own mysterious schedule. I would have happily neglected the training indefinitely, however, my visions began to assert themselves more and more forcefully and their frequency began to resemble my pre-Sophia era. My visions demanded to be brought under control. It felt as though my visions were jealous of my success elsewhere, and demanded attention.

I held out for a week before I admitted I was hopeless at controlling my visions and returned to Delphine for assistance.

"I am ready to try something that will work," I told Delphine.

"Finally," her tone conveyed her impatience. I sat at the bar, my head down, mindlessly scrolling news headlines, scanning for kidnapping and murder. The bar was empty, I had cleaned every surface twice. My new boss was lax to begin with, but on days like this she seemed to expect little actual work out of me.

"I decided we are going about this all wrong. We are going to do things my way."

I asked myself, *haven't we been doing things your way since the start?*

"You need to relax," she explained.

Delphine dropped a stout glass of amber liquid on the table, startling me. The smell overpowered my senses. "Is this whiskey?" I asked. I wasn't much of a drinker; alcohol didn't mix well with my vivid, often violent hallucinations.

She confirmed, "Yeah. And it's pretty good. I'll switch over to well whiskey when you are too drunk to notice the difference."

I held the glass nearer my face and sniffed it delicately. "I don't know if I can drink this." So close to my face, the smell made me shudder. I explained, "I had a bad Fireball experience in college. Woke up in a bathtub."

"There's a bathtub upstairs if that is a normal part of your process." Delphine clapped me on the back, "Drink."

I hesitated, looking back over my shoulder to plead my case. "I can relax on my own."

"You want my help or not?"

I returned my attention to my glass. I drank it in one gulp.

And I paid for it immediately, coughing, sputtering, and nearly vomiting. I emitted an unintelligible sound of disgust.

"Nice," I could hear her smiling approval. She put another glass in front of me.

"Seriously?" I choked. I could feel the trail the whiskey took through my throat. I felt it spreading into my abdomen, into my blood, and charting a path to my brain.

"Seriously?" She shot back, "You're still questioning my method?"

I took a deep breath. I wasn't making progress on my own, and I didn't have a better idea. Or even a *different* idea. "Okay." I exhaled.

The second drink followed the first, and the resulting reaction from my body just as I predicted: coughing and gagging.

The liquor made short work of me. The world moved differently around me and I felt more connected to my body.

Delphine set another glass before me, "I can tell you are not an accomplished drinker. You can sip this one."

"Can I? Really?" My response earned narrowed eyes and pursed lips. "It doesn't taste good," I complained.

"Yeah, and that glass will be worse, that's the well liquor."

I tasted the new whiskey, it tasted better.

"Why don't you put some music on? Drink that glass, slowly. When you are finished we will get started."

I obeyed. Halfway through the glass, I found myself swaying around the bar to the music, carrying a bowl of crunchy bar snacks. Those tasted better than normal, too. It took determination to eat. I held the bowl and glass to my chest with one hand and reached into the bowl with the other, requiring a careful balancing act occasionally threatened by my desire to continue dancing. I wondered how long it would be before I was drunk.

Delphine watched me with detached amusement. When I finished my drink, she called me back to her. I shuffled to the bar in time to the music, dropping my glass and the bowl on the well-worn counter.

"Have a seat."

I complied. Sitting down, fatigue crept into my body and my mind. I rested my elbows on the bar, and put my head in my hands. Delphine poured me another drink.

"Slowly," she advised. "Think back to trivia night last Tuesday."

"K," I nodded.

"You collected the answer sheets. You were totaling the scores."

"Yup," I agreed.

"Look up. What is the woman in the pink beanie doing?"

"Oh! She took her friend's drink. Uncool."

Delphine rolled her eyes at me. "Behind you, in the corner table, the man with the glasses put something in his pocket. What is it?"

"It's a folded piece of paper. I think it is his answer sheet."

Delphine bowed her head to me. "There you have it, Win. You just decided what you would see. And you saw it."

I gasped. "I did, I saw it. Something specific, and it wasn't scary."

"Now you just need to do it sober."

CHAPTER 35

Sober visions proved more challenging than drunk ones. On two subsequent occasions I summoned visions while intoxicated.

I informed Delphine, "I don't think this is healthy."

She shrugged, "It's fine. Your generation is always so worried about your health."

"Yeah, okay, kids today, sure, I will get off your lawn." I shook my head. "But you are about ten minutes older than me."

Delphine laughed. "You understand that I am immortal, right? I haven't even tried to pretend I'm human."

I flushed in embarrassment. "I know that. I just don't think about it all the time. This is all new to me." It didn't feel new. It felt normal and easy. I accepted what Delphine was, but it didn't really matter, so I disregarded it. Leaving me in a state where I both knew she'd lived for hundreds of years and I thought of her as a peer.

She continued chuckling to herself. Ignoring me as she prepared the bar for the evening crowd.

I continued wiping down tables. My retort came too late, but I offered it all the same. "And anyway, my generation didn't invent liver disease."

"You got me, there," she grinned. "I guess you better figure out how to see when you're sober. For the sake of your liver."

I mumbled a response that was more of a suggestion about what she could do with her advice. She laughed again.

I heard her quiet response, "I'm not being hard on her."

Delphine often talked to herself. Sometimes, I overheard entire conversations. Or at least half of entire conversations. For although she talked to herself frequently, she rarely responded to herself. Or at least, sometimes she responded to herself, but only when she asked the question in her own head. It concerned me at first, but like her inexplicable ardor for instant oatmeal, I grew accustomed to it.

Delphine interrupted my thoughts. "What's your story, Win?"

"Huh?" I didn't realize at first that she addressed me.

"Your story. Before you got here. I'm interested," she explained.

"Nothing exciting. I clean houses. I *cleaned* houses. Now I work in a bar."

"Give me a break. You have visions of the past. That is a part of your story, pretty unique feature of your story, I think."

I sighed. People rarely pushed past basic demographics. I didn't like sharing my past. Even Sophia never asked me about my past and she had learned more about me than most.

"Tell me," Delphine insisted. I joined her behind the bar.

"Okay," I agreed, and I told her a story, "Once upon a time, there was a little girl named Win. Win had a mother and a father, two older brothers and two older sisters. A perfect family. They lived in a nice house, in a nice town. Her family was accomplished, respected, even popular."

"But Win was different. Win saw things that no one else could see. Her visions terrified her family. Her condition separated her from her family. They were afraid. Win never knew why. She thought maybe they were afraid she could infect them with her condition. Or maybe that people would judge them for having a daughter with a serious mental illness. So, they taught her to cover it up. To pretend. And she did. Win's family was well-off and fiscally responsible. When she grew up, they paid for her to go to college out of state. She packed her car, went off to school, and never returned home." I shrugged, "That's it."

Delphine patted my arm, her eyes sympathetic. She meant well, but executed the gesture a little awkwardly. "They didn't call or visit?"

I poured myself a beer; I could thank Delphine for that new, healthy habit. "We talked on the phone periodically for the first few years. Holidays, birthdays. I made excuses to stay at school, they never tried to persuade me to come home. Eventually, I decided to wait, to see if they called me. They didn't. That was about ten years ago."

"Nothing since then?"

"I sent a thank you card when I graduated. For paying for college. Wished them well. But they didn't respond."

"There was no one you were close to growing? One of your parents, one of your brothers or sisters?"

"No, they didn't like me. Sometimes, I thought maybe my dad liked me a little. But only when we were alone. He kept his distance when anyone else was around. With five kids in the house, there was usually someone else around. It was obvious to everyone I didn't fit. Neighbors, kids at school, they picked up on it too. So I was pretty much just on my own. One time, when I was fourteen or fifteen, I stayed out all night. I didn't have any friends, so I just wandered around. I convinced some guy to buy me one of those big cans of cheap beer. I drank it in the park. I drank the whole can, even though it was disgusting. I came home in the morning, when I thought everyone would be awake. I walked into the kitchen with my empty beer can, in yesterday's clothes. My mom said, 'If you want anything to eat before lunch you better eat quickly. We have church and you need to change.' I only had one brother still at home. He didn't even look up from his eggs."

"And your father?"

"He noticed the beer, he asked if drank beer, now. I didn't even have the will to lie, to pretend I had a serious drinking problem. I just said, no, that I didn't like the taste. I made myself a bowl of cereal and got dressed for church. I just thought, they had one too many. Should have stopped at four."

"I'm sorry." Delphine placed her hand on mine.

I pulled my hand clear to take a swig of my drink. "It's not a big deal. I don't really think about them. I never belonged with them. It is better for all of us this way." I watched little bubbles of carbonation escaping my glass. "I like beer now, though."

"It matters what kind." Delphine shifted the conversation back, "Did anyone in your family have your gift?"

"Not that I know of. My father didn't talk about his family much, we didn't really know them. And my mother's family seemed normal."

I didn't have the impression from Sophia that my ability was genetic. In fact, the way she described it, it was almost random. But Delphine didn't know that. And I never discussed Sophia with Delphine. I distrusted Sophia, but I couldn't escape a lingering sense of loyalty to her.

"That's a sad story, Win."

I shrugged. "Everyone has a sad story. Mine's not that bad."

"It's not that good, either."

I seized the opportunity that presented itself. "What's your story?" I asked.

Delphine shook her head, "Not today."

It wasn't the response I wanted, but she stopped asking about my past.

CHAPTER 36

Between Sophia and Delphine I had learned several important truths about mystical, immortal beings.

Truth Number One: It is almost impossible to discern when Immortals are joking. Their humor is ancient and strange. Delphine expected me to understand her sense of humor, and sometimes became offended when I mistook her amusing banter for serious conversation. Sophia never had been bothered when I couldn't discern the difference, and made no effort to mitigate my confusion.

Truth Number Two: Immortals do not employ demonstrative facial expressions. This attribute exacerbated the first truth, and in addition, made it difficult to ascertain the seriousness of a given situation. When I mistook serious conversation for amusing banter, Delphine was equally offended as when the opposite occurred. Sophia took these mishaps in stride, as was her wont.

Truth Number Three: Immortals almost always answer rhetorical questions. On one occasion, I asked Delphine, "If I had to have a super power, why did it have to be a confusing one?"

"I don't know," she answered, "That *is* unfortunate."

Sophia answered rhetorical and regular questions in the same ways, she answered with perfect candor, or she ignored them.

And then, finally, they all collided in one culminating truth.

Truth Number Four: Immortals had limited understanding of the concept of mortal danger. It was logical that they would not worry overly much about death, having no natural lifespan. And it was never made clear to me if immortal also meant invincible. Their indifference to existential threat was exemplified in my interactions with both Sophia and Delphine. When Sophia insisted, "go into that cave and retrieve a magic mushroom" or more recently, when Delphine tasked me with "picking up a few odds and ends from an insane purveyor of illicit, underworld goods." Those weren't her words exactly. Her exact words included phrases like, "it's so busy at the bar" and "you'll be careful, it will be almost safe."

After the cave and the witch, mystical errands presented themselves as dangerous and potentially lethal.

"You worry too much," Delphine told me. "Follow my directions, do exactly what I say, it will be fine."

My head swiveled to stare at her. "The last time I heard that I got chased by a tree."

Delphine cocked her head to one side in contemplation. "Weird. I don't think that'll happen this time." She looked back to the paperwork spread out on the bar. "Anyway you're a better fighter now, I'm sure you could defeat a tree in combat."

"Great," I shook my head.

Like the last time, the directions were simple enough. I had also learned that even simple directions eluded me when faced with threatening shadows and terrifying monsters.

After a few days of light, consistent pressure from Delphine, I surrendered and agreed to the task.

The assignment took me fifty miles out of town. When Angus and Kya learned that I would be spending hours on buses to complete an errand, they insisted I take one of their cars. I could see it in Angus's eyes, I expected he would find me something cheap and reliable within the week.

The drive was pleasant. It reminded me of my time on the road with Sophia. I didn't want to miss her, we didn't know each other well and I liked being upset with her. But I did wonder what became of her after she left me. I wondered if she found someone else to bait her trap.

When I arrived at the shop, I followed Delphine's instructions precisely. I ignored the front entrance and walked around the building to the side. Hidden from view, the building offered a side entrance, I knocked in the pattern Delphine taught me. It felt ridiculous, I wondered if the knock was another example of Delphine's sense of humor.

The door opened promptly. "You the errand girl?" A gangly, middle aged man opened the door. His bearing expressed boredom. He looked like the embodiment of ennui, lifeless and thinning hair, long and lean with a thickening midsection, gray and hoary and nondescript.

My nose wrinkled in protest, *errand girl*, but I said, "Yeah, sure."

"Follow me," he signed.

Delphine prepared me for this. She also told me I would "see things" and it was "best not to react to anything." I looked around discreetly, prepared for awe-inspiring mystical artifacts.

The shop contained artifacts, to be sure, everything fell short of awe inspiring. Vials, figurines, and vessels of all manner crowded the shelves, fighting for space more than prominence. Nothing too exciting. I might have imagined a sense of power radiating from a few objects, certainly many things looked unusual, but nothing stood out as something I might "react to." I saw an earthen tablet displaying incomprehensible bifurcated lines. It might have been the Rosetta stone or it might have been the work of a child scratching out invented letters in clay. I wondered how much someone would pay for it.

One shelf contained a series of wax figures with indistinct faces, lined up in order of height. That gave me the chills. I imagined a nefarious destiny awaited each one of them.

The shopkeeper led me to a counter against the wall, midway through the store. The back wall caught my attention immediately. Shelves lined the wall, extending nearly to the ceiling. Amassed on each shelf were jars of varied shapes and sizes. Some held fluids and shadowy carcasses, some contained powders, some were simply opaque. Two jars drew my eye, on each end of the display. One container glowed slightly, golden and somehow dark. Though it felt impossible, I sensed evil in the jar. The other container, seated on the opposite side of the same shelf, accommodated an amorphous material moving swiftly within the glass enclosure. I divided my attention between the jars, until I sensed movement in the periphery of my vision.

Next to the counter, I spotted the "thing" Delphine warned me "not to react to."

A cage sat next to the counter, within it sat the largest cat I had ever seen. The cat's size exceeded the ideal capacity for the cage, it could barely turn around in the space.

"I have the package ready," the man's monotone voice broke through my fascination with the cat; I looked back at him swiftly, hoping he didn't notice what I noticed. If he did, he kept quiet about it.

"That's great," I smiled. He turned his back and started looking through labeled parcels on the back wall. I returned to study the cat. I disliked its confinement. It seemed docile enough. The size of the enclosure was cruel. The cat met my eyes, startling me. Its eyes glowed slightly, I sensed an intelligence, and maybe a plea. *I can't help you,* I thought. I half expected a response, instead, I heard nothing, but its gaze intensified. I noticed abrasions on its shoulders and legs. Someone abused the cat and shoved it into the cage. I noticed a heavy combination padlock holding the cage door closed. "Cute cat," I said.

"I had to drive it all the way from Tennessee," he spoke with a lack of wonder that hinted he had seen everything, and approved of none of it. "Here it is," the man dropped a box on the counter. "Will that be all today?"

A bad idea formed in my mind.

I asked, "There is one other thing, it's a fungus. It's sort of blue and it glows. I'm embarrassed to say I don't know what it's called."

"I know it. I might have it in the back." I nearly giggled at my luck. Still a bad idea, but one that might work.

"Could you check? It would save me a lot of trouble." I offered a charming smile. The shopkeeper grunted and trundled away. Immediately, I examined the cage. The only way out was the door, and the padlock made that option impossible. I looked around for an enchanted sword or some magical bolt cutters. Nothing stood out.

I focused on the combination lock. For a moment, I thought I saw something moving in front of the lock. I imagined the shopkeeper's hands, long thin fingers with knotted knuckles and bulging blue veins. Watching the lock, I gasped as his hands appeared, turning the dial right and then left and then right again. I recorded the sequence in my mind as I saw it.

I shook the vision away and looked around. The man remained safely out of sight. I remembered the cave, and recognized that I might have something to do with the peril I found myself in then, and I definitely courted danger as I reached for the lock.

I turned the dial without hesitation, following the sequence. I felt the scrutiny of the cat. I pulled the lock open and removed it as quickly as I could, opening the door while surveying the room. Still in the clear.

Upon exiting the cage, the cat stretched to its full length. For a moment, I wondered if I should be afraid of the cat, it may have been incarcerated for good reason.

The cat stood on its hind legs, easily transitioning into a biped. Standing, it was about the size of a small human. I waited, ready for an attack or a handshake. The cat nodded.

I interpreted the response as positive, "Um, you're welcome."

It blinked at me, and I felt a message.

"I should go, right?"

The cat didn't nod this time, but it nearly did.

I took Delphine's requested item from the counter, dropped the cash, and hurriedly followed the cat out the door. The cat melted into the shadows, disappearing in an instant. I ran to the car and lost no time speeding away from the shop.

After thirty minutes on the road my heart slowed to a normal rate. After sixty minutes on the road, I realized that I had finally summoned a vision on purpose, while sober.

I whispered, "Thank you cat creature."

CHAPTER 37

"It'll just get hungry and go back." Delphine responded to my confession with a complete lack of support.

"I don't think so. It didn't belong in a cage. Nothing does."

"You can't just go freeing things in cages, because they don't want to be in cages!" Delphine often expressed frustration at what she considered a lack of mystical acumen on my part.

I did not care. I asked, "Why not?"

Delphine didn't have an immediate response for that. She opened her mouth, then she listened to the silence, then she closed her mouth. After several seconds, "Because I don't want to have to find new suppliers, there are very few."

"Do your research. Select more ethical suppliers," I suggested. "What kind of cat was it?" I asked.

"How the hell should I know? I wasn't there."

Delphine shook her head and walked away.

I followed her, "What's in the package?" I asked.

"It's not your concern."

"I could have just opened it in the car."

"But you didn't. Missed opportunity."

"Aren't you going to ask me how I freed the cat?" I knew she wouldn't ask.

And she didn't. "I don't care," she replied.

I followed her into the office, though she clearly wished to escape me. "I focused on the lock and I saw the shop owner unlocking it. I saw the combination."

Delphine paused, "You did?"

"I did," I grinned.

"You didn't have a fortifying swig of whiskey or anything like that?"

"Nope," I confirmed.

Delphine nodded slowly. "That is very good news. We should celebrate."

"Yeah," I agreed.

"Later," she gently pushed me back through the door. "It's your day off, get out of here."

I was halfway home when I began to question Delphine's insistence that I leave. She kept secrets from me. She had every right to keep secrets, I kept them too. I wanted to respect her privacy, just as I had once asked Sophia to do for me. But I wondered, *what if her secrets are dangerous?* I didn't have the right to pry, I knew it. Yet, to stay safe, I had few options.

When I arrived home, I discovered another error I'd made in judgment. Angus didn't wait a week and he didn't wait for me to buy it. A reliable, gently used car waited for me outside the garage.

"It was a good deal," he explained. "If you don't want it, I can flip it and make a profit. I won't charge you anything extra, just what I paid for it. You can make payments if you need to." He continued to add excuses for the unexpected purchase.

I considered objecting to his generosity, to his kindness, but I appreciated it. And I wanted the car. I stopped him before he talked himself into making it a gift. "Thank you Angus, I have some money saved. And I need a reliable car. I am really grateful." On impulse I hugged him.

He accepted the hug with as much grace as he could muster. Then he pushed me away, took his keys from my hand, and gave me the keys to the new car. "We can deal with the title transfer later." He hurried into the house.

After the success of the day, I began to accept that I might, in fact, be lucky.

CHAPTER 38

I practiced at every opportunity. I learned quickly that I could call up a vision tied to a location that was pretty easy for me. I could conjure a vision connected to people too, however I struggled to control it. And so I tried it whenever I could. I hesitated to practice on the regulars, it felt like an invasion of privacy. Strangers felt like fair game, so I took every opportunity to see into their pasts. Sometimes I found things I didn't want, evidence of crimes or disturbing behaviors. Mostly I saw prosaic, normal lives.

Though I avoided looking into the pasts of the regulars, I did not extend the same courtesy to Delphine. Delphine served as my most frequent subject. I didn't mention it to her. The strangeness of her preoccupied me. More than just the obvious, conversations with herself, obsession with oatmeal, preoccupation with fighting styles. Her secrets plagued me; I didn't want to be caught off guard like I was with Sophia.

Looking into Delphine's past felt like staring into water. Everything appeared clear beneath the surface, but then any movement created a rippling distortion and the forms I saw lost meaning. One form appeared often enough I came to expect. It looked human. Still, the closer I looked, the more opaque it became until a gray shroud swallowed my vision. I never knew exactly what I was looking at. I kept trying anyway.

Day by day, I improved. I struggled with Delphine, so I looked for her in the places in the past I was certain to find her. Direct visions of Delphine eluded me, instead I searched adjacent to her.

Poking around in Delphine's past became an ordinary pastime, I stopped paying close attention to what I saw. I expected to see the regular bar operations, which stretched back years. And expected to see a shadowy figure. In some moments, the figure resolved itself into a girl, her face obscured. I knew she was more than just a girl. But when I caught her, her image rippled until it lost shape. Sometimes, I thought she might be me, perhaps that was how I looked when I saw myself in the past.

Spending so much time with Delphine, I habituated, her peculiarities became invisible. Still, I noted a number of her habits. She talked to herself a lot. It annoyed her when I answered, I learned the subtle difference in tone when she spoke to me and when she conversed with herself.

Delphine's speech and manner combined an interesting mix of old-fashioned and trendy. She commented frequently on food related innovations, but took for granted most of the technology I would consider worth discussing. I found her a pressure cooker at a garage sale, she received it with overwhelming gratitude.

After a few weeks working at the bar it occurred to me that Delphine never left the property. I had never seen her farther away than the parking lot, and I had only seen her at that distance a handful of times.

I also determined where I might find her secrets. I spent enough time in the bar to know every corner. In the office, stood one door that never opened. It reminded me of the basement where I found Twain's body. Delphine didn't seem the type to keep a body in the basement below her business. Of course, to my knowledge, there were no physical markers that distinguished people with subterranean repositories for illicit human remains. So, how would I know?

After asking myself that question, and several related ones, I realized that I had an unusual ability that allowed me to see into the pasts of other people. I still struggled with attaching a past to a person, Delphine more than anyone. But I was becoming quite adept at seeing into the past of a location and I spent a lot of time in places Delphine occupied. I saw three available options.

Option one: Ask Delphine what was behind the mystery door. I considered this option carefully. She might simply tell me what was there. Or tell me to go look for myself. Or tell me to stay out of it and to keep my special seer abilities to myself. And that last possibility was why I didn't select option one.

Option two: Wait for Delphine to exit the enigmatic room. From there, I would have to try to peer into Delphine's immediate past. There were two problems with this plan. I never saw Delphine near the mystery door. If she ever used it, it was after hours or when I was away from the bar or when I wasn't looking. Which led to problem two, when it came to Delphine, I could see into her very immediate past. However, the farther I got from the present, the more obscure the view became.

Option three: Focus on the history of the bar. Locations were my strength. I could sit in the office, and stare at the door, working my way backwards until I saw if she took anything in or out of the mystery door.

Option three meant I might have some explaining to do when caught staring at the door at regular intervals. As a drawback, not too bad.

I chose option three, acknowledging that if option two became available, I would try that too. I justified the endeavor by classifying it as practice. Delphine instructed me to practice. I knew it was also prying, but Delphine had no compunctions about me snooping around into other people's lives and I decided that she wasn't a hypocrite and she probably had nothing to hide.

Option three required a lot of staring at the secret door, and attempting to see some event worth noticing. I took all of my breaks and meals in front of that door. Delphine took the decision in stride, as she did most things.

The first time I caught sight of Delphine in the door's past, I nearly fell out of my chair, startled by her sudden appearance. I exclaimed, "I was thinking about an old episode of Iron Chef! Have you seen that show?" It was my prefabricated, feeble excuse for staring blankly at the door, designed to distract Delphine with conversation centered on food. I admitted to myself, strong concept, rough delivery.

But Delphine was not really there, just a shadow of her past. And because of my loss of focus, her specter trembled and shattered and faded away before I saw anything at all.

It took weeks to see anything interesting, but, eventually, I learned a little more about Delphine's habits from watching the door. Not what was behind it exactly, but I saw enough behaviors to justify my suspicion.

Delphine kept cases of food behind the door. She periodically brought cases of protein and nutrient shakes through the door and into the room beyond. There appeared to be stairs behind the door. Another basement. That gave me chills. I caught Delphine headed down the stairs with medical supplies on two separate occasions. A disturbing certainty began to grow in my mind: Delphine was keeping someone in the basement.

An alive person, there was reason to believe the person in the basement was alive. I appreciated the difference between keeping a living person in a basement and keeping a deceased person in a basement, but I wasn't really sure which was worse.

I thought again of the cat in the cage. Delphine reacted to my decision with irritation, forcing me to question if her response had nothing to do with finding a new supplier for magical, mysterious commodities. Maybe Delphine worried about losing her own captive.

CHAPTER 39

Surveillance of Delphine's recent past intensified. I became determined to get a better view of the girl I saw, when I tried to see her past. I never saw her for long, but the flashes of images became more and more distinct. As I began to see the girl's features, I knew she was not me, as I originally supposed. The image of the girl connected to the mystery of the basement. I had no evidence to support the theory. I also had none to refute it. Delphine shared nothing of her past. I knew she could fight. I knew she was strong. And I knew I had reason to be afraid of her.

Delphine noticed my distraction. She said little more than to comment that she was happy to see me taking my practice more seriously. I thanked her for noticing and hoped that practice explained my distraction. I had a lifetime of experience making excuses for my bizarre behavior. If Delphine noticed that I was becoming increasingly frightened of her, she said nothing. The more I searched the past, the more I came to accept that I would need to gain entry into the basement.

The task presented an impossible puzzle. Delphine never left the premises. She lived above the bar. She rarely slept. She noticed everyone's comings and goings. I was afraid there was nothing I could contrive to convince her to leave the bar on an errand. Short of burning the place to the ground, I imagined there was no way to get Delphine farther than the dumpster out back.

Her near omnipresent status left me with short windows of time when Delphine was too occupied with her work to notice where I was. Most chores that occurred outside of the building Delphine assigned to me, or one of the other two employees. Delphine oversaw deliveries directly, the only task that she insisted on handling herself. Fortunately, between my physical training and my seer practice, Delphine had come to expect that I might show up at any hour.

Deliveries were early. Which meant that I had to get myself together, and start showing up first thing in the morning. I couldn't go for the door on my first early arrival. Instead, I chose to practice my physical training. Delphine gave me free access to her gym equipment, located upstairs in her apartment. It delighted her that I was finally taking her prescribed exercise regimen seriously. By my third morning workout she promised to schedule me a "bout" so that I could practice my new fighting maneuvers. I groaned internally, and externally thanked her for the opportunity.

I let my early arrivals become a routine. The pretense forced me to improve my physical stamina. Because I arrived early nearly every day, far more frequently than the morning deliveries, Delphine began to rely on me as a sparring partner. She was a skilled fighter, and though she didn't expect me to be, she wasn't easy on me.

Delphine genuinely enjoyed this new routine. And though she liked me to begin with, the time together began to deepen our friendship. She talked occasionally about the old world. It was unclear if she simply meant Europe or if she meant the distant past. I listened, I attempted to understand. I felt incredibly guilty. However, no matter how wretched it made me feel, the more I watched the past, the more I became convinced that there was someone held captive beneath my feet.

CHAPTER 40

I nearly gave up on the door. It wasn't a lack of opportunity. Once Delphine grew accustomed to my appearances, she frequently ignored me, it would have been easy to slip downstairs and find a way into the basement. I felt terrible for doubting Delphine, for believing that she was the sort of person who could keep a person locked up against their will. I considered that my amateur investigation of abductions and murders left me paranoid, seeking intrigue and finding conspiracies only because I wanted to find them. Not because they were there.

Still, I watched the door. I took most of my dinners in front of it. Frequently staring intently with a fork stuck in transit to my mouth while I focused on seeing more. I cast wildly into the past, trying to see into the basement, trying to understand its secrets. And one quiet evening, without ceremony, and with no special effort, I saw her.

It was only for a moment the first time. I saw the girl, the one who was attached to Delphine in so many visions. She was young, and I saw her staring into nothing, her eyes empty of thought. She slipped away. I reached out again, and she appeared to be tied to a chair. I forgot my gratitude toward Delphine, I forgot the loyalty and the trust, as I grew in certainty that Delphine was a captor, and the girl her captive.

Once the girl's face was in my head, it became easier to call her past forward. Her face often appeared to glow with an inconstant light, hues shifting across the spectrum from full white lights to blues and reds and everything between. I couldn't see who she was or how long she had been kept in the basement, but I could see that she was bound, held firmly to a chair. I never saw her speak or struggle. She appeared vacant, defeated.

I considered calling the police. I could leave a tip, that the owner of the *Sleeping Dragon* held a girl captive beneath the bar. What information I had cobbled together about law enforcement from true crime documentaries and court dramas, led me to believe they would need a warrant to search.

And I would have to come forward and say that I had seen her myself because I had no proof. That lie risked too much. I didn't know if the girl was there presently, or fifty years before. I saw little more than her bindings and a vacant expression. Selfishly, I knew that if I was wrong, I lost everything. I would be out, on my own again, with no idea what to do. That fear slowed me. I needed proof.

I didn't have a clear path into the room. I could try to steal the key, but if that went badly, I could do more harm than good. I could break the door down, but Delphine would hear that and again, more harm than good.

The idea came from Delphine herself. I hadn't shared much with her about my experience with Twain or about Sophia's belief that I could do more than just see the past. But I told her that I believed I once had a conversation with someone who was in the past.

"Let's do it," She suggested.

"What do you mean? I don't really know how I did it."

Delphine waved her hand dismissively. "Just try it."

"How exactly?" I asked, frustration clear in my tone.

She rolled her eyes. "Go into the office. Set a timer for, say 30 minutes. Wait 30 minutes. Then come back 30 minutes into the past and talk to me."

"But, what if I see myself in the past? Or my past self sees me now? Won't that start a paradox that could end the world or something?"

Delphine shrugged, "I don't know." Typical immortal response.

As I walked into the office, I called back, "What am I supposed to do for thirty minutes?"

I heard her reply, "Read a fucking book, I don't care!"

We tried it, with fingers crossed that we didn't destroy the fabric of reality.

I spent my wait time doom scrolling on my phone, believing the endeavor to be pointless.

When the timer went off, I dutifully reached into the past. I was getting better about pinpointing a time to view, but my skills were hardly precise. Surprisingly I got the timing right. I returned to the bar floor within a few minutes of when I left. I attempted to talk to Delphine, but she didn't respond.

When I caught up to the present, I learned an important fact about my ability.

Delphine explained, "You were gone, about thirty minutes. Then you came out of the office. You talked to me, but you couldn't seem to hear me."

While I was seeing the past, I was interacting with the present. I was in both places, though at the time, I could only see one.

"Maybe you're the problem," Delphine suggested.

I conceded, "I'm the problem. It's me."

"Exactly! You're doing it wrong."

I returned a deadpan stare, "That is not helpful."

"Let's try again. This time, I will lock you in the office."

My first thought arrived in an instant, *She knows, she is going to trap me in the basement.* I shook my head clearing the thought, "Nope. No, thank you."

Delphine seized my shoulders, and shook me.

"Why?" I asked.

"Win! Pay attention." From where she stood she had to look down nearly a foot to make eye contact. "You are using your body. Try just using your mind." She turned me around and pointed at the office. "Go!" She insisted.

I complied. This time, per her suggestion, I attempted to reach out with my mind. After several attempts, I made it into the hall, where I saw Delphine, sitting in a chair against the door. When I returned to the present, and my body. I was standing in the office, pressed against the door. Progress.

More importantly, I discovered a way into the basement.

CHAPTER 41

I practiced for days, each time getting farther from my body. Counterintuitively, it was easier to reach out with only my mind, the further back in time I traveled. I worked on familiar locations first. But then, as that became easier, I started to attempt to enter places I had never been, like the neighbor's house. I forgave myself these invasions of privacy, I figured being a seer, minor infringements were probably forgivable. And I needed the practice.

Once I had built up some confidence, I made a plan.

I decided to try to enter the basement from home. In the event that Delphine was a dangerous kidnapper, I preferred to learn that fact from the safety of my living room. Even though my skills improved, I still had a tendency to move around while I was attempting to reach a different location in the past, so I cleared the breakables from the room and placed furniture in front of each entrance. When the room felt secure, I seated myself on the couch and focused a half mile up the road, on the door to the basement. I concentrated on the day before I arrived at Delphine's.

I opened my eyes to the basement door. I looked around. No sign of Delphine. I didn't expect that she would see me, even if she were in the room, but I was just uncertain enough to be nervous.

I reached for the door, then remembered I didn't actually have hands. I moved through the door and down the stairs. I felt myself moving as though I had a physical body, though I knew, my body remained in my apartment.

The basement was not what I expected. I couldn't quite escape the image of the root cellar that had become Twain's final resting place. I expected to see the same unfinished walls and low ceiling, darkness and shadows.

Instead, I entered an apartment room filled with light and cheerful decor. The girl sat in front of a giant television, her face in profile to me.

From where I stood, I could see she was strapped across the chest to a wheelchair. Her head cocked to one side, resting against the chair. Her face was blank and empty, she stared vacantly at the television.

I watched her. She appeared to be well cared for, she was clean, her hair was neat. The binding held her upright rather than restricting her movements. My guilt reasserted itself. It was weird, it seemed that Delphine secretly cared for a young woman with a disability. I wondered, *Why keep it a secret? Why hide a person in the basement?* It was wrong, but maybe not the same kind of crime as originally suspected.

Why not just ask me, a strange voice sounded in my head.

My jaw hit the floor. I looked at the immobile girl in the chair.

Yes, the voice said, *it's me. I've been waiting for you, Seer.*

I moved to stand in front of her. "Can you see me?" I asked.

Yes, she said, *You are standing in the middle of your living room. And you are here.*

I looked into the girl's eyes. When I had seen her in my visions I thought her eyes looked empty. Moments ago, I observed her as vacant, like a body with no soul. But face to face, I saw something very different. Her eyes were so busy with thoughts they appeared nearly opaque. What I had seen as absence, I realized was abundance.

"Who are you?" I asked. "Are you okay? Do you need help?"

She answered my questions out of order. *I am well,* she told me. *I could use some help, I would like to watch a different television program, but you are weeks and miles away. I am the Oracle.* She added, *You ask many questions, Seer.*

The Oracle. "I thought..." I stammered, "Sophia said... what?"

We are believed to be gone. We are not gone. We hide.

"Delphine didn't kidnap you?"

I heard nothing, but I thought she laughed. *Delphine is a dragon. She is my protector.*

"Wait, Delphine is a dragon?!" I would have needed to sit down if I had been in a corporeal form.

It is a title, not a species, the Oracle explained. *Her position is to serve me, to guard me.*

"Oh yeah, of course," I said, unconvinced. "You said you have been waiting for me. How did you know I was coming?"

I am an Oracle, she explained.

"Okay," I replied, "but how did you know?"

I am an Oracle, she repeated. *I See.*

"Right... Makes sense." I said; it did not make sense. "I'm really happy to meet you."

Come see me.

145

CHAPTER 42

I spent almost two days agonizing about how I would tell Delphine that I knew about the Oracle in the basement. I thought of every option. I could lie, say that the Oracle reached out to me, but I had no reason to believe the Oracle would back up what I said. I could engineer a situation where I discovered her, one that didn't involve me snooping. Once again, the Oracle could rat me out if I tried that. Finally, I decided that I would do the right thing. I would ask Delphine what was behind the door, and give her the opportunity to tell me. It was slightly dishonest, but mostly it was not. And, from a certain perspective, Delphine hiding a person in the basement was slightly dishonest.

When I stood in front of Delphine, I lost my nerve and blurted out. "I used my power to go back in time and I found the girl in the basement."

Delphine looked hurt. "I would have told you. If you had asked."

"I'm sorry," I said in an attempt to repair any harm. "I wasn't sure how to ask."

"'Who's in the basement?' would have been an option."

"Yes," I agreed, "That was an option I did not consider."

"I knew Penny would talk to you when she wanted to talk to you. She doesn't exactly take direction from me." She added quietly, "You don't."

"I do!" I insisted, "Who's Penny?"

"The Oracle. And I wasn't talking to you." Delphine's look indicated that it should be obvious.

"How would she have contacted me?" I asked. "She is strapped to a chair."

"I don't know how." Delphine continued with her bar prep. "She is very mysterious. She won't tell me how any of it works. She can talk to me, I figured, when she wanted to talk to you, she would."

"So Penny told you I was coming?"

"Yes, the day you arrived."

"You said George texted you."

"I lied." She shrugged, "Penny told me to say that. Who is George?"

I shook my head, "Just a guy I know." *Who isn't a guy, but I don't know what he is.* I added, "If Penny wanted you to know, she would have told you."

Delphine nodded, "Yes, she would."

"Penny. The Oracle, magical, immortal, omniscient, omnipresent, Penny."

"I call her Penny. Or Penelope."

"What's her name?" I asked.

"She won't tell me."

"She's okay with Penny?" I couldn't keep the skepticism from my voice.

"She says she likes it."

"Okay." I prepared for Delphine to dispute my next request. "She told me to come see her."

"Alright." Delphine removed a necklace from beneath her shirt and handed it to me. "The key."

"Really?" I asked. "Just like that?"

"It's a relief, honestly. I am tired of training you."

"Oh." I tried to sound casual. Delphine had never before implied that I was a burden to her.

"Except in fighting. Because that *is* really important."

"Okay. Still have to learn to fight."

I walked toward the office. I stopped at the threshold, "You're not going to train me anymore? Does that mean I am done?"

"I doubt it. You are still pretty bad at it. But it was never me training you. It was always Penny." Delphine smiled in gratitude. "She can handle that directly now."

My mind flooded with a multitude of incoherent, incomplete conversations I witnessed Delphine have with herself. "Wait, when you talk to yourself, are you talking to Penny?"

Delphine sputtered indignation, "I do not talk to myself."

"Oh, no of course not."

Penny waited for me below, as promised.

I began to despair that you wouldn't come, she said. Her clothes were new, she still sat in front of the television.

I asked, "Do I talk to you outloud, or in my head..?" Breaking the rules of etiquette with immortals became more and more common for me.

Speaking aloud is fine, Penny told me.

"If you're an oracle, didn't you know that I would show up?" She knew weeks ago that I would arrive.

It doesn't work that way. The future is not fixed, I see many possible futures. Things become more certain over time. Some doors close, and sometimes new ones open. Until this morning most of the alternatives had you leaving town. As she spoke to me, she moved very little. Her head moved a bit, she blinked. I could see how anyone looking at her might see a person who was completely unaware of her surroundings. The opposite proved true. Penny saw everything, felt everything, her brain inundated with information from all directions.

"I have questions."

I know. You always do.

"Where are you from? How did you get here? How old are you?"

Eastern Europe. A boat, then a wagon. Very old.

"Do you know Sophia?"

I know of her.

"How old is she?"

Older than I am. I could answer all of your questions, Win. It may satisfy your curiosity for a moment, but you will only think of more questions.

I considered her point. I could think of a lot of questions that an oracle could answer. "You're right. But I have a few more."

Penny thought, *sigh.*

"Why hide? You could just live in the world. There are plenty of people who use wheelchairs now. No one expects them to hide in their homes."

Interesting. I imagined she nodded her head, thinking through my suggestion. *How many of them are immortals who do not demonstrably age?*

I admitted, "I don't know. Maybe none?" I sensed a smug reaction. "So maybe don't live a public life. But you could come upstairs. Or go out occasionally. Most people pay no attention to the people around them. The modern world is super anonymous."

I will consider that.

"Delphine says she is done training me. Am I done learning?"

Penny's head shifted. *One hopes one is never done learning.*

"Okay, yeah, *and* I think you know what I mean."

I will teach you.

"Can I call you Penny?"

You may.

"I am going to keep trying to convince you to go upstairs," I informed her.

I know.

CHAPTER 43

Training with Penny changed everything. First, she knew more about me than anyone I had ever met. I made the mistake of telling her so once.

She responded, *Win, that makes me sad. No one knows you so well as you know yourself.*

Penny's perfect absence of expression left me guessing. I could never figure out when she was joking. I knew she joked. I knew she often made jokes at my expense. Delphine regularly laughed at them. Somehow, Delphine distinguished earnest Penny from humorous Penny. I had no idea the subtle differences in tone that communicated Penny's intentions. Especially as she remained a voice in my head. It was like interpreting tone in writing. I assigned the tenor and inflection without real evidence, and often in the ways that incensed or insulted me. As a result I rarely asked questions about myself, as the discussions left me irritated and dissatisfied.

The inherently deceptive nature of telepathic communication was the only thing dishonest about Penny. She had great depth, of emotion, of thought, of character.

Under Penny's expert guidance, my growth accelerated. Penny could explain what Delphine struggled to articulate. She understood first hand what it felt like to initiate a vision and how to prevent the visions from overwhelming my senses. She steered me when I was stuck.

As we got to know each other, I found that I liked her.

First, Penny approved of my setting the cat creature free. She said, *I am glad you let her go. She is a great protector.* Mostly, the immortals I met gave me grief for my impulsive decisions and poor choices. Penny affirmed my actions, understood why I took the risk.

Second, I enjoyed her company. Once I knew she existed, I showed up at the bar to keep her company. She enjoyed an eclectic variety of television. She wanted someone to talk to about it. Delphine didn't care much for TV, I graciously stepped in. She forced me to watch a great many bizarre shows. I introduced her to audiobooks and podcasts. Determined to get Penny out of the basement, I recommended podcasts about adaptive technology and speech generating devices. In my mind, there was no reason why she couldn't interact with the world. I understood if she and Delphine hesitated to be out in the open, but she could spend time in the bar, maybe take the occasional outing.

Penny didn't comment on these seeds I planted, still, I suspect she considered them.

Finally, Penny became the first person to answer nearly all of my questions. Sometimes, her responses were vague, and sometimes she refused to answer out of respect for the privacy of others. But mostly, she answered my questions.

Penny felt like the first person I could trust, in my life. Penny liked me as well. She responded to me with genuine warmth. She held me accountable to my goals. She treated me like an equal, even though I wasn't her equal.

I still questioned Delphine's motivations, I would never know Sophia's, but I believed in Penny. It wasn't that she was incapable of deceit, I suspected she could lie as well as anyone. She existed beyond duplicity. She needn't lie, because she had access to every truth. She was fearless.

After working with her for weeks, Penny helped me to see that I belonged at the bar. One day, I might reclaim my name, but I would never return to my old life.

CHAPTER 44

At Penny's insistence, we were watching a dense, twisty television show with subtitles. I was curled up in the armchair in front of the television. My chair and Penny's formed a V, allowing us to alternate between conversation and companionable television viewing. I leaned toward the screen, fully engrossed and waiting eagerly for the next reveal. As such, I was unprepared for Penny's question.

Why did you come here? She asked.

I looked at her and pointed at the television in confusion.

Not today. She clarified, *To the bar. When you first arrived, why did you come here?*

It took a full minute to drag my mind from her engrossing show and consider her random question. To buy time, I pointed out the obvious, "That's a random question."

As she often did, Penny responded only with the information she felt pertinent. *You don't have to see the connections for them to exist, Win.*

I sighed. No getting out of it. "I didn't have anywhere to go. People were after me. I thought if I could control my power, then maybe I could use it to help Twain. It's not one reason, no one does anything for just one reason."

Twain is the dead boy? She asked. *How can you help a dead boy? Is he a restless spirit?*

I flinched at the plain terms Penny used to describe Twain. "What do you mean restless spirit? Ghosts aren't real."

Of course ghosts are real. I recognized the subtle change in her expression, exasperation tinged with condescension.

I resisted responding with, "Sophia said…" and instead asked, "You can see ghosts?"

There are many things I cannot see that are real. Penny replied, haughtily.

I gave in and responded with, "Sophia said ghosts aren't real."

In her silence, I felt her indignation. Her reply arrived, curt and a little petulant, *Well, I believe they are real.*

I let that sit, and returned my attention to the television.

Penny stayed quiet for a few minutes before continuing, *If you don't believe he is a ghost, how will you help him? He is dead.*

"I'll go back and warn him. Tell him to run away." This time I sounded indignant.

How? He has been dead for a long time.

"However I did it before, I guess. I would just find him in the past and tell him what was going on, so he doesn't try to hide or fight or whatever it is he did."

I watched Penny's expression carefully. I noted skepticism, doubt. She told me, *I have known many seers. I have not known them to talk to the past.*

"Well I did," I insisted, "I think I did. Unless, your ghost theory is correct. If I didn't then I am back to not knowing what the hell is going on. Which sucks."

I do not know. When I try to look back, I only see you. Penny conceded, *However, I struggle to see and interpret the past. My gift is the future.*

"Is it possible that some of my visions are real and some aren't? Maybe I have hallucinations and visions," I cast about for any explanation. I didn't want to go back to feeling like I had no idea what I was, what was true.

Maybe. Penny tried to help me. *I don't know much about hallucinations.*

"Are you sure I am a seer?" I barely knew what it meant to be a seer, but I knew very well what it was to have symptoms and no identifiable condition. I liked being a seer better.

I am confident you are a seer, Penny offered. Not a yes, but better than a no.

I could think of only one way to find out for certain. "How are you at the present?" I asked, "Could you find someone?"

It depends.

I threw myself back against my chair. "That's your favorite answer," I sighed.

It is the most common answer to questions, Penny admitted. *I would need a way to find them. Like a beacon. If I know them, I can look. If I have an object they are connected with, I might be able to use that connection. Who are you trying to find?*

"Another seer." I had abandoned any serious attempts to find them. But, they might be able to help me. "I know I need to find the other two."

Do you know anything about them?

"I think one sees the future, and one sees something else, I don't know." I also didn't know if they could help. They might be living in complete ignorance, just as I did. Or maybe they would know everything, and know that Sophia was wrong about me. Maybe I had stumbled upon this magical world, but I wasn't really a part of it.

Insufficient, Penny's pithy response interrupted my spiral into self-doubt.

"Yeah, of course it is." I struggled to decide which misery to follow, the possibility that I would never find them, or the possibility that finding them would upend my newly formed identity. I chose the former, and then chose to laugh it off, because it felt better than existential crisis. "I'll probably need to propel myself down a mine shaft or climb some remote mountain peak or fight a sphinx to find anything out."

Penny alerted, *Do not fight a sphinx. Even if it tells you it will help. They are not to be trusted. Never speak to a sphinx.*

I noticed that mythical beings regarded each other with a lot of distrust. Oracles disliked sphinxes, and whatever Sophia was disliked by witches. I asked, "So, sphinxes are real?"

Yes, and dangerous.

Out of curiosity, I persisted, "The Greek girl ones or the Egyptian boy ones?"

Penny's head adjusted a few degrees to look at me. Her eyebrows remained stationary but I sensed she intended to raise one.

"I read stuff," I shrugged.

Her supercilious reply followed immediately, *The eternal sort, that may help you or may kill you depending on their mood and character.* Penny's eyes returned to the television. The way her mind worked, she had probably been paying attention the whole time. For my edification, she continued, *They don't fit well in this world anymore, and they probably avoid it all together. But if you do come across one, turn around and walk away. It will ensnare you, first with irresistible promises, then with a lethal claw.*

"Got it. No sphinxes." I tried to return my attention to the show, knowing Penny would quiz me later. My mind rejected the words on the screen, and I considered my new predicament. Whatever came of it, I had to find the others. It might be the only way to settle the question. As frightening as it was to think I might not belong with them, wondering was worse. "I need to find them," I whispered.

If you need to, then you will. You always seem to find yourself where you need to be.

"What do you know about seers?"

Seers are humans, blessed with sight. A trio is born in every generation, a gift to guide humans if they have the wisdom to listen.

"You know me, listening to me about anything, probably isn't wise." I hesitated to discuss Sophia with Penny, especially after the ghost conversation. But I had no alternatives. "Sophia said that I'm probably not entirely human. That seers probably have some magical ancestor. Are you saying that's not true."

Seers are human. Penny confirmed, *I have seen nothing to suggest they are related to immortals or magical beings of any kind.*

My temper flared at her casual comment. "You know, the intentionally vague, non-committal responses are irritating, but I am really over the contradiction. All of you immortals need to sit down together and get your stories straight."

There is no one who knows everything, Win. Penny's tone shifted to sympathetic. *It would be very comforting to believe that the truth is waiting in someone to be discovered and shared. But realities are personal, stories hint at histories, and we all cling to the beliefs that comfort us.*

"Well that's stupid. I just want to know the truth." My tone shifted to petulant.

I want that, too. Penny agreed. *The best we can do is share what we know and be open to being wrong. There are no guarantees.*

"That sounds nice," I acknowledged, "but I am not ready to benefit from this lesson. I will think about it later. Right now I want to be mad." Penny let me be after that. Demonstrably, returned her attention to her program, and commented only rarely when the story truly surprised her. It was nice that something could still surprise her.

I couldn't think about the show. I only thought of Penny's words, designed to help, to gently introduce facts I needed. There are no guarantees.

Even so, I wanted to find another seer.

CHAPTER 45

The conversation with Penny stripped away all of my illusions about my new life.

Though I had learned to control what I saw, and I continued to push the limits of my reach, little had changed. I remained mired in the same uncertainty that surrounded me when I arrived at the bar. Only now, it was worse. Penny unwittingly resurrected my doubts about my nature. If she didn't know exactly what I was, then probably, no one did.

When I arrived at the bar, alone and afraid, Delphine and Penny helped me. They offered safety and belonging and confidence and purpose. They didn't owe me peace of mind or certainty. Penny sharing her doubt was clinical honesty, and kindly meant. However devastating.

Maybe my power was a delusion, there was nothing I could do for that. But if my power was real, then it was useful, whether or not I was a seer.

Whatever I was, I still faced the same alternatives that presented themselves months ago, before I had ever heard of the Sleeping Dragon. I could go home and resume my old life. I could confront Sophia's cultists, if I could find them. I could search for the seers, possibly forever. Or I could save Twain. And for the first time, I could do nothing. Stay at the bar. Safe and anonymous. And occasionally sift through other people's pasts.

My dilemma shone through in all of my interactions. Penny treated me like I might break. Delphine started with sympathy, but ran short of it quickly. Then she was put out by my preoccupation. Angus noticed, too. He didn't push me, but he watched me more closely, and clearly with concern.

What I told Penny was true, no one does anything for just one reason. Three separate catalysts informed my decision. First there was a body. The second body in my life to force a decision.

The man was found only a few blocks from the bar. Authorities believed that he died in another location, but if they knew where, they did not say.

They asked the public to share any information that might be helpful in their search for answers. News reports hinted at murder and satanic rituals. He had gone missing weeks before. Some keen investigator noticed a similarity to a murder hundreds of miles away, in another state, and made the mistake of making a public comment. Almost immediately, reporters suggested connections and conspiracies and cults. I wondered if the public revelation would help or hinder Sophia's investigation.

I considered renewing my own research. I contemplated sneaking into the hospital, questioning potential witnesses, scouring the internet for clues. It took an embarrassing amount of time for me to realize that I had access to information almost no one else did.

The murdered man's body was found in an alley downtown. The streets downtown reflected a recent revitalization of the century old boom town. The city council had peeled back decades of overlays, each representing a different era of style. The original, early twentieth century charm was polished and painted, creating a welcoming picture of small town paradise. The downtown storefronts faced streets lined with hawthorn trees and planters overflowing with a collection of carefully selected flowers. Each attractive element assembled into a priceless tableau for setting up multiple, lucrative narratives, ranging from "blame an outsider, this doesn't happen here" to "dark, unearthly powers scheme to preserve the idyllic facade." Ample photographic opportunities awaited local and national news media ready to pick up the story.

On my day off, I found myself standing across the street from the alley. The alley itself was still cordoned off, and there was a small media presence nearby. I stayed back, I wanted a clear view, but I had no desire to be seen or questioned or filmed. Particularly not, since I was in hiding and using an alias.

I leaned against the wall behind me, keeping one hand against the roughhewn brick. The jagged edges against my skin helped me stay grounded. I was less likely to drift out into the street if something physically connected me to the spot. I focused my mind on the alley in front of me. I reached back, looking for the night the man's body appeared.

As always, I was a little startled when it worked.

Darkness engulfed me as night replaced day on the street. A man ambled down the road on an old fashioned bike, pulling a fully enclosed bike trailer. The street was empty, save the man on the bike. Even in the dark, I could see the peeling yellow paint on the bike, at odds with the sleek, modern trailer. He stopped near the alley and got off the bike. The hood of his jacket obscured his face in profile, and when he turned to access the trailer, he turned his back to me. I considered letting go of the wall, moving to the other side of the street. But then I remember, whatever I saw now, it was midday, there was foot traffic and car traffic. I still struggled to remain still during my visions. If a car didn't hit me, I would hit a pedestrian. I stayed rooted to my spot, and hoped the mystery man would turn to face me.

The man unzipped the trailer. I didn't need to see in it, as he wasted no time in reaching in and picking up a lifeless body. He threw the body over his shoulder and carried him around the bike and into the alley. My heart raced, the desire to intervene threatening to overwhelm my reason. I reminded myself, *this isn't happening, it's over.* The only time I had ever interacted with the past was with Twain, and I still didn't know how I did it. I dug my hand into the wall, something real, something to cling to in the maelstrom of emotions.

I waited for the man to leave the alley, hoping for a clear view. I half expected a semi-truck pulling a long trailer would appear in the street, and the man would be gone before I saw him. But my luck held out, and the man reappeared, his face turned toward me. The darkness made it difficult to discern his features. I squinted my eyes to sharpen my view. A sudden gust of wind pestered the man, pushing the hood from his face. For a few seconds, I saw him clearly. His hair lay in perfect waves, neatly maintained and precise. He looked friendly, if a little stiff. I imagined him leaving the alley and heading home to his family, spraying down his kid's bike trailer with disinfectant and deodorizer, hitting the shower, then joining the daily commuters off to the office.

The man pulled his hood up and returned to the bike. He quietly pedaled away, back to his life, away from his crime.

I didn't recognize the man. But I knew he wasn't human. After spending a considerable amount of time among magical beings recently, I was getting better at spotting them. He didn't move like a human. Humans felt their bodies, they moved like they wanted to avoid pain and feel comfort. The magical beings of my acquaintance moved as though they occupied their bodies, but with a detachment. When the mystery man heaved a lifeless body on his back, there was no attempt to mitigate the weight, no attempt to brace himself or catch his breath. He just took the pain of it and completed his task.

And of course, there was the super human strength. Also, a good indicator that the man wasn't human.

I let go of the vision and I let go of the wall.

The street returned to normal. A shop owner up the street halfhearted washed her windows, and watched me with curiosity. I wondered how long I had been there. And what my face did as I watched the past. It hadn't occurred to me that immersing myself in a vision in public might make me a spectacle. Or that staring too long at a crime scene might look suspicious.

I checked my phone, then looked around impatiently. Maybe it would look like I was waiting for someone. I sold the story by pretending to get a call and leaving in a hurry.

I reflected on my progress. I had seen the face of the killer, or at least an accomplice. And per usual, I had no idea what to do with that information.

CHAPTER 46

The next antecedent to push my decision making was far less dramatic than the first.

In a rare occurrence, Penny, Delphine, and I all sat together. The bar was closed, and I convinced Penny to join us upstairs. Delphine dutifully brought first Penny's chair, then Penny herself to sit in the bar.

It looks the same, was Penny's only remark about the barroom.

Delphine's posture slipped a little. "I've improved some things," she muttered.

Internally, I marked the strange, interdependent relationship between Penny and Delphine. Penny occupied a permanent position in Delphine's mind offering information and secrets, and no privacy. In truth, Penny was powerless, and wholly reliant on Delphine for survival. Yet, Delphine remained ready to command, following every direction from Penny, without hesitation. I couldn't say that it was entirely mutualistic, and I didn't know who had the better of the deal.

With the three of us settled, I caught the two of them up, as briefly as I could. I didn't think they would approve of my intention to learn about the murders, but I still wanted their advice.

"You know there are people looking for me," I began. "And it's possible there are others who are in danger, from the people who are looking for me. There are people who are disappearing. And they end up dead. I think they are connected…"

Delphine interrupted, "How do you know?"

"There is a pattern, similarities between the men who are abducted and later found dead."

You're not a man. Why would they want you? Penny asked.

"I don't really think they do, not anymore," I explained. "But other than not being a man, I have a lot in common with the men who have gone missing."

"You think there is someone out there who wants to kidnap and kill you and a bunch of men you don't know?" Delphine asked.

Before I could dismiss Delphine's absurd question, Penny interjected another series of questions, *What makes you think there are connections between the murders?" People are murdered all the time. And why would that be connected to you?*

They didn't understand, their response made that clear. I felt the connection deeply, and certainly. "Because I just know," my reply sounded worse out loud than when I briefly auditioned it in my head. I began to regret wanting their advice. I added, "And I know what is happening is connected to me in some way. I just know."

Penny stilled eyed me askance, but Delphine accepted my explanation. Delphine asked, "Could it have something to do with your friend who was murdered? Maybe he was a victim."

As obvious as her suggestion was, it had never occurred to me. I paused to consider it. "But he died thirty years ago. That means this has been going on for decades."

"So what," Delphine returned.

Penny slowly blinked in what could only be irritation. *Let's not encourage this.*

"I guess, if they started young…?" I wondered aloud.

Delphine shook her head. "Not everyone lives short little mortal lives, Win."

I thought back to the man I had seen. My initial impression was that he was not human. Sophia never said how long she had been looking into the murders. Maybe the connection I felt was Twain. "I saw someone," I admitted. "I went to where the body was found, and I looked back. I saw the man's body dropped off in the alley. I saw a face."

"But you didn't see who killed your friend," Delphine confirmed.

"No," I agreed. A plan started to coalesce in my mind. I wasn't ready to speak it into existence, and I certainly wasn't ready to commit to following it. I sighed and slumped in my chair. Every action seemed to take me deeper, but no closer to a real understanding of what I was or why I found myself on this path. I muttered, "I wish I could just go back to my safe, simple life. I didn't recognize it at the time, but it was better."

Penny returned to the conversation, *Mortals often long for a time that was safer, better. But there aren't such times. They are longing for the time when they were ignorant of the dangers. Unaware of the suffering and torment outside of their immediate view. They ask to live in foolish ignorance, not relative safety.*

"Wow," I looked at Penny, "that was judgmental."

Delphine glanced between us, taking stock. "Why don't we play cards?" She proposed with uncharacteristic enthusiasm.

I nodded absently. Delphine had inadvertently given me too much to think about.

CHAPTER 47

The conversation with Delphine and Penny loitered in the back of my head for days, attempting to gather conviction.

I continued to search half-heartedly for clues relating to the murders, combing headlines and social media posts. It should have brought me closer to a decision. But I remained stuck.

Despite my best efforts, the scheme went from inclination to impulsion accidently, as the result of a vague and unrelated conversation with Angus.

Angus responded to my increasing despondency by demanding I allow Kya to feed me. Kya laid out a sumptuous feast, far more food than three people might eat. I noticed a fourth place setting at the table and raised an eyebrow at Angus.

"My nephew is in town," Angus explained.

The panic must have been all over my face.

Angus quickly added, "Don't worry. He's an idiot. I wouldn't even consider it."

His response made me uncomfortable in a different way. "I didn't know you had a nephew," I remarked.

"Yeah," Angus grunted. "I have a million of them. Mostly worthless."

Kya emerged from the kitchen with wine. "Angus," she warned.

"He knows how I feel about him."

"Yes, Uncle, I do." A young man materialized behind Kya. Like Angus, he was tall and lanky. Unlike Angus, his appearance was crisp and polished. He looked like a member of a staid secret society at an Ivy League school. In thirty years, I expected I would see his face in the news, a handsome, buttoned up politician mildly disgraced after controversial pictures surfaced online, calling his respectability into question. I shook off the image, and smiled a greeting.

Angus's nephew returned a smirk, and his smile contained a question.

Angus frowned, looking between us. "This is Ginny. Stay away from her."

The question followed his smile to his melodic voice, "Sure."

Angus completed the introduction with, "This is one of my nephews."

"Mac," the young man supplied his own name.

"Nice to meet you," I replied awkwardly.

"Sit, sit," Kya instructed us. Conversation was sparse during dinner, limited to requests for food or wine and appreciative phrases here and there. Angus, Kya, and Conan approached the meal with great reverence and a small measure of ceremony. They savored each bite, as they worked their way through an impressive volume of food and wine. Plate after plate, glass after glass.

I drank a glass of wine, and I ate a plate of food, as prosaically as one could. Even with consideration for the superior quality of the spread, or adjusting for my general state of malaise, there was no way I could not muster that sort of veneration for a meal. For the first time in Angus's home, I felt out of place.

The bizarre meal effectively distracted me from my troubles, as I could do little more than observe Angus's unusual behavior. I had come to expect eccentricity from Kya, but Angus's reliably ordinary behavior was one of his best traits.

As their eating slowed, Kya reopened discussion, "Ginny, how are you feeling?"

I was slow to respond, both because I was preoccupied with curiosity about the unusual meal, and because I needed to consider the question. I took note of my relaxed internal state. A tentative serenity had found its way into my mind. My questions and mysteries remained, but felt less threatening before. "Pretty good, actually," I replied in wonder.

"Wonderful," Kya smiled. "A good meal makes all the difference. Conan is such a tremendous cook."

"You made this?" I asked. Angus's eyes narrowed, he watched the interaction carefully.

"I helped," he corrected, humility ringing false in his liquid voice.

"And you can help me clear it away," Kya added.

I stood, reaching for my plate.

"No, not you," Kya nodded at the dining room door. "Why don't you and Angus take your drinks into the living room? We can take care of this."

I nodded gratefully and left my plate behind. I might have insisted I help, but likely, I would have lost the battle. And I preferred Angus's comforting presence to the unusual dynamic between the three of them.

Seated on a plush sofa, I luxuriated in the security of the moment.

Each small glimpse I had into Angus's life beyond the bar confounded me. First, his enigmatic wife, then his exquisite taste, now his arrogant nephew.

"I didn't know you came from a big family," I commented.

"I do," Angus confirmed, "One big obnoxious family."

"Me too," I commiserated.

Angus nodded sympathetically. "How about I don't ask about yours if you don't ask about mine?"

I grinned, "Deal."

Alone with Angus, it was easy to relax. We talked of nothing important, and shared a few effortless silences. In the stillness, my mind wandered back to my great conundrum. I thought again about the other seers. It tempted me as surely as the murder mystery. But I had no idea where to start.

For no reason at all, I asked Angus, "What if you lost something irreplaceable? And it's almost impossible to find. Do you take the time to look for it?"

Angus considered the question carefully. "Well," he offered, "Do you remember where you saw it last?"

I nearly said, no, I'd never seen it at all. But then I remembered. I knew exactly the last place I'd seen a seer.

All of my puzzles crashed together: Seers, Twain, murders.

A plan propelled itself forward without my permission. For the first time, in a very long time, I knew exactly what I needed to do.

PART FIVE: THE HOUSE

CHAPTER 48

"I need to go back to the house." It was the first clear path I had seen since the journey began.

"What house?" Delphine asked. "Your house? I thought you lived in an apartment."

"No, the house where it started."

"The house you were born in?"

I wrinkled my nose at her. "I was born in a hospital."

Delphine shook her head. "I'll never understand why it became fashionable to send healthy women to have babies in the same place you send sick people. Pregnancy isn't a disease."

"That's where the doctors are. And anyway," I interrupted myself, "We are way off topic here."

"Can't the doctors leave? Meet them somewhere? Why would they even want a doctor? Doctors spend all of their time with sick people."

"They're a special kind of doctor," my retort expressed my exasperation. "Delphine, I am leaving for a few days. I need to go home, I think I know what I am meant to do."

"Oh, purpose is always good. So you are coming back?"

"Yeah, this is the first job I've ever had that I like. Unless you fire me." I was a little worried she would fire me.

"Why would I do that?"

"You wouldn't," I agreed. "So, it's okay if I take a few days off?"

Delphine shrugged. "Sounds important. I ran this place for years before you came along. I can probably manage a few days without you."

"Thanks, Delphine. For everything."

"Don't make it weird." As she walked away I heard her mutter, "That wasn't mean."

I smiled broadly. After only a few months at *The Sleeping Dragon* I felt like a different person. I was stronger and in control. I wasn't "Clumsy Win" or

"Spacy Win." I felt like I could stand on my own two feet. I understood my power, and I knew how to use it. And now, I knew what I had to do.

I took time to prepare, tempering my eagerness to begin with thoughtful planning.

I let Angus and Kya know that I would be away for a few days. So they didn't worry. Angus and Kya had become surrogate parents. They interfered with my life and directed my actions and disapproved of my poor choices and took pride in my accomplishments. That relationship meant more than friendship. Angus's nephew still lurked around the house and the yard. To appease Angus, I stayed away from him. When I told them of my plan to return home, they expressed concern. They each pulled me aside to ask if I was alright, if I needed anything. Angus blamed his nephew Conan and offered to kick him out of the house. I reassured them that I was fine and everything was fine. As I said it, I hoped it was true.

Penny didn't like me going. She said nothing, per usual, but I sensed it in her. She tried not to interfere with the normal course of events, unless I asked her. I didn't want her to dissuade me, therefore, I did not ask. I spent more time with Penny before I left. She acted tough and disaffected, I knew her to be bored and lonely.

After we met in person, our friendship grew quickly. Sophia was too far above me to be a real friend, she felt like a colleague. Or a supervisor. Delphine and I were friendly, but she kept everyone at a distance. Penny said that Delphine's training isolated her, that Delphine couldn't fulfill her purpose if she grew attached to others. Once again, I felt the imbalance in the relationship between them, and I disliked it for Delphine.

Penny, better than me in every way, mostly treated me as an equal. She liked hearing my thoughts, even as she probably knew them better than I did.

When I decided to go, I knew I would miss her. And I knew she would miss me, too.

I shared my decision with Penny after the conversation with Delphine. Penny saw it coming.

I told her, "I know you know, and I know you won't agree. I need this. I might be able to make a difference. And I won't be okay until I try."

I know you have to go. She could see if I might be successful, and said nothing.

"Thanks for not making this harder."

You have a path to follow, Win. We all do. I can't live your life for you.

I smiled at her fondly. "But you would be better at it, if you did, right?"

Yes, of course.

I had the money to fly, and it would be a great deal faster, so I used my real name and my real credit card to buy a plane ticket home.

The day before I left, Delphine voiced what Penny would not, "Are you sure this is a good idea?"

"Nope," I owned my uncertainty, when before I might have tried to feign confidence.

As I packed, I reflected on the mixture of trepidation and fortitude that accompanied me home. I might have to look over my shoulder for the rest of my life, but I didn't want to look back with regret. Returning to help Twain would be a balm to my soul.

Angus insisted on driving me to the airport. He remained characteristically gruff, but after he took my backpack from the trunk of the car he pulled me to him for a quick hug.

"I'll be back," I promised him.

He replied, "I know."

I watched him drive away until I couldn't see him in the traffic.

After an uneventful flight, I arrived. Miles away from home. I considered the options. I could reclaim part of my life, return to my apartment, take the things I wanted, pay off any obligations. I didn't want it, my real life felt a poor fit. My new life, the bar, Penny, Delphine, replaced what came before.

I decided I would go directly to the house. I saw no point in drawing out the trip.

I chose rideshare over rental. I was in the habit of conserving funds, a difficult habit to break. This time, I fully charged my phone.

The ride out to the house was heartbreakingly familiar, yet distant, another lifetime. I passed the same open fields. Animals grazed casually on their daily fare. The people appeared here and there, attending to mundane, daily chores. No one here seemed to know how much the world had changed.

My heart skipped a beat at the sight of the distinguishing red mailbox. The driver maintained his speed, I suggested, "That's the turn." He nearly missed it too.

As his car bumped along the gravel drive, I noticed his eyes studying me in the rearview mirror. Our eyes met. He asked, "Are you sure you want me to leave you out here?"

"Yeah, it's fine. I set up a pick up for later." He looked skeptical. "Thanks," I added.

The house looked the same, derelict with hints at a stately past. I focused, attempting to find the house before peeling paint and a mossy roof. For just a moment, it appeared dressed in crisp white paint accented with a cheery yellow door and matching yellow shutters standing open beside each window on the ground floor. I smiled ruefully, watching the past fade into today.

My car remained in front of the house. Clearly, the homeowner did not concern themselves with abandoned property in their front drive. And, probably, they didn't concern themselves with the dead body in the basement.

I made it only two steps into the house before I realized I made a mistake.

CHAPTER 49

Okay, Win, you have been abducted. Remain calm, make careful prudent decisions.

Rope cut into the skin of my wrists. My hands were tied together behind me to the hard wooden chair. My ankles were secured to the chair legs. A bag surrounded my head, preventing me from seeing where I was, or who had taken me.

When the black bag disappeared, I found myself facing a young woman. She seemed familiar, but I couldn't place her exactly.

"I have been waiting for you, Win. For a very long time."

My eyes narrowed in response. I had just about reached my limit on strange people making cryptic, unsettling statements. "I am supposed to feel honored? Impressed?" So much for prudence.

"Well aren't you a lively little thing?"

"Aren't you a condescending medium sized thing?" It wasn't smooth, but I still felt a little proud of my defiant response.

The woman smiled broadly. "I've waited for you for more than thirty years, and you do not disappoint. You've been looking for me, too, I think."

I sighed. After running and hiding and turning my life upside down, I sat, tied to a chair, in the place it all began, with the person who began it. And I only felt tired. "You killed Twain," I stated. I didn't know what she was, but she reminded me a bit of Sophia, I assumed she was immortal.

"No," she replied, interrupting my thoughts. At first I thought that, like Sophia, she could read my mind. But then she continued, "I did not kill him." Either she didn't have Sophia's talents, or I had gotten better at guarding my thoughts. She finished, "My husband killed him."

Her dismissive tone broke through my exhausted indifference, fury appeared in its place. "Why? Why kill him?"

"Because of what he was. Because of what he could do. I needed his power to fulfill my purpose. Just like I need you to fulfill my purpose." I felt a strange pressure in my head. Like the beginnings of a headache. I held it back.

"Do you hear how unhinged that sounds?"

She looked at me sharply. "Are you trying to provoke me? You think that some child seer can goad me into losing my temper and slipping up?"

I came right back with, "No, I'm pissed, and probably being more candid than I should be. I don't think you realize how crazy it is to murder people to 'fulfill your purpose.'"

She took a moment, visibly retaking her composure. Her mouth formed into a kind smile. "I don't expect you to understand, yet. But I hope you will. It isn't fair that I was willing to sacrifice Twain. I know that. But I am willing to sacrifice myself too if it means saving the world pain and suffering."

"That doesn't sound sane, either." I looked away from her and examined my surroundings. We were still in the house. In one of the upstairs bedrooms. The one Twain and I entered together. I wondered if I could still save him, if I could find his time and find him in it.

The mad woman and I were not alone in the room. A man stood solemnly by the door. He didn't look at me. He wasn't the man from the alley, but I'd seen him somewhere before, I felt sure of it. When I looked at him, an unfamiliar mix of energy and certainty washed over me. I wondered if he projected his internal state outward, like Sophia did.

"Win," she said. "I know I am not the nicest person. And I know you take issue with the way I have handled all of this." I refused to look at her. I fixed an impassive stare on the far corner of the room. The headache threatened again. "But I know you are a good person. And I think if you understand the stakes, you will understand why I did what I did. You might think there was another way, and you might be right about that, but I don't believe that you would question my purpose."

I looked at her long enough to roll my eyes. Then my gaze returned to my chosen corner.

"Would you bring me a chair?" She asked quietly. She added, "And get the box." I felt the man leave the room. With him went my calm, and a little of my strength. "I would like to be able to untie you. Maybe we can work toward that. Once we understand each other. Once we have established some trust."

The man returned with a chair and I felt better once again. He placed the chair in front of me, near enough to make conversation easy but out of striking distance. I strained against the bindings. I couldn't strike if I wanted to, and I did want to strike her.

The man placed the box beside the chair. For a moment, our eyes met. For that moment, I knew he felt it, too. His eyes registered surprise, and then became guarded, harder than before. "Thank you, Max," she said. Her attention returned to me. "I want you to think, Win, think of the way the world is changing. The world is getting darker, scarier, more dangerous." Her voice compelled me to look at her, to listen. "I have watched it for nearly a century. Again and again I see the influence of the exiled immortals. So much evil, sown to divide humans. They show up everywhere, they live among ordinary people, they hold public offices, and they interfere. They don't belong in this world. I once hoped to expel them, give the world back to the people who deserve it. But now, with the state of the world, I don't think that is enough.

"Win," she leaned in, her gaze intensified along with the nagging pressure in my head. "What if there is a way to prevent the pain and suffering of today *and* all of the unnecessary suffering of the past? The immortals forced themselves into our world, even if we got rid of all of them, their imprint is left on the world. But there is a different world waiting. A world without them. I need your help, Win. We can prevent them from being here, remove them from time." My head throbbed. "You can change the past. *"*

My body tensed reflexively. "Why do you say that?"

She gave me another kind smile, "I told you I have been waiting for you for thirty years." The woman picked up the metal box next to her chair without standing. She took a key from her pocket, unlocked the box, and opened it. She looked into the box and sighed with contentment. I leaned forward, too curious to feign indifference. From the box, she lifted a sweatshirt, shaking it out and releasing a small cloud of dust. Even without the word "WIN" printed clearly across it, I recognized it. Only the top third resembled the original gray, the rest discolored into the rusty brown of dried, very old blood.

She set the box on the floor and let the stained garment rest on her knees. "When my husband told me he saw a girl in the basement, I thought he had lost his mind. He was spooked. He said, 'She was there and then she was gone.' He wasn't the brightest fellow, but it wasn't like him to imagine such things." She smiled slightly, in fond remembrance, "I was trying to complete the ritual, to subsume Twain's power. His death was regrettable, I didn't want it to be wasteful as well. Sadly, the ritual didn't work." She turned away from me, for a moment returning to the past, "I made a mistake. I've made plenty of mistakes." She sighed heavily and looked back at me. "When my husband returned upstairs, I was not thrilled and I didn't particularly want to hear about his flights of fancy. But he insisted I follow him downstairs, 'in case the girl is still there,' he said. He sounded so afraid. A man of his size, and his strength, can you imagine? Afraid of a slip of a girl? I went down stairs with him. Of course, I didn't see anyone. But I saw this. None of us had a sweatshirt. Twain wasn't wearing one. I pulled it from under him and took a good look at it. I saw this on the back." She pointed to my name. "But it was the front that interested me." She turned the sweatshirt around and indicated the print there, the name of my high school, and the year of my graduating class. "Maybe it was a joke, a graduating class more than twenty years in the future. But I didn't think so. And of course, where did it come from?"

For weeks I worried that I was the reason Twain was dead. And maybe that was still true. But it never occurred to me that his death endangered me. I swallowed a laugh as I realized, *I have been hunted since before I was born because of a half-hearted graduation gift from my parents, who hate me.*

"You left it for me, Win. I have been watching this house for decades. Because I needed to find you. Because I need your help. We can save the world together."

She moved closer to me. I stared at the sweatshirt, transfixed by Twain's blood. The sweatshirt had stayed in the past. He gave me an apple. I gave him a sweatshirt.

"I wish I had known better," she told me, "I wish it would have worked out differently. But here we are Win. We have the opportunity to make a better world for everyone."

In spite of myself, I asked, "How is that?"

I saw the relief spread across her face. It was the opening she wanted. "You can go back, and prevent the exile that corrupted the world. Think of it like, preventing original sin."

Whenever she leaned in, the pressure in my head grew. She was trying to influence my thinking. Like Sophia did, but clumsier. I brushed away her effort. The sweatshirt moved as she shifted in her seat, catching my attention. "You said the world is getting darker, scarier, but I don't believe that. We have problems, some new ones maybe, but I think there are lots of ways the world is better now. And if we can get this far, we can get farther."

She nodded, "Maybe. Maybe not. That is quite a risk to take." She moved closer again. "Think of all of the suffering, Win. We could prevent that."

I saw the man watching me closely. Somehow, his scrutiny emboldened me. "I have questions," I told her.

Irritation appeared and disappeared on her face, stifled quickly enough that I might have missed it. "Of course," she replied. For a moment, I thought of Sophia. The way she answered every question without judgment, without irritation.

"What are you?"

She didn't like the question. And her friend Max saw that too. I had his attention. "I'm a type of guardian."

"Are you immortal?" I asked.

"It's complicated."

I met her gaze with skepticism, and then looked to Max. We locked eyes. "Were you born?"

Max looked at the woman and she at him. She shook her head to communicate her waning patience with my questions. "Yes, of course."

"For the sake of clarity," I looked back at the woman. "You are possibly immortal, it's complicated, so if you are human, you are not completely human. And you were born. So you are an exile..?"

"Technically, I am."

"And what is he?" I pointed to Max with my head.

"I don't see why that matters," she responded, resolutely.

"I want to know. And you want my cooperation." The woman considered the question. I offered an alternative, "Is he completely human?"

"No," she said.

"To be clear, you want me to stop the exile. Which would erase you, and me, and your brooding friend over there?" Max watched this conversation with suspicion. I sensed surprise from him. I could almost feel what he felt.

"It's the right thing to do," she whispered.

"Oh," I said. I made eye contact with Max, and held it as I explained, "I guess I'm not as good a person as you thought." I thought of the sweatshirt. I gripped the chair, and I focused backwards. I felt myself reaching out to Max, gripping him with some invisible hold. And I thought back to the moment I first arrived at the house. I watched the room shift around me, the strange young woman was there, and then gone. I held on to Max with my mind, and the chair with my tied hands. I focused on the ropes, pushing against them with my arms and my ankles. The room shifted around me.

My wrists and ankles felt the air of the room in place of the burning ropes. The woman came back into focus. She sensed nothing. "Win?" I heard her say, and I thought she might be repeating herself.

I leaned toward her, shifting my gaze from Max to her. "I really didn't expect that to work." She hadn't yet noticed that I had taken my bindings on a trip to the past, and left them there. I tucked my chin down, darted forward, and I cracked my head against hers.

Before she could recover, I kicked my leg out, knocking her over in her chair.

Max watched with shock. I pressed my advantage and rushed him. Pushing him into the wall. As I made contact, I felt a surge of strength. He was bigger than me, he was stronger than me, but for the moment he was shocked and I had a boost of adrenaline.

I ran out the door and down the hall. I knew the layout of the house, I explored it top to bottom with Twain. My heart thrummed in my ears nearly drowning out the sound of my pursuer. I hurried down the steps, leaning hard on the bannister so that I didn't trip. With his superior height and greater physical confidence, he took the steps two at a time and by the bottom step he reached out and caught my shirt in his hand.

Once he had the shirt, he gained the advantage. He pulled me to him, lifted me, and threw me over his shoulder. I kicked and punched and landed a few solid blows. "Hey!" He shouted, shaking me for emphasis. "Don't make me knock you out."

I stilled at once. Couldn't defend myself if he beat me to death. He brought me back upstairs.

"She just wants to talk. You need to listen."

"She wants you dead," I pointed out. "Both of us. She thinks we shouldn't exist."

"Consider the possibility that she is right." He set me on my feet in front of him. "No one wants to hurt you, Win. But we need your help."

"Why do you trust her?" I whispered.

"I waited for her for a long time. A guardian. I knew she would come for me. And I knew she would show me the truth. The truth isn't always easy."

"Thank you, Max," the woman said. I peered around Max to see her. Her nose was red and swollen. I smiled a little. "Win, this is your chance to make your own choice. You can choose the easy way or the hard way."

CHAPTER 50

"What's the easy way?" I asked.

The woman smiled, more to cover her irritation than in joy. "We work together. And we save the world. Return it to the way it was meant to be."

I nodded, "What's the hard way?"

The woman frowned. "We make you do it." Max looked a little uncomfortable with this option.

"You've given me a lot to think about. I need some time."

Her fists clenched. "You may have a few moments to yourself." She left the room stiffly, gesturing for Max to follow. "Max will know if you go for the window."

"What is he?" I called after them. The door closed.

Alone, I looked around. No chairs in this room. I glanced wistfully at the window. "No," I heard from the other side of the door.

"Damn," I mumbled, impressed. I tested it. I thought about the woman's crazy plan, and I stepped toward the window.

"No!" More adamant this time.

"Damn."

I wasn't going to help them, no matter what they said or did. I wondered if Max could read that in my mind. And I wondered if Max would report it to the boss. He didn't seem entirely bad. I felt certain I'd seen them both before. With time on my hands I wracked my brain. Everything about her was familiar. I felt as though there was a fog around my memory.

I shook myself. Now I was stalling and procrastinating at the same time. I couldn't get out through the past, Delphine and I had tested it, I stayed in both places. Maybe I could scan for a time before the house and fall through the floor. Or maybe I would stay suspended in the air. Possibly not a good time to test that out. Before I could talk myself into a daring escape plot, they returned.

"What have you decided, Win? Will you help me?" The woman was all business now. No more warm smiles and flattering entreaties. I considered playing along until I found an opening to escape. But without knowing her plan, I could find myself backed into a corner. And I wanted a fight.

"I don't think I can help you." Before she launched into a warped pep talk, I continued, "Have you thought about inpatient treatment? That might help you."

Her rage crested and broke across her face. I was going to get a fight. "Do it," she said.

Max was on me in an instant. He wrapped around me. I couldn't breathe. My body strained for air and my mind became vulnerable. They attacked there too.

I could still hear the woman muttering to herself, "I should have just taken you from the library. I had hoped to convince you, I had hoped you might be reasonable. We could have saved so much time."

The room around me faded. Her rants became garbled. My lungs burned. Shadows overtook the light and it was over.

CHAPTER 51

I floated below the surface.

I heard people talking, their words indistinguishable and just out of reach. I tried to pull myself toward them, to break through but my body remained unresponsive. Time passed here. It might have been minutes but it felt like hours. I'd never felt so alone.

Days passed this way. Alone, separated from the world by an invisible barrier. Motionless, held in the insecure embrace of nothing. At first, I was angry. Determined. But nothing erodes will power as well as time. And I began to grow frightened. *Can they leave me like this forever?* And I began to wonder if it would be better to fade out of existence, than to suffer alone in this void for eternity. Some part of me shouted, *No! This is my world!* And held on to that.

I started a conversation with myself, because that is who I had. I said, *the world cannot be remade to satisfy the designs of one small group.* I felt fairly certain that this woman represented the zealots Sophia had described to me. *They have one voice, but they don't get to drown out or erase all of the others.* Whatever they did to me, I wouldn't work with them.

I told myself, *Let the doubts come, I can handle it.*

In the blink of an eye, the void became a room. The room was bright, my eyes should have needed adjustment but they accepted the change without protest. I felt less solid here. I could feel my body somewhere far away, held motionless. I looked around my new prison.

Max stood watching me.

I tried out my voice, "Hi, Max."

"Hi, Win."

"Are you doing this?" I indicated the room.

"Yes."

I nodded. "Is this a thing you regularly do? Trap people inside their own minds?"

He shook his head. "I've never done it before. It's new."

"Huh, wow." I thought of how long it took for me to control my abilities, and how many drinks. Whatever he was, he was good at it.

"I've been more powerful recently," he confessed.

"Oh. Wow. The last few years? How long has this been going on?" Talking to him about anything was better than the void.

"Today."

"Is it still today?"

He confirmed, "It is still today."

"Why are you helping her?"

"I told you. I saw her coming in a vision of the future. I knew she had an important purpose, and that I was supposed to help her."

Interesting. Hope flared within me. "You see visions of the future?"

"No. It was someone else's vision. I just saw it too. That's the only time I have experienced that." I nodded, disappointment killed my hope.

"She send you in here to recruit me? To threaten me? Or did you just feel like stopping by?"

"I wanted to talk to you because I thought I could make you understand. I know it seems crazy. It seems crazy to me too, sometimes. But I know that following her is the right path."

"Maybe for you," I conceded. "We've met before."

"No." His certainty kindled a flame of doubt.

"You weren't following me?"

"No."

"But I have seen you."

He shrugged, "If you say so."

"We are in my head, right?"

He looked around. "I don't really know. Like I said, this is new."

I thought hard about a chair, even closing my imaginary eyes to help my concentration. I opened my eyes and looked around. An armchair manifested a few feet from where I stood. "Cool," I set myself down. "You want one?"

He shook his head. "Have you ever noticed that you don't really belong anywhere?"

"Sure." I closed my pretend eyes again and imagined a foot stool. It worked. I kicked my feet up.

"And you have never wondered why?"

"I assume most people feel that way," I yawned.

"Maybe just the ones who don't really belong feel that way."

"Max, you seem like a decent person. I don't think there is anything you can tell me that will convince me that the people I have met over the last few months shouldn't exist. Because we do exist. I am here. You are here. Your friend is crazy, but she is here. You can leave me locked in here until my body wastes away and dies. Maybe I will change my mind. But I don't think I will." I conjured a blanket.

"I guess we'll find out." And he was gone. My bright, empty room became my dark, empty void. My chair, foot stool, and blanket disappeared.

And days passed. I found ways to fill the time. I tried to recite poems memorized as a student. I got a few right. I sang songs, both remembered and invented. I told myself stories. Occasionally, I tried to reach out with my mind to Max. But I couldn't find him.

Truly alone, I panicked, I could not feel my body, I knew it was out of breath. Or maybe they were suffocating me. My throat constricted tighter. I sensed it but couldn't feel it. I tried my breathing exercises but my lungs did not respond.

This is in my head. I repeated, *This is in my head,* until I started to believe it. And slowly, the breath I could not feel seemed normal, even as it remained distant. Distant, and still connected. I began to wonder if I tried hard enough, would I be able to climb out?

CHAPTER 52

Max pulled me from my prison and back to my empty, bright room. My chair had gone; I made a face at that.

"Are you ready to have a serious talk?" He asked.

"So," I began, "trapping people in their minds is a new skill for you. What kinds of things could you do before?"

"I can't do what you do."

"Cocktail waitress?" I asked.

"Change things in the past. Fix things in the past."

I conjured my chair and dropped into it. I enjoyed the luxurious sensation of fabric and softness. "You mean the genocide thing. Like if you wanted to commit genocide, you have to do it manually? And you think I can do it automatically?"

"You can change the past."

I nodded. "Let's explore that. So far, the sorts of things I have changed in the past are the equivalent of minor historical errands. For example: I moved a rope back in time, to a time that was only a few months away." I thought my chair into a chaise lounge and spread out. "However, what I have not done is change the entire course of history. For example: I have never murdered countless innocent people. That seems pretty advanced. I don't even know how I would begin."

Max was determined. "Maybe we could help each other."

"You think?" I asked.

"You came here to change the past, right. To save your friend. So you must have believed you could do it." He stepped closer to me and thought he would reach out to touch me. I wondered if I would feel it.

I didn't want to find out. I moved more quickly towards the inevitable conclusion. I said, "Oh, sorry. I am not being clear. It would be a 'no' even if I knew how to do it."

He sighed.

"I just want you to know, it isn't going to happen for a lot of reasons. I want to like you Max, but you have got to start thinking for yourself." On impulse I added, "You can send me back to my void now."

And he did.

CHAPTER 53

This stint in the darkness was the most challenging yet. It lasted longer than the other two. And that was hard. Distantly, I thought I sensed my stomach growling. And that was hard, too. Max's single-minded attempts to sway me kept returning to my thoughts. And that was hardest of all. Because I wanted to believe in him. And I didn't know why.

All of these challenges coalesced into anger. The anger vulcanized and became resolve.

I began to push outward. Reaching for my body. I couldn't feel it, I couldn't find it. I wasn't even sure that I really was pushing. But I kept trying anyway.

After days and days and days, Max summoned me to his visiting room. "Win," he said, he liked using my name, "I am worried for you."

I thought, *ditto*. I said nothing. I created a much more extravagant chair. I planned to enjoy it while it lasted.

Max made several more attempts to engage me. I ignored him and waited for the void. He exiled me after two or three pleas for reason, and one stern warning that his insane, murderous friend could be dangerous.

It became a routine. Max called me forward. I ignored him and enjoyed the light. I added furniture based on predetermined themes. I sang songs meant to insult him. I danced. And less overtly, I reached out to my body. A few times, I thought I could almost feel it.

Then it was back to the void. I amused myself as much as a person could do while completely inert. And I kept pressing myself toward my body. The effort exhausted me, but I kept trying. What's exhaustion to an incorporeal mind, anyway?

And then to the room. Max grew more and more desperate. Begging, near tears, then demanding with shouts. I gave him nothing. He was my only company so I looked forward to our time together.

Back to the void. Periods in the void grew longer and longer. I found myself walking back through old memories. Thinking of people I haven't thought of for years. Thinking a lot about Sophia, who may have been my protector or may have been my betrayer. And now I would never know. The last time I saw her, at the diner, I was so angry I couldn't appreciate anything she had done for me. And I regretted that. The diner. And then I remembered when I had first seen Max. He was in the diner. He and his homicidal friend, both. Running through that moment again I recognized that he hadn't seen me for good reason. I wasn't there yet.

And Max returned. I wanted to share my discovery. And I wanted to stick to my plan. The plan superseded the discovery. I felt closest to my body in the room. I could nearly reach it.

Max tried a new tactic. "Win, this is getting serious. The guardian, she is losing patience. You know she needs you. She won't kill you. But..." he hesitated in genuine concern. "She wanted me to tell you, you don't need hands or feet to live."

Dismemberment gave me pause. I looked at him with surprise. And disgust. "You would let her do that to me?"

"I don't think I could stop her."

With the conservational seal broken wide open, I shared, "I figured out how I know you. I saw you two. At a diner a few towns away. You were sitting alone, pretending to read a newspaper. And she joined you. You looked annoyed. But you left together."

He shook his head. "Impossible. I would have remembered you."

How flattering, I thought. "I wasn't there yet. Could have been days or weeks later that I was there. But I saw you."

"Win, she is serious. She will hurt you."

"So what if she does? She wants to erase me. Either way, I lose my feet."

"Please, Win." He meant it. In some twisted way, he wanted to protect me. And for a moment, I had an opening.

An idea took shape.

"Listen, this is pretty effective torture." I leaned toward Max. My eyes grew sad, desperate. "And we both know, I won't ever give in. So she is probably going to ask you for a hacksaw." I staged a dramatic scoff, "Hell, she's probably going to make you do it." I shook my head. "It's inevitable. She is going to hurt me and I feel very alone," I imagined tears forming in my eyes. "Will you hold my hand?" I added, "While I still have one."

The moment his hand touched mine, I felt it. And he realized his mistake.

I pushed in all directions with all of my strength. Pressure built within me. For a moment, I thought I would shatter with the power that radiated outward. I felt my body.

Real eyes opened, on a real room. I lay on a cot, in an otherwise bare room. Max sat next to me on the edge of the cot. Still stunned by his own error. I jolted upright. Max let go of my hand. For the second time in our acquaintance, I knocked him over. This time, I threw all of my weight behind my left fist. I connected to his nose with a sickening crunch. Then, I ran.

Also, for the second time in our acquaintance, he pursued me.

This time, Max bled from the face.

Also this time, I failed to take care on the stairs.

I tripped three steps from the bottom. Max caught me and we both went tumbling to the ground. He landed on me, knocking the breath from my body. After so much time away from my body, the feeling reassured me that this was not a new room in my mind, but the real world.

I tried to recover, to breathe. He used the time to pin my arms. Once again I felt a surge of strength. I wondered if I could take him to the past and leave him there.

"You will need to remove yourself from Win, before I remove you from this world." Sophia's quiet, confident voice filled the room. I looked toward the sound. Sophia stood near the door, fully composed, watching us, deadly serious. Max looked, too.

I smiled at Sophia, I didn't know if I could trust her, but she'd never tackled me, or pinned me to the ground, or asked me to help commit genocide. I looked back to Max, ready to gloat about the ass kicking he would soon receive.

Max's face conveyed remorse, mortification, fear, and a little hope. As I saw them I felt them. He sat up, letting go of my hands. His emotions faded in me a little.

He whispered, "Lamassu."

She almost smiled at him. "Lama, is what it was, once. But no one has called me that in a long time."

"Sophia," he said. "You go by Sophia, now." I wriggled beneath him to get free. Realizing that he still sat on me, Max shifted to sit on the floor. "She told me.." He trailed off, pain evident in his voice.

"Yes," she sounded genuinely pleased to be recognized, "How did you..?" She stopped, comprehension spread across her features starting at a sobered mouth moving up into steely eyes. "Not again." Apparently, she could read his mind, too. "Dolores!" she called.

I sat up rubbing my shoulder where it had bounced against the floor. "Sorry," Max offered.

The heeled boots tapped against the wooden floor upstairs as Max's guardian casually made her way toward the stairs. She spoke before her face appeared, her voice too loud compared to Sophia's quiet command. "Well, well. I should have known you would show up sooner or later."

It wasn't until I could look back and forth between them that I noticed the resemblance. "You must stop assuming my identity. This time you have caused Max harm. It never ends well."

The woman's eyes darted to Max, seated on the floor. "You fucking lied to me," he said. She stopped on the last step.

The woman looked worried. "I told you Max, I would have to do things, difficult things, even immoral things if we are going to save the world."

"You told me that you are the guardian, that was a lie. You told you wanted to save the world, that was a lie. I believed I was fated to follow you. That your purpose was true." He sounded hurt, devastated. Thinking back to my time in the void, I thought, *he should be*. He repeated, "You lied!"

"No!" She interrupted. "I told you what you needed to hear. Because I needed your help. Once I knew Sophia had Win, I knew I would need you. Because together we can convince Win to do the right thing. *We* can make this right."

"Enough Dolores." Sophia interrupted, "It looks like they have no interest in your mad scheme. You'll need to go back to your cultists for that."

Max and I watched the exchange from the floor like children wrapped up in Saturday morning cartoons. Dolores scowled. "Did she tell you what she is, Win?"

"Max thinks she's a guardian," I replied definitively. With Max next to me, I felt a confidence I had not earned.

"She calls herself that," Dolores spat back, "but she is a demon. That is what she really is. The demon spawn of the first forsaken immortal."

Sophia shrugged, "Jinn is more accurate than demon, but demon is a somewhat reasonable description. There isn't really one word to describe us. I *am* the spawn of the first forsaken immortal, that part is true. I was the first of many, in fact."

"She is evil!" Dolores growled. "Her existence creates Chaos, corrupts the world." Dolores turned to me with desperate eyes. "I know the truth about her, I will tell you everything. You must trust me."

"Lady," I said, "I appreciate all of your 'villain reveal' monologues, but I am just not interested. And at this point, I am in no mood." I looked to Sophia. "How do you know each other?" I asked, now more curious than afraid. Somehow between Max's solid presence beside me, and Sophia towering above us both, I felt safe.

Sophia looked expectantly at Dolores. "Not mine to tell," Sophia said.

Dolores glared daggers at Sophia. "Sophia's father, The Deceiver, is my grandfather."

"Dolores is mostly human," Sophia added, for my benefit, no doubt. Sophia held her hands out to Max and to me. "I think we have a lot to discuss."

We looked at each other, then each reached out to take a hand. Sophia pulled us to our feet with surprising strength.

"It seems that you lost some acolytes for your cause, Dolores."

"No," Dolores said, "Mortal or Immortal. There is no in between, no both. It isn't right. We will prevail."

"You base all of this on an old story, from a religion that disappeared centuries before you were born. It is possible your followers have become an echo chamber. You might benefit from learning more about different perspectives." Sophia seemed to be issuing genuine advice. "This is our world, Dolores. We have been in it as long as the humans have. We belong here. And you don't have to agree with it, for it to be so."

"This isn't over," she threatened.

"I know, that is how zealotry works," Sophia chuckled. "For today, though, it is over."

Max and I followed Sophia out. I hesitated at the threshold. I thought of the last time I walked out that door. I whispered, "I'm sorry, Twain. I'll find another way. I'll be back."

Sophia and Max waited for me by her sensible, luxury vehicle.

"Sophia," I said. "I have questions."

PART SIX: THE END

CHAPTER 54

The car ride felt like a return to normalcy. Though normal looked nothing like it used to look. Max sat quietly in the back, watching us converse like it was a tennis match.

I began, "Your niece," Sophia shot me a look, "your niece said her husband killed Twain." I added, "Because she told him to kill Twain."

"You found the killer. That's good, right?"

"Damn that witch," I muttered. It wasn't satisfying. "No one is going to believe that woman killed him. She looks younger than me."

"No," Sophia, "I am afraid if you are imagining a resolution involving the criminal justice system you are bound to be disappointed."

From the back, Max timidly offered, "What about her husband?"

I turned to him. "Wouldn't we have the same problem?"

Max shook his head. "He's human. I know where he lives. I've taken So… Dolores there."

"Then, yes, we have to go," I said, with conviction. "Maybe he will confess."

"Are you certain this is wise?" Sophia asked.

I shrugged, suddenly introduced to doubt. "Not anymore. Not when you ask questions like that. Why do you think this is a bad idea?"

"I don't think you will really get what you want out of this, Win. And I would like to protect you from additional pain."

I shrugged again. "Well, if that's all." I watched out the window for several minutes. "Let's go."

"Are you..?"

"Sophia," I said, determination clear in my tone, "things have changed. I can protect myself now. I appreciate that you came to rescue us. It was helpful. But I might have escaped on my own. I was close. And I think Max would have switched sides when he had a hacksaw in his hand, anyway."

"I don't follow," Sophia looked at Max in the rear view mirror.

"I don't think I could have gone through with it," Max admitted.

Sophia turned a concerned look to me. "I'm so happy to hear that."

"I knew it," I said for Max's benefit. *Later,* I mouthed to Sophia.

I thought about the confrontation to come. Finally, Twain's murderer would answer for what he had done.

The witch was wrong. I would have satisfaction.

Chapter 51

"Damn that witch."

The address Max provided was for a senior living home.

We checked in at the front desk. Max provided his name. We all signed in under our own names, I missed my name and enjoyed writing it. Max was on an approved list of visitors. The receptionist brought us to a door leading to the left wing of the facility. She unlocked the door and ushered us in.

"Why do they lock him in?" I asked.

"This area of the facility is secured for the safety of our residents in the memory care program. We want them to experience as much freedom as possible, while still ensuring their safety."

"Oh, of course." I thought, *Damn that witch.*

The receptionist handed us off to a nurse. "Jay will show you to Mr. Landry."

We followed Jay to a withered octogenarian, sitting serenely by a window, clutching a worn teddy bear. "Mr. Landry, you have friends here to see you."

"Oh?" He asked. There were hints of the man I saw in the basement, a bulk that age had diminished. "Hello," he said, "There are some chairs." He shakily gestured to seats in the area. We pulled a few chairs over.

Jay told us, "Find me when you are ready. The door can be tricky."

"I remember you," Mr. Landry looked directly at me. "Who is your friend?" He gestured towards Sophia.

"She's not my friend… We're working on something together."

"That was hurtful." Sophia interjected.

Her response caught me off guard. "Uhhhh," I stammered for far too long. "I didn't," *I didn't what?* I tried again, "I mean, I thought…" *What did I think?* Not that we were friends, certainly. Co-dependent? Co-workers? Finally, I surrendered and asked, "Are we friends?"

"I thought so," her reply arrived with no hesitation and no emotion.

"Oh," I wasn't sure I could believe her, "Okay. But I thought you were using me."

"Yes, I don't see how that precludes friendship."

"Alright. We're friends." Max and Mr. Landry watched the exchange with great interest. "This is my friend, Sophia and my new friend, Max."

"That's not Max," he said, "That's Trip. I know him. He's my friend."

OUT OF THE WAY THINGS

I looked at Max. He nodded regretfully.

"Wait, what?" I asked, "Your name's not Max? Should I just distrust everything everyone says to me from now on?"

"Not everyone," Max answered.

Just as Sophia said, "Probably a good idea."

"I've gone by Max for a long time," He explained.

I returned my attention to Mr. Landry. There would be time to find out if there were any other major lies we needed to explore as a group.

"Mr. Landry," I began. And stopped, I wasn't really sure what to ask him. I knew Dolores's would have aged substantially in the intervening years since Twain's death. But I didn't think about how old he was at that time of the murder. In my mind, he was older, sure, but not so old that I might hesitate before yelling accusations at him, threatening him Law and Order style to get a confession. I hadn't seen the show, but I had a feeling I would have been really good at that.

He saved me the effort when he said, "I didn't know if I'd ever see you again. You looked so scared in the basement. I don't like it down there. I am glad you came up here. Do you want some coffee? Jay makes the coffee the best."

"No, thank you." I looked at Sophia. And I knew why she wanted to spare me this.

Sophia pulled her chair directly in front of Mr. Landry. She reached out and took one of his hands in hers, and she smiled, one of the rare genuine ones that radiated outward and filled all the open space with joy. "Mr. Landry," she said gently. "Do you remember Twain, the boy Dolores needed. The one she told you to put in the basement?"

Mr. Landry nodded. He leaned forward fearfully, "He's still down there."

"He's safe now, Mr. Landry. We will get him out. But can you tell us what happened to him?"

Tears filled Mr. Landry's eyes. He held tighter to his stuffed toy. Yeah, Sophia was my friend, she was doing this to help me, nothing in it for her. I put my hand on Sophia's arm and I shook my head. Sophia released him at once.

"It's okay, Mr. Landry."

"Don't go back in that basement," Mr. Landry insisted.

"I won't," I agreed. "I promise."

He whispered, "She hurt that boy."

"Yes, she did." I said it to placate him, as I did, I heard the truth of it.

"Stay away from Dolores. You're the one she really wants."

"I will, I promise."

He asked, "Will you come see me again?"

"I'll try," I said. And I meant it.

"Jay!" Mr. Landry called out. "My friends have to go, but they are going to come back later!"

Damn that witch.

Chapter 51

"So much for vengeance, "I pouted.

Sophia insisted on taking us to a diner to regroup. "What's with you and greasy diners?"

She shrugged, a very un-Sophia-like gesture. "I simply like them. The menus are almost always the same. They have too many options to be believed. The food is always ready quickly. It's a modern marvel."

"Okay." *A modern marvel.* "Wait until you hear about air travel."

Sophia shook her head in polite disapproval. Max could hardly contain his shock.

Thinking of Delphine, I added, "Instant oatmeal will really blow your mind."

At the suggestion, Sophia eyed me with skepticism. "I can't imagine being impressed with any kind of oatmeal."

I snorted. "Naturally, she who loves greasy breakfast would eschew a wholesome classic. What a snob."

Max's jaw nearly hit the table.

"What's with him?" I asked Sophia.

"I don't know. Max, are you well?"

Max got a grip of himself. "Ye… yes," he stammered, "I'm fine."

"You two get a table," Sophia instructed, "I need to make a quick call."

Max and I entered, leaving Sophia to her call. We were seated near the window. I watched her pace delicately.

"Why are you so disrespectful to her?" Max inquired, indignation plain in his tone.

"What?" At first I didn't comprehend his words, transfixed as I was observing Sophia.

"The way you speak to her," Max said. "Do you know who she is?"

"She's Sophia."

"That is the name she uses. Yes." He leaned across the table. "But that is not who she is." Max's tone conveyed an urgency, his eyes darted to the window. It looked like he wanted to set me straight before she joined us.

"Dolores said she is a demon. She said she is a Jinn. Like a genie? I think."

"That is *what* she is. Not *who* she is."

"Oh, for God's sake. Will you just tell me? We are running out of interrogative pronouns."

"She is the Guardian." I blinked in response. "She is an eternal goddess worshiped by the ancient world." I had nothing. "She is known for protecting humans from other gods, she is a great champion."

OUT OF THE WAY THINGS

I really didn't know what to do with that information, so I said, "Okay."

"You should speak to her with more respect."

"Okay," I repeated. I remembered, Max had mistaken Dolores for Sophia. "So, you thought Dolores was an all-powerful guardian goddess?"

"I didn't say 'all powerful,'" Max corrected. "But yes. I told you, I saw someone's vision of it. That I would meet her, and aid her. But it was in someone else's mind and I didn't see her clearly. She said she was the Guardian and I believed her. Usually, I can tell when people are lying."

"Shielding one's thoughts is a common practice among exiles." Sophia explained. She took the seat beside me. "We know how easily we can hide among mortals."

"Does she have a lot of the same powers you do?" I asked. "Because you are related?"

Sophia nodded, "Dolores is more human than not. We share some abilities, however, her skills are lesser, watered down with ordinary, mortal blood."

"Was that some shade, right there? Are you bragging about your superior power?" Max's eyes grew wide in warning.

"I was pointing it out, definitely." Sophia agreed. "What's wrong with him?"

"I dunno." I dismissed her question and asked, "What was your call about?" Max kicked me under the table. My jaw fell open. I mouthed the words, *Ouch, Why?* He urgently indicated Sophia, and his eyes grew even wider.

"I was talking to the police. Did something happen while I was gone?" Sophia looked back and forth between Max and me.

"What were you talking to the police about?" I asked.

"Twain. I could find out, you know. Win prefers privacy for her thoughts, but this seems important."

Max shook his head vigorously, suddenly embarrassed by the attention.

"He's fine." I waved my menu dismissively. "You promised," I reminded her. I responded to her question about Max, "He doesn't like my tone."

My menu gesture caught the attention of the server and she returned to our table. Sophia ordered her usual, pancakes, eggs, hash browns, and toast. I ordered breakfast as well. Max, who I was learning valued convention, ordered a burger, because it was dinner time.

After the server left, Sophia informed Max, "That is a very normal tone for Win." An uncharacteristically fretful look crossed Sophia's face.

Max blushed and nodded.

"What?" I demanded.

"I'm concerned you will be mad at me, and we've just made amends."

I heaved a sigh, "What did you do?"

"I took care of things. A few of them." She evaded.

I asked, "What does that mean? The phone call?"

She responded in a nervous rush, "Yes. And I had your things packed up and securely stored."

"Wow."

She added, "And I made sure your bills were paid."

"Wow," I repeated.

"I didn't want anyone to be able to search through your possessions. It might have endangered you." Her face reflected consternation. "It seemed like a good idea at the time."

"Sophia, we have talked about boundaries."

"I know. I'm sorry." Max watched the exchange in wonder. I ignored him.

Her decisions baffled me. "Why did you keep the apartment if it was empty?"

"In case you wanted to go back, I wanted it to be ready for you. You didn't choose this," she clarified.

"And they just let you do that?"

Sophia admitted, "I said you were my cousin."

Despite Sophia overstepping, her thoughtfulness touched me. "You're a good friend." I amended, "And you seriously need to work on boundaries."

"I know. It's still a pretty new concept." Max observed it all in astonishment.

I asked, "Boundaries are a new concept?"

"Yes," Sophia adopted the tone she often used when instructing me about the ways of the world, "People used to accept that powerful individuals exercise power."

"Wow."

Sophia shrugged, a rare gesture from her. "I didn't create human society. I just live in it."

"Well, Sophia, human society changes. And self-determination is real big right now." I got the conversation back on track. "You called the police about Twain. Why? What did you say?"

"I anticipated you'd want that. Closure, to ensure that his body is found."

"I do. But this was between Twain and me. I wanted to decide. And to handle it myself. For closure." I didn't care if it sounded childish. Twain was mine, and I didn't want Sophia making the decisions where he was concerned. And there was still a chance for me to save him. I wanted to explore all of my options.

Sophia explained, "How would you have convinced the police to look into it without implicating yourself in some sort of wrongdoing? And of course, we have to think about Mr. Landry. I had the impression you didn't want him arrested."

"I don't. But you are just deciding for me again. You decide what risks I should take. You decide what happens next. You have to stop doing things like that for me."

"I'm sorry, I was trying to help."

"I know, but if we are friends, really friends, you have to let me decide what I want help with. When it comes to Twain, I am the one who has to make things right. And as for crazy adventures in which I am being hunted by your crazy niece, I have a say. I get a seat at the table."

Max stared in awe. Sophia remained contemplative for a long time. Long enough that our food arrived before another word was spoken. Before taking a bite, Sophia said, "Alright. That seems reasonable."

"Thank you."

"You've come a long way, Win. I look forward to hearing about it."

"On that topic," I hesitated, "I may have done a little independent investigation into the missing persons you and George were looking into."

Sophia shook her head. "That sounds dangerous."

"No, mostly just internet searches. But I did see a face, someone involved." I monitored Sophia for signs of rage.

Ever the pragmatist, Sophia accepted the confession, and said, "Tell me everything."

CHAPTER 55

Sophia dropped me at the airport parking garage. Even with our solid plan to meet at the bar, Max hesitated, unsure if she should stay with me or go with Sophia. "Stick with Sophia, I'll see you at the bar." He agreed nervously.

I understood. I was nervous, too. Delphine might have fired me, I was quite late returning. She almost never answered the phone at the bar, so I had been unsuccessful in contacting her. And then, I had to consider the looming question: What now?

Dolores remained a threat. Max was set adrift. And I didn't really know what Sophia did when she wasn't trying to protect me.

When I got home, I spent a little time on a few ordinary tasks to settle my mind. And when inconsequential chores started to make me anxious, I headed into work. Depending on Delphine's interpretation, I was either quite late or very early. It would be another hour before Sophia showed up.

I entered the bar prepared for anything.

"Look who decided to show up for work," Angus called to me. I heard relief in his voice.

I stuck my tongue out at him. "I only came because I heard you wouldn't be here." Angus laughed too hard at the comeback. It felt like everything was right in the world.

"Hey," Delphine said. She was in her usual spot behind the bar, setting up for the evening service. "Everything okay?"

"Yeah," I realized after I said it, it was true. "Sorry I'm late."

Delphine waved her hand dismissively. "Penny said you would be late. It couldn't be helped." I sent a silent "thank you" to Penny, she always had my back.

"I owe her one," I smiled, "My next day off, I'll binge whatever weird show she wants."

"Be careful before you make that commitment. Last time I agreed to that, the show had eight seasons. And they were long ones." I joined Delphine behind the bar, taking over her prep. She watched me for a moment and then asked, "What's going on? You look nervous."

"I have a few friends coming by in a while."

"You have friends?" Delphine sounded earnestly surprised. She continued quietly, "It wasn't meant to be mean. I didn't know."

"You're my friend. Penny's my friend."

"We're already here."

"I have friends!"

Angus looked at me with surprise, "Okay."

As if summoned, the door opened to Sophia and Max. "That's them."

Delphine's jaw dropped. "Those are your friends?"

"Uh-huh." I waved Sophia and Max to the bar. "Sophia, Max, this is Delphine. She's my boss."

"Sleeping Dragon," Sophia remarked, "clever. This place is nearly invisible from the outside."

"Nearly?" Delphine uttered, taken aback.

"Yes," Sophia asserted. "Very well done."

Delphine appeared to be pleased with Sophia's assessment. She also seemed reluctant to address Sophia directly. She said to me, "Why don't you take a break. Enjoy some time with your... friends." The word "friends," she spoke with more incredulity than before.

Max looked around curiously. I thought he might be searching for Penny, her presence would be obvious if he knew what he was looking for. When we were seated, Sophia turned to me and said, "This is a good place for you."

"Yeah, I feel good about it. I feel like I belong." I smiled.

"I meant The Dragon." Sophia interrupted. "She has the place well guarded. You'll be hard to find here... Gin." She smiled at my pseudonym, as though she had made a joke. "Her secrets are dangerous, so she will keep yours."

I nodded, "I think that's reassuring?" I knew there would be a great deal to discuss, probably plenty more important than what occupied my thoughts.

"Go ahead and ask," Sophia prompted.

"What will happen with Twain?"

"If his body is still in the basement, the police will find it. If Dolores is still there when they arrive, they will find her too."

"How did you do it?" I asked.

"Anonymous tip from a day laborer. Couldn't come forward for personal reasons."

It was a good plan, but that assumed the police took it seriously. "How do you know it will work?"

The question amused Sophia. "I can be very persuasive."

"Over the phone?!" Angus looked up from his beer with interest. I repeated in quiet surprise, "over the phone?"

"Yes. Over the phone. Are these really the answers you want?"

I considered that. There were plenty of answers I wanted. But more than any, I wanted to know what would happen to Twain. "Yes. I owe him."

PART SEVEN: LATER

EPILOGUE

Sophia collected me and we traveled together.

She worried about me being alone on Dolores's turf. Sophia drove. I suggested we fly, that it would be faster, but she dismissed this as easily as if I suggested that we walk. I spent the first day of the drive asking Sophia questions about her preferred methods of travel. She had never been on a plane. That revelation inspired a commitment from me, to get her on a plane. She once enjoyed train travel, but now found it too utilitarian to be interesting. She enjoyed driving, and anything relating to cars. She was happy to consider travel by horseback; she often missed that particular form of travel. She also admitted to enjoying all forms of sea-faring vessels. I admitted I had never been on a boat, and she vowed to change that. I almost wished Max was in the backseat, so that he could marvel at the easy banter between an ordinary seer and a goddess. Sophia remained oblivious to his hero worship, a circumstance that provided me with endless amusement.

By the second day the solemnity of the occasion changed the tone. Even the weather displayed appropriate reverence, respectfully overcast but dry. Sophia demurred, allowing me to lead conversations where I wished, when I wished, and otherwise remain silent.

Twain's service was graveside. I was touched by the number of people present. He had family. His parents were alive, siblings, nieces and nephews, aunts and uncles. They spoke about him as though he had been gone 30 days rather than 30 years. Except when they talked about the opportunities that he missed. In those moments, there was longing and regret.

I wondered, if it had been me, would my family show up? Doubtful.

When the service was over, we held back. I didn't have the right to be there, but I wanted a moment with him.

I shared my plan with Sophia for the first time, "I think I can save him. If I warn him. Maybe I can get him to run out the back?"

Sophia released a long stream of air. "I had hoped you would realize that you can't save Twain."

"I might be able to, I can do more than just talk to people in the past, I can, I did. I can take things back and forth. This is easier than that," I insisted.

She stopped me, placing a hand on my arm. "That's not what I mean. You know what you can do better than I do." She took a deep breath. Her reticence took hold of me. "Win, I told you once. The three of you are tied together. You must feel that. With Max?"

I nodded.

"Twain was a seer. I believe he saw the future. I think I mentioned that?"

I nodded again.

"Win, Twain had to die for you to be born."

I knew it was true. And I knew that maybe that was okay. I could trade my life for his. He was missed after thirty years. He had people. When I left my life behind, I didn't even know if anyone would notice. I told her, "I could try."

"Maybe it would work, and Twain would live another hundred years. But you and Max would not exist. If you wanted that, you would have joined Dolores."

"You don't really know how long mortals live, do you?"

Sophia lifted a shoulder in a near shrug. "I don't. And they are all so different. Who could keep track?"

"You're right." I would be taking Max out of the world, and some stranger who wouldn't even see it coming. I concurred, "I can decide that for myself. But not for Max. And not for whoever the third seer is, either."

"Did you know about Max from the start?" Sophia asked me.

"I think, sort of. I feel more powerful with him near. And he said there are things that he can do now, that he couldn't do before he met me."

"Did you tell Dolores that?"

I snorted out a laugh, "I don't know if you picked up on the vibe, but Dolores and I didn't really hit it off."

"Do you think Max told her?" Sophia was serious, intense.

"I don't know," but I thought I did know, so I amended, "No. I don't think so. He kept things from her. He believed in her, but he didn't trust her completely."

"Let's hope she doesn't know. She'll be that much more desperate to have you."

"What about the third seer?"

"The third seer must be found." Sophia had a plan, I saw it in her.

I considered the life I left behind, the life before the house and the forest and immortals. I no longer considered going back. "You mean, we need to find the third seer."

"Yes," Sophia said simply.

"I don't want to quit my job at the bar." I told Sophia.

"Of course not," she agreed.

"Okay." I took a deep breath; I prepared as much as I could. "So now what?"

ABOUT THE AUTHOR

Kendall McNutt is a story enthusiast from way back. She has been authoring stories since she could hold a pen. She loves stories in all forms, and takes every opportunity to jump into them wherever they occur, in whatever capacity is available.

Kendall lives in the Pacific Northwest, known for breathtaking landscapes and Seasonal Affective Disorder. When she is not consumed by a story or toiling away in the public education system, she can be found adventuring with friends and family, or snuggling cats. Her cats. Not all cats. Certainly not strange cats.

Catch up with Kendall at
kendallmcnutt.com

Made in United States
Troutdale, OR
11/30/2023